The Caper Brothers

A Novel by

Tom Tozer

Copyright © 2014 Tom Tozer

All rights reserved.

ISBN-13: 9781495247897
ISBN-10: 1495247899

All characters appearing in this work are fictitious. Any resemblance to real persons, living or dead, is purely coincidental.

This book is dedicated to my wife, Dana, my son, Jordan and his spouse, Beth Lyn, their son, Ford, and my daughter, Merris, and her spouse, Todd – friends for life.

I want to thank my sixth-grade elementary school teacher, Jewel Rafferty, for challenging her class with a short-story writing contest. I tied for first and discovered my love for writing. This book could not have been possible without the guidance of my New York City book editor, Alice Peck, (www.alicepeckeditorial.com). Her focus and encouragement made the project a challenging achievement. I also have to mention Mark Ethridge of Charlotte, author of "Grievances," "Fallout" and the movie "Deadline." His feedback was key to improving the story. And to the many good colleagues at the *Charlotte Observer*, thanks for 30 years of inspiration.

About the Author:

Tom Tozer retired in late 2013 after a forty-year career as a newspaper journalist. He spent thirty years at the *Charlotte Observer* in numerous leadership roles. He directed and encouraged hundreds of reporters and designers in the art and craft of storytelling. He keeps his love of a good story alive now as a freelance writer and editor in Charlotte, NC. *The Caper Brothers* is his first novel. To learn more, go to: www.tomtozer.com.

CHAPTER ONE

A single beam from a lamp illuminated papers and photographs spread across a desktop—the contents of a thick manila folder that was stamped in bold, black type:
Official Business
Marietta, Ga. Police Department
Detective Sean Gerard

The digital clock on his desk shone red: 3:45. Sean slumped in the old wooden chair that had been a Christmas gift from his first wife, while Connie, wife number three, snored softly in the next room. He tugged open the top drawer of his desk and took out a bottle of Lorazepam and a half-empty pint of Makers Mark. He popped two pills, fully aware the prescription indicated he was only supposed to take one at a time, and washed them down with the dregs of the bourbon.

He began to study the photo on the top of the stack of papers. It was a school portrait of a teenage boy with hair so lavishly red it clashed with his bright blue eyes. The hair and freckles were too familiar—the boy reminded Sean of someone he had known a long time ago.

The next picture from the pile was the same boy, flat on his back, those blue eyes open to the sky. His nude body had been staked to the ground and surrounded by yellow police tape. The kid's arms were at right angles to his torso and his legs tied together, his body forming a perfect cross. Strangulation bruising around his neck was evident.

A bolt of lightning lit up the backyard. The wind picked up, rain pelted the house.

He gathered up the investigation file and wrapped the bundle with a large rubber band.

"I never, ever should have taken this case," he whispered. Realizing that he'd been crying, he wiped the snot from his nose.

There was a small, black book on the corner of his desk. Unsnapping the plastic cover, he reread the inside page: *Remembrance of first Holy Communion, February 1960, St. Joseph's Catholic Church.* Thumbing to a red satin bookmark in the middle of the children's missal, he took out a prayer card. After staring at the image of Saint Jude for a moment, he turned the card over and fell to his knees on the shag carpet that should have been replaced a decade ago. He read aloud: "Most holy apostle, St. Jude, faithful servant and friend of Jesus, the Church honors and invokes you universally, as the patron of hopeless cases, of things almost despaired of. Pray for me, I am so helpless and alone."

He repeated the words into the morning light, "helpless and alone… helpless and alone."

He blessed himself with the sign of the cross and stood up.

"It's time to confront the perpetrator."

He checked on Connie who was still sleeping with a peace he had never known, and then headed for the shower. He was shaved, dressed, and out the door in thirty minutes, heading straight for the police station. He saluted as he drove past.

An hour later, he was two drinks into his breakfast.

Sean squinted into the morning sun that blazed through the open door into the smoky bar. He raised his arm to protect his eyes. "Shut the damn door," he shouted, sweeping his detective badge off the mahogany counter and dropping it into the side pocket of his corduroy sports coat, where it clicked as it landed on his Glock 9mm.

He drained his glass as he tried to focus on the figure in the door. "Lou, let me have another one," he ordered, rubbing his eyes. His hand trembled slightly as he slid his glass forward.

The bartender nodded. He tossed a scoop of vanilla ice cream into a silver shaker, added some milk, two shots of Jack Daniels, and a dash of Kahlúa. The blender did its job, creating a frothy concoction that the bartender placed on the counter.

The detective slurped deeply.

"Little early to be drinking breakfast, wouldn't you say lieutenant?"

He slowly turned his slight frame to face the new arrival, wiping the last of his drink off his gray moustache. "My, my, if it isn't the dutiful Patrolman Incorn, the department's top toady."

"The day you made detective was another celebration of how God loves a loser," said the patrolman as he flicked a small piece of lint off the sleeve of his gray uniform shirt, disgust contorting his face.

Sean looked straight into the face of the young officer, extended his arm, and jammed his middle finger against the cop's nose. "Run along," he said, and turned back to the bar.

The officer tapped his shoulder. "The chief wants to see you. And the fact that he knew to send me here says a lot about where your career is going. So if you are serious about staying on the—"

"Tell the chief I'll be along shortly."

The officer slapped his handcuffs.

"Don't even think about it, Incorn." He took out his handgun and placed it on the bar, then spun around on his stool so fast he ended up hitting the floor hard with his backside. He stood up slowly and grabbed the bar railing for balance before facing the patrolman who stepped back and started walking towards the door.

"Do you really think you can make up your own rules all these years and get away with it?" said the patrolman. "Judgment day is coming."

"Well, today is not that day." He pointed to the exit.

As the door slammed Sean cocked his head in the bartender's direction. "Nothing worse than a young cop who thinks he's special 'cuz my boss sends him on an assignment," he said.

He dug a twenty out of the back pocket of his jeans and placed it on the counter. "Thanks for breakfast, Lou."

The bartender grabbed his arm. "Take care of yourself, you little bastard.

Are you sure you are okay to drive?"

Sean nodded as he picked up his gun and headed to the exit.

"I need to see the chief and get this over with." He cleaned his aviator glasses with his shirttail and put them on before stepping out into the Georgia morning.

CHAPTER TWO

It was cold for Marietta in November, just above freezing. The steady breeze blew some of the sweat from his nose as Sean surveyed the parking lot. He walked to his black Mustang and clicked his remote ablaze with the Atlanta Falcons logo to spring the locks.

When he arrived at the police station, he passed his desk and walked straight into the chief's office.

John Templer pointed at his computer screen as he crossed the threshold. "I got your email this morning. If I grant your request for a leave of absence you will be giving up the Doyle murder case?"

He pulled a chair up next to the desk.

"You are a public servant, for God's sake," said the chief. "You just can't walk away. You're not working for the public library. This is the police department!"

"You don't understand."

"You're right; I don't. And I might never understand. We have a pervert running around killing young boys and you have suspects. I know it in my bones. Did you think I've worked with you all these years and wouldn't know?"

"Look, I can't. I just can't."

Chief Templer reached over and placed his hand on his shoulder. "Well, you can't blame me for giving it one more hard sell. We've been cops a long time," he spoke softly. "If you honestly feel that you can't continue, then Sean, I believe you. I'm approving your request and putting you on administrative leave starting immediately."

"Thanks, John."

"Still seeing the therapist?"

"Yep."

"Sean, follow her advice. I need you with us and on this case. But this is your last chance. Get sober."

He shook John's hand like he meant it.

As he navigated the side streets home through traffic, he lowered his window, sucking in the cool air. He pulled a pewter flask from under his seat, placed it between his legs and twisted off the top with his right hand. He sipped until the flask was empty, timing it just right as he pulled into his driveway.

He lurched through the side door and into the kitchen. Connie had left for work, so he scrawled a note to his wife: *I'm no good to you and I'm no good to the force until I confront the truth about my life. I have to go to Ohio. There is no other way. I will call often. Wish me luck. Love, Sean.*

CHAPTER THREE

Decades away from the Midwest had thinned Sean's blood. He had forgotten the gray of the Ohio winter, especially the ashen sky. There was no escaping the gloom around the Great Lakes this time of year. This shroud of frigid air wrapped Sean in its misery, yet the grim garment seemed appropriate for what he was about to do. The landscape matched the bleak cold at his core.

Beyond the picnic benches and swing sets, down the walkway to the beach, Arctic temperatures transformed the lake into a solid frozen slab. Near the shoreline, the constant motion of the currents created a wall of twisted cakes of ice, some the size of small mattresses.

Off in the distance, snow clouds scudded towards Cleveland. His breath formed into small crystals across his moustache, the snow lashing his face did not slow the hot salty tears coursing down his cheeks.

He remembered the tone in his father's voice the day he had marched into his bedroom to warn about this particular section of shore. "Sean Gerard, this is a direct order: no matter how alluring that blue ice is out on the lake, don't you dare go on it," cautioned his father. "On this coastline, the current moves mile-long sections of ice without warning. If you fall through, young man, the current sucks you past the hole. Then the freezing water does the rest.

"Two years ago, the Stewart kid thought he'd go for a joyride and pedaled his bike out on the ice," said his dad. "When they pulled his body out, his fingers were frozen to the handlebars."

He looked at the snow blowing over the ice just as a large section broke free, the crack echoed off the cliffs like cannon fire.

The wind howled as he shuffled off the bench and headed to a large evergreen tree for protection. As he labored through the snow, he tried to recall all of the details of the event that had changed his life. Time flew away like swallows fleeing the cold.

He knew the futility of yelling into that wind—it stole the sound of your voice and threw it back down your throat, but still he screamed. His fear and anger had been bottled up long enough. His secret had to be revealed.

He pulled his ski cap lower and headed toward the parking lot, scraping his mustache clean. He crunched through the fresh January snow towards St. Thomas Aquinas. The flurries had given the granite steps a fresh coat of white, making them look as if the stone had just come from the quarry, but Sean knew that for over a hundred years, hardworking parishioners had worn the granite steps to a fine luster. The faithful were pulled to this place like the iron ore lifted off lake freighters by massive magnets for the nearby steel mills.

Sean paused, his panting created small clouds that hung in the waning light. He knew from his days as a Catholic schoolboy that the Saturday service at St. Thomas Aquinas commenced promptly at four p.m. Officially, it was called the "Sacrament of Penance." A parishioner must confess all "serious or mortal sins" at least once a year. Failure to do so was a mortal sin. If the rule was broken, other sacraments could not be received, and then the sinner would be no longer considered a practicing Catholic.

He wanted his confession to be the last one the priest heard that day.

Entering the church through big wooden doors, he strode to the side of the vestibule, keeping his eyes locked on a spot about halfway down the right wall. Off to the side, he could avoid attention while monitoring everyone entering and leaving the church.

He slid into a pew, removed his cap and parka, and glanced at his watch. Only twenty minutes left in the scheduled confession. As he knelt to pray, he noticed a Bible, open to the Book of Psalms. He began to read, "Psalm 40, Thanksgiving for Recovery."

Happy is he who has regard for the lowly and the poor; in the day of misfortune the Lord will deliver him. The Lord will keep and preserve him; he will make him happy on the earth, and not give him over to the will of his enemies. Even my friend, who had my trust and partook of my bread, has raised his heel against me. But you, O Lord, have pity on me, and raise me up, that I may repay them.

Fresh tears fell as he closed the Bible.

The church was almost empty.

When Sean studied the front of the room, he panicked for a moment. The confession would not play out as he had hoped. Penitents were not using the confessional booth for privacy. A gray-haired priest sat in a chair facing the altar. A padded kneeler was positioned to one side. The priest wore a purple stole; the vestment looped around his shoulders and fell across the front of his black suit. Sean stared at the next-to-last sinner approached. The priest shielded his face with his left hand and kept his eyes locked on the crucifix that dominated the far wall as the parishioner knelt by his side.

He examined the priest's muscular frame. This was definitely the man he was looking for. Even after thirty years he recognized Father Ken Wasowski's sloping shoulders and thick neck.

It was almost five p.m. as the last parishioner exited down the center aisle. Father Ken rose from his chair. A loud cough and the rustle of feet caused him to sit back down. One more sinner approached the altar. Sean knelt, laid his jacket on the marble floor, and made the sign of the cross. "Father, I have not been to confession in a long time," he began. "I've come seeking God's forgiveness and your understanding."

Father Ken picked up his Bible as he folded one leg over the other. "Do not fear, my son, God will hear you," assured the priest. "It's time you rejoined your Catholic family. Welcome home."

"I hope you feel that way after I confess. I've come a long way to talk to you."

Father Ken shifted in his chair.

"Why have you sought me out?" he demanded.

"Father, I committed a crime many years ago," he said softly, not looking up. "My actions resulted in innocent lives being damaged beyond repair. I was never caught, never tried, never punished. I feel tormented to this day. Father, you know about my sins."

Father Ken moved his chair closer to the kneeler. "My son, we all make mistakes," he counseled. "Trouble is part of life. God cares about how we handle adversity. True character is revealed in times of trouble. Your soul is not lost."

"Father, I broke the Ten Commandments."

"Which ones?" blurted Father Ken, his voice rising.

"Major ones, Father. I tried to protect myself and someone I loved and it all went wrong."

"Who calls himself a Catholic, or a decent man for that matter, and doesn't seek immediate redemption?" exclaimed the priest, his six-foot frame shaking as he rose off his chair. He placed the Bible on the seat, pointing a large finger at Sean's forehead.

He retracted his finger as his eyes widened. "Raise your head so I can get a better look," he ordered. "Do I know you?"

"Father, I was an altar boy when you said your first Mass at St. Joseph's Church. When I was a teenager, you came to dinner one night at my family's home."

Father Ken slammed a meaty fist into the palm of his hand. "Oh, I recognize you," he announced. "Your mustache can't hide that round face of yours. And you haven't grown much taller either. So it's you, Sean Gerard, after all this time. I wondered when you'd show up."

"Father, I don't understand."

"We were all in denial in those days. Now the memories are with us for life, no matter how hard we try to forget."

Father Ken picked up his Bible and placed his arm around Sean's shoulder. "Let's move next door to the rectory," he said. "The Saturday evening mass will start soon and we'll get run out of here."

"Father, keep your stole on, I still want to confess."

The two men walked in silence. The housekeeper ushered them into an office, and promised to return with coffee.

"No interruptions," directed Father Ken when she brought a tray holding two steaming mugs. He waited quietly until the woman closed the office door.

Father Ken poured cream into his cup, and then studied Sean's face as he slowly stirred.

"Well, Sean, here you are finally," mused Father Ken. "I'm ready to listen, my son."

Leaning back in the leather chair, he faced the priest and took a sip of coffee.

"Finding you, Father, took several weeks. But I'm a police detective; tracking people comes with the work. Telling you the truth is going to be the hard part. Returning to Ohio is my first step. My job, my marriage, hell, even my soul are all in jeopardy. My therapist says I must confront the trauma that controls me, it's the only way to break free."

"You better start at the beginning."

"It all began in the summer of sixty-seven."

"Vineyard Beach," sighed Father Ken. "How I've tried to forget what happened there."

CHAPTER FOUR

The garage windows shook violently, startling the boys. "It's that damn helicopter again," yelled Sean Gerard, throwing down his cards. The four friends scrambled to pull up the door, knocking over the card table in their mad dash out into the morning sunshine. Nickels and dimes rolled across the concrete.

For two weeks, the Plexiglas-bubbled chopper had flown over the tree canopy of Vineyard Beach with the regularity of newspaper delivery. Every morning and every afternoon the silver craft broke the silence of summer in Vineyard Beach.

The whirlybird drove the pals wild with curiosity, especially Sean, whose two older brothers were away in Army boot camp training for Vietnam. In the summer of 1967, the evening news overflowed with black-and-white images of death and shuddered with the thumping sound of helicopter blades chopping through the Vietnamese sky.

The boys scurried for their Schwinn Stingrays each time they heard the helicopter. They feverishly pedaled their bikes with the swooping handlebars and the long, thin seats down the middle of the street in the direction of the noise, hoping the pilot might notice their enthusiasm and slow down so they could see it better. It never worked. But the experience did help Sean and his friends develop a keen ear for the sound of approaching aircraft.

In time, the village gossips flushed out that the helicopter belonged to the DeLanes of California, the most-talked-about newcomers and only residents to ever commute over Vineyard Beach. Mr. Mark Delane had relocated his electronics factory to the southern edge of the village's boundaries. Why he chose Vineyard Beach for his new enterprise did not interest the boys. Their fathers went to work in mundane ways—in the family car or by bus. Mr. DeLane flew in a helicopter every morning and back to his lakefront home every afternoon.

The helicopter, with its chrome trim and big red "D" on its side, was a sign of change. Vineyard Beach's sleepy days as just another village on Lake Erie were ending. Local leaders pointed to the sky and declared industry and better jobs were on the way.

The DeLane's new residence reigned over Lake Boulevard, the demarcation line between the haves and the have-nots in Vineyard Beach. Each mansion was set back far enough to be invisible to passing cars. Local folks could only imagine a home said to cost $100,000 with its view of the water, and piers below the cliffs where pleasure boats were tethered. Those who did not reside on Lake Boulevard—and that was most of the other residents of Vineyard Beach—lived in modest frame ranches built in the cottage style of the 1940's. To see the lake they went to the public park or rented a 16-foot aluminum dinghy by the hour from Dell's Fish & Tackle.

The approach of the helicopter that Friday morning had broken up the monthly poker game of The Caper Brothers—the name Sean's friends have given to their little gang. Jimmy Moran had just shuffled the cards for another hand of five-card poker, nothing wild, and was expounding on his favorite subject, namely shoplifting, when Sean yelled the alert. By the time the boys raced outside, the helicopter had darted over the tree line at the end of the street.

"I don't care if we just saw that stupid helicopter again, we're finishing this hand and then we're going to go out and steal something," declared Jimmy. "I'm tired of that damn helicopter."

Sean flushed, whirling in Jimmy's direction with clenched fists.

"The rest of us just want to play cards," uttered Sean. "You are such a nutcase, you have to steal something every day just so you can brag about it."

Buddy Trotz and Johnny Pasquale looked on in silence. They had seen the Gerard and Moran competition play out too many times. It all started in the seventh grade over a girl. Eventually Sean and Jimmy decided not to make a big deal over Mary, although they later regretted it when her chest swelled delectably. Catching a glimpse of Mary's naked breasts was the fantasy of every boy in the parish. Now just months from entering high school, Sean and Jimmy were locked deep in a rivalry that invaded ball fields, ice ponds, and their studies in female anatomy in the dark basements of the village's little houses.

"Your problem, Gerard, is you're a goody-two-shoes," proclaimed Jimmy. "You strut around like a little general. You think you know more than the rest of us, so you try and order us around."

"Yeah?" challenged Sean. "I am smarter than the three of you combined, and that's why I'm the leader of this group. So stop your crap."

"Stop my butt," laughed Jimmy. "Giving Mister Leader Boy crap is what I live for. You're just pissed because we voted three-to-one to call our group, The Caper Brothers. Not getting your way just drives you nuts. And besides what's wrong with a little stealing?"

"If it was just a little stealing, I might understand," said Sean, shaking his head. "One of these days you're gonna get us all in trouble. Don't you think you might have a problem?"

Sean was right; Jimmy's conscience just didn't seem to bother him. He woke early every morning, seven days a week, to deliver the Cleveland *Plain Dealer*. Being out before the village kicked into life afforded Jimmy ample time to rifle the unlocked cars and garages of his neighbors. He often rode home with his *Plain Dealer* delivery bag bulging with a prize or two, which he later sold to neighborhood kids.

Jimmy's scheming extended to the contests the *Plain Dealer* staged to attract new subscribers. The newspaper enticed its paperboys with the mother of all awards, an all-expense-paid, one-week trip to Expo '67 in Montreal. The first one hundred paperboys to sell fifty subscriptions automatically earned a seat on the chartered bus.

"You just watch me, I'll find a way to get to Canada," Jimmy had declared to his friends at the start of the summer. True to his word, he concocted a devilish sales strategy, offering the same pitch at every home he visited.

"I only need one more subscription order and I'm on my way to the World's Fair," Jimmy would plead. "Don't you want to be the one to send

15

me on the trip of my lifetime? You will always be in my prayers if you say yes."

For added effect, Jimmy would hold up the brochure depicting the architectural wonder of the United States Pavilion, a sparkling geodesic dome two hundred feet tall. In time, Jimmy persuaded fifty Vineyard Beach families that they were the ones responsible for helping him achieve his goal.

The boys continued to argue as they walked back to the garage.

Jimmy got under Sean's skin like a hungry mosquito.

"My old man was a bomber pilot in World War II and he's told me a hundred times, there's only one captain on a mission," declared Sean. "And I'm that captain."

"Well, we didn't name our group the 'Boy Scouts' on account of that name was already taken and we're not the scouting type," countered Jimmy. "We voted in 'The Caper Brothers' and that's that. And you guys better live up to our name or you're all a bunch of candy-asses."

"Deal the cards, Moran," interrupted Johnny as he picked up the overturned card table. "I'm feeling lucky and besides, you both talk too much."

"Everybody seems talkative around you Pasquale," challenged Jimmy as he shuffled the cards. "That's the first damn thing you've said this morning."

Pasquale faced Jimmy and crossed his arms over his chest to show off his bulging forearms.

"Okay, Pasquale, everybody knows you do one hundred pull-ups every night hanging from the pipes in your basement," said Jimmy. "The problem with you is you walk around like some big snake waiting to strike. You like to scare people with those arms, but it doesn't work with me. That's an Italian thing isn't it, being a tough guy?"

"And it's an Irish thing being all covered in freckles," chided Johnny, pointing at Moran's face.

"We need to all get along," offered Buddy, his booming voice echoing off the garage walls.

"We sure as hell don't need your big mouth flapping right now," said Sean in disgust as he stared at Buddy and pressed a finger to his lips.

"Can I help it if I was raised in a house with deaf mother?" whined Buddy, pulling his t-shirt down over his flabby stomach. "I don't talk loud on purpose, it's the only way I get heard at home."

"We know, we know, but you're not at home, you big jerk," said Jimmy covering his ears and writhing in mock pain. "And Gerard," he continued, slapping a card in front of Sean, "so what if your father was a pilot and got his picture in the local paper. That was before we were born. Hardly anybody remembers he was a hero."

"At least my dad has two balls," said Sean. "Your dad's only got one good one and that's why you're an only child."

"You're always pissed off and I know why," said Jimmy, looking down at his cards. "When your brothers headed off to the Army you thought your dad would go easier on you. Hell, he doesn't even call you by your real name. It's always, 'Buster this' and 'Buster that.'"

"Shut up."

"Here's what I want to know," taunted Jimmy, pushing his chair back from the table. "How can a little, hairy shit like you have two brothers so tall and bald. Well, Leader Boy, got any theories?"

"What's that move you do again when your brothers pick on you about your size? Come on, Leader Boy, let's see it."

Sean forgot his anger, the thought of his latest tactic to shut up his brothers bringing a smile to the corner of his mouth. "You mean this," said Sean, shooting a mock look of rage at Jimmy as he ran his fingers through his hair. "How's that, Caper Brother!"

"Pretty nice touch with the hair, Leader Boy," laughed Jimmy.

The Caper Brothers were a cross-section of Vineyard Beach, the sons of the blue-collar families that dominated the villages of northern Ohio. The boys also shared a common heritage. They were Catholics. They confessed together, received First Communion together, were confirmed together, even studied to be altar boys together. This brotherhood, and the fact their homes were just blocks apart, made the friendship feel bulletproof.

In the late 1960's, the village, located halfway between Cleveland and Sandusky, boasted only 2,000 residents. On the western edge of the village, squatted the town's most important landmark, the Cleveland

Power Plant. The brown brick building constructed in the '20s, featured four stacks that belched smoke day and night from coal-fired steam generators, but Vineyard Beach's source of pride centered on the Concord grapes grown in the rich farmland nearby. Abundant fall harvests provided the red wine consumed at Sunday Mass all over the state.

At the center of the village, across from the Lake Boulevard mansions, stood St. Joseph's Catholic Church. For the faithful, life revolved around the church and adjacent school, which was run by Ursuline nuns, a teaching order founded over 400 years ago. Their ranks adhered to a strict dress code of black habits and an even stricter code of discipline for their students.

The talk in the garage turned to the summer of freedom unfolding for The Caper Brothers.

"We are free from those crazy nuns for three months," said Sean. "We should be celebrating. "It's summer, and our folks don't know a damn thing about what we do all day. All we have to do is show up on time for dinner."

"Ah, dinner," mused Buddy. "I wonder what my mom is making tonight."

"Will you shut up about food?" ordered Sean, rising from his seat. "And just shut up in general."

Sean pointed a finger at Jimmy. "Of course, if you had your way, Moran, we'd be out trying to steal something right now."

"Yeah, and if you had your way we'd spend all day riding through town with our eyes peeled for that helicopter," retorted Jimmy.

"I'm tired of this poker game, let's go throw the football around," said Buddy, his voice muffled slightly by the remnants of a candy bar he was chewing. "It's gotta be more fun than this. Last one out of the garage is a pussy."

The boys raced their bikes the two blocks to the new football field outlined in chalk next to St. Joseph's.

"See those construction guys working on the new high school?" asked Jimmy, gesturing to the edge of the field. "It looks like they're packing up for the weekend. I wonder if they leave any of their tools out. It could be easy picking."

"And so would sticking a finger in your nose, Master Thief, and picking out a juicy booger," teased Sean.

The boys peeled off their t-shirts to catch the breeze coming off the lake. Pasquale fished a nickel from his jean's pocket and flipped it expertly into the air. He smacked the coin against the back of his hand.

"Your call, Moran," he said.

Sean and Jimmy won the toss and opted for offense. Sean walked across the field and took his position at quarterback. Jimmy crouched over the ball, snapped it smartly to Sean, and took off down the field, Johnny in hot pursuit. At the end of his route near the sideline, he looked back over his shoulder expecting to see the football. Instead, all he saw was the quarterback standing still holding the pigskin at his side. The ball slipped from Sean's hand. He tilted his head at a sharp angle towards the tree line.

"It's coming," screamed Sean.

The chop of the helicopter approached with the speed of a summer storm.

"That thing doesn't sound like it usually does," warned Sean. "Something's not right."

Sean tried to yell at his friends but his voice was drowned in a sudden explosion of wind and dust. He quickly shut his mouth to keep out the flying debris. Trailing a thin line of black smoke, the helicopter bore down on the boys, lurching from side to side as it attempted to clear the trees on the edge of the field. They dove to the ground as the helicopter swooped directly overhead. The powerful down draft pushed their faces into the fragrant summer grass. The helicopter descended at the far end of the field near the goal posts. It spun completely around before landing with a thud, the blades slowly coming to a stop.

The pilot jumped from his door cradling a fire extinguisher. He raced to the back of the craft and threw open the engine hatch. His image was quickly engulfed in smoke and white foam. The passenger door opened and a tan leg emerged, its hue enhanced by the afternoon sun. Securing a foothold on the helicopter's steel running board, the passenger swung out another brown leg. The owner of the tanned appendages then stepped clear.

Tom Tozer

The boys lay in the grass, eyes frozen on a girl unlike all the girls in Vineyard Beach. Sean scooped up the football, stood and punched his arm into the air.

"What are you, the Statue of Liberty?" cracked Jimmy. "Why are you standing there holding the football up?"

"I want that new girl to see me," gushed Sean. "And, besides, you all look like a bunch of chickens lying there in the grass."

Still holding the ball aloft, he trotted away, leaving his friends prone on the ground.

As Sean approached, the girl moved to join the pilot near the back of the helicopter. Even from a distance, Sean could see that her small frame had luscious curves, the kind boys study with primal awe. She wore a white sleeveless top, cut-off corduroy shorts and open-toe sandals. The sun had streaked her light brown hair, which was parted in the middle and fell down the length of her back. Sean's eyes widened as the girl stooped to look into the engine compartment. As she bent at the waist, her shorts scooted up, exposing the skin at the top of her leg. The whiteness of her flesh, just where her bottom began to turn up, made all the hormones already racing through him pick up speed. The sight of her tan line made Sean lower his arm. He broke into a run.

"The nuns were right, there really is a God who cares about us," sighed Sean.

The girl with the tan threw her hair to one side, tucking it neatly behind her ear. She looked over in the direction of the boys. Her eyes fell on Sean as he sprinted towards her. She waved.

The afternoon breeze blew the last of the smoke clear of the helicopter. As he got closer, Sean could see that the girl's features were as sharp as a porcelain doll's, everything in perfect proportion. Her face was a blemish-free oval, marked by lips of a prominent fullness, with a chin that jutted out just slightly into a perfect point, giving her an air of character beyond her years. Her forehead was accentuated by arching brown eyebrows that set off the paleness of her blue eyes.

"Hi, I'm Sean Gerard," he announced with a wide grin as he came to stop in front of the girl. Sean brushed off the grass kicked up by the helicopter that stuck to his damp skin. The girl returned his smile then studied the boy in his shorts and sneakers, the football tucked under his arm.

Sean scratched his chest. "It's the grass, it's kinda of itchy."

"Here, let me help you, after all if it wasn't for my father, you wouldn't be such a mess," she replied. "I hope we didn't scare you too much when we flew over you and your friends."

Sean froze. He couldn't summon the courage to say anything. The girl walked behind him. Sean tingled as she brushed her hand across his shoulder blades and down his spine knocking off the debris.

The girl stepped around Sean to look him directly in the eye, her gaze not wavering. She winked. Sean tried to clear his head, hoping she didn't notice his blush of embarrassment. He coughed nervously.

"Oh, darn, I forgot my manners in all the excitement," declared the girl, extending her hand. "My name is Candace DeLane, my friends call me Candy. And that man over there with the troubled look on his face is my father, Weldon."

Sean grasped Candy's hand and was about to start a conversation but lost his train of thought in the commotion caused by the arrival of his three friends.

"Is everybody here okay?" asked Weldon DeLane, walking up to the group. "It looks like a fuel leak caused a small fire. I'm just thankful we landed and everybody is all right."

All four friends nodded in unison.

"You sure you boys are going to be fine?" wondered Weldon, his gaze moving from boy to boy.

"We'll be just dandy," said Sean, letting go of Candy's hand. "We've been trying to get a closer look at your helicopter for a long time."

"Well, here is the darn thing," said Weldon, pointing to the helicopter. "I'll have to send somebody over to fix this thing later. We're heading up to the house for supper now. How 'bout you boys lend a hand with something I've got behind the seats."

Weldon opened the side door, pushing the pilot seat forward to reveal two blue surfboards in the back of the helicopter.

"What are you doing with surfboards?" inquired Sean.

"I've been surfing all my life and I wasn't going to leave my prize possessions behind in California when we moved east," said Weldon pulling out the boards. "They were shipped to my office by mistake. We were getting them home when we were forced to land."

Weldon stacked the boards against the side of the helicopter.

"You boys ever try surfing on the lake?" probed Weldon. "I understand the lake can get pretty kicked up."

"Yes sir, when that happens it means a storm's coming down from Canada and then you can see the four-foot waves," answered Sean in his most helpful voice. "We've body surfed on those big waves but you have to watch the undertow. Last week four guys drowned down near Huron trying to rescue a friend. She made it out but they didn't."

"Thanks for the warning," said Weldon.

"You'll have to be careful with those boards on this shoreline too," advised Sean. "I'd hate to see these beauties damaged. There's really not much sand here at all, just plenty of flat stones left behind as the lake's fallen over the years. That's why we have those big shale cliffs hanging over the water. We can help though."

Sean tossed his football to Candy.

"Come on guys, let's lift them up and get moving," ordered Sean.

Soon the little troupe was heading towards the DeLane mansion across Lake Boulevard from the church property. Weldon led the way. Each boy held an end of a surfboard high over his head. Candy walked next to Sean, whistling and swinging her arm with the football.

"That sounds like 'Take Me Out to The Ball Game,' why are you whistling that tune?" wondered Sean.

"That song's been kicking around in my head all day," answered Candy. "I've been going to baseball games with my dad since I was a little girl. My dad thinks I enjoy them. Heck, I just like to go and watch the people."

"Does your mom like to go to the games too?" asked Sean.

"You sure do ask lots of questions," said Candy, frowning coquettishly. "My mom died when I was small. My dad's raised me pretty much by himself. We're pretty close though. I sometimes feel more like a son. He's taught me lots of things beside baseball and surfing."

"Maybe we can go out on the lake sometime," interrupted Sean, glancing at Candy.

"Maybe we can," she said, tossing the football from hand to hand. "But for now, you better keep your eyes on where you're walking."

"I'd rather keep an eye on you," whispered Sean, blushing at his boldness.

"Are you trying to impress me or are you always such a charmer, Sean Gerard?" challenged Candy.

"Usually I'm pretty shy, but today is kinda different, considering you plopped down in the middle of our football game," replied Sean. "I've never met a girl that flew in a helicopter before so I guess this makes our meeting real special. At least that's how I'm looking at things."

"Are you sure you're not just another pushy boy trying to impress someone new?" kidded Candy.

"Maybe we were supposed to meet like this, did you ever think of that?" offered Sean, smiling in Candy's direction. "I like that idea. Maybe this was meant to happen."

"Don't get your hopes up, mister," declared Candy. "This wasn't destiny."

Candy stepped closer to Sean and lowered her voice.

"What I'd really appreciate is someone helping me understand this place," she confided. "I'm not great at meeting new people, especially other girls. I've spent so much time doing guy things with my dad that I prefer hanging out with boys."

Sean looked at Candy and nodded in amazement.

"It's just that girl talk and the whole makeup thing and all that stuff is a puzzle to me," said Candy. "If you know what I mean."

"I'm not sure exactly, but for you, I'll definitely try my best," declared Sean.

The party reached the end of the DeLane driveway where it widened to accommodate the three-car garage.

"Let's put your haul in the back of the garage," instructed Weldon, pulling out his keys to unlock the door.

When the boards were stored away, the boys started to head back down the driveway.

"I'm going to put some steaks on the grill," said Weldon to the group. "Would any of you like to stay for supper? It's the least I can do to repay you for toting my surfboards."

"Sorry, I can't," said Sean, sadness creeping into his voice. "My folks are having the parish priest over for dinner and he's bringing his new assistant. It's a big deal for my folks to have them over and I was ordered not to be late. But I sure would rather eat steak."

The other boys declined the invitation, promising there would be a next time. Candy walked alongside Sean as the group moved off the property.

"Let me know when you want to go out on the lake," she whispered, squeezing Sean's hand before turning towards the house.

Sean looked over his shoulder as Candy jogged up the drive, her tan body moving effortlessly, hair glinting where the sun struck it through the canopy of trees. Sean wanted to run after her. At the first step of the front porch, Candy whirled, cocked her arm and launched Sean's football skyward in a perfect spiral. It landed softly in Sean's hands. Candy waved to the guys in triumph and ran up the stairs. Sean's eyes followed the girl until she disappeared behind the big double doors. His spirits rose as he made for home, the image of Candy's athletic body burning into his memory.

Sean could see himself eating steak, watching the sun dip into the lake, while he sat beside the alluring girl from California. However, when his dad said 1800 hours for dinner, he meant business. There were consequences for being late.

As Sean pedaled down Maple Street, a shrill whistle pierced the air. The boy's spirit plummeted. Most families rang a dinner bell or just shouted, Chuck Gerard whistled for his sons to get to the table.

CHAPTER FIVE

The white house with black shutters at 203 Maple Avenue stood out from the other clapboard-sided cottages lining the street. The structure featured an impeccable lawn and gleaming windows that on this June day emitted the faint scent of ammonia. The four brick steps leading up to the screen door were lined with pots of red geraniums, each plant pruned to perfection, not a brown leaf or wilted flower to be seen. Next to the front door, under the mailbox, hung a brass plate with the word "Gerard's" in raised Roman letters, a small trace of polish remained in the curve of the "G."

Upstairs, Chuck Gerard, former bomber pilot in the old Army Air Corps, put down his brush. Standing in his starched boxers, he peered into the mirror to inspect his crew cut. Known around town to friends and co-workers as "Lieutenant," Chuck spun on his heels with a quick kick, sticking out his chest with martial pride. He marched across the carpet, singing to the music drifting up from the stereo console in the den.

"Many men came here as soldiers, many men will pass this way," he bellowed with his favorite movie score. He pivoted his paunchy frame at the far end of the bedroom and stomped across the room. "Many men will count the hours, as they live the longest da-ay." He drew out the last word for impact, his voice rising in volume.

Chuck's blood raced with the music. His love of the military had inspired the purchase of the first record album for his new stereo, the soundtrack of "The Longest Day." Five years earlier, he had dragged his sons to the three-hour, black-and-white tribute to the D-Day invasion, calling it "the greatest movie ever made about World War II."

Chuck now felt primed for putting on his uniform. He sat on the end of the bed, rolling up dark nylon socks over his calves. He picked up his folded black slacks, snapping them sharply to remove any dust, then slipped them on one leg at a time. He reached for the short-sleeve white dress shirt with the initials 'CG' on the pocket. The light starch of the shirt felt good against his clean skin. He threaded his favorite belt, the one with his squadron's insignia on the buckle, through the loops of his trousers. He then knotted his dark tie. Finally, he laced on his black wingtips that were ablaze in new shoe polish applied with a bit of spit.

"Sean Gerard, front and center Buster, right now, that's an order," Chuck yelled down the hall.

Sean knew that tone. He approached his father's room with trepidation.

"Atten 'shut," ordered Chuck, examining his son as he entered. "Straighten up, get your shoulders back for God's sake. Excuse me, soldier, but did you hear me say 'at ease?'"

Sean pressed his arms against his sides and tucked in his chin.

"That's better. Now snap off a clean one, soldier," barked Chuck.

Sean saluted with the precision of a palace guard.

"Has your mother seen what her youngest son is wearing for tonight's dinner?" inquired Chuck, shaking his head. "You're not going bowling with your friends. We've got the priests coming for Christ's sakes. Of course, your mother will come to your rescue. Hell, she adores the ground you walk on. The way you're going, if your relationship to that woman gets any closer, I'm going to have to buy you a dress."

Chuck returned his son's salute. "Now, Buster, get out of my sight," he ordered.

"Wait. Wait. *Wait.* Hold it right there," yelled Chuck. "I forgot something. Get in here a minute and close the door."

Chuck sat on the edge of the bed as the oak door swung shut.

He pointed his finger at his son's forehead.

"I want to make sure of something," he said lowering his voice. "Do not, under any circumstances, bring up the gossip tonight that keeps circulating around this little town."

"You mean the Miller boy?"

"Yes, exactly the Miller boy."

"Dad, that boy was real quiet and hardly anybody knew much about him."

"Just don't be like those old bags who meet up at St. Joe's every morning for Mass," said Chuck. "For every piece of gossip there's always a back story. You remember that."

"I don't know about any back story but people say all of a sudden he started hating school and just stopped going. Just like that."

"I have it on the highest authority in this town, and you know who I mean without me having to use his name," said Chuck, rising to his feet. "That boy needed some help. He just ran off that's all there's to it."

Sean blushed.

"Now, let it go. And that's a direct order! Go see what your mother needs. Do it immediately."

Chuck turned away as Sean raced from the room.

Downstairs, Lorraine swept the kitchen one last time. The hardwood floor had already been mopped and waxed but she did not want her husband to find a speck of dirt during inspection. She groaned when she bent to pick up the dustpan. The stabbing pain between her shoulder blades was her reward for a day of hard work.

Sean rushed into the room. Lorraine straightened her aching back as she reviewed her son's attire. She winced.

"*Mon Cher*! Didn't you see the black slacks I ironed hanging on your closet door?" she clucked with aggravation. "Why did you put on those old brown things? And no socks. What were you thinking?"

Sean sighed.

"Come here to your mother," Lorraine demanded, putting aside her broom.

Sean stood still as Lorraine raked his disheveled hair into some semblance of order with her stiff, arthritic fingers.

"Please, be on your best behavior tonight," she whispered. "Your father is … tense."

"No kidding. He's always worked up about something," answered Sean. "I've already failed inspection, of course, that's nothing new for the Lieutenant. He's usually got some gripe about me."

Lorraine smiled weakly and patted her youngest son's check.

"Don't take it too hard," she advised. "You are trying your best. Your father loves you in his way." She gave one last motherly tug to the collar of his knit sport shirt and pushed him gently in the direction of the den.

Sean stopped in the doorway to the kitchen and looked backed at his mother. "Mom, you look lovely tonight," he said, blowing her a kiss.

Lorraine Gerard was an alluring woman, still trim after three pregnancies. As she approached forty-three, time had kissed her softly. The stoop in her back was becoming more pronounced, but her skin was a delicate shade of cream, which Lorraine credited to her nightly application of Oil of Olay. Only the small wrinkles around her sparkling eyes divulged her age. She wore her hair short, a luxurious jumble of dark curls that barely touched the collar of her simple cotton dress. She smoothed the front of the white outfit, her freshly painted red fingernails a perfect match for the collar and trim.

"Don't stand there staring, your father will be down in a minute," warned Lorraine, applying a fresh layer of matching lipstick to her full mouth.

"What exactly did you see in the Lieutenant that day he showed up at your farm house?" joked Sean. "You must have been in shock from the war, or something, to fall in love with him."

"Sean, my darling, that was a long time ago. Stop worrying about such trifles," replied Lorraine with a wave of her hand. "Besides, you are too young to understand the ways of love. There were many French girls in my village who thought your father was charming. He was rather dashing in his day."

"It amazes me how calm you stay around him," marveled Sean. "Come to think of it, I don't remember a single time I've ever seen you sweat."

"I am a lady, we do not perspire," said Lorraine smiling at her son. "Enough of your questions, Sean. Everything is not so simple in life."

The doorbell chimes interrupted the conversation.

"Hurry up now, we must greet the priests at the front door, it is the proper thing to do," said Lorraine, clapping her hands together.

All three Gerards collided in the foyer. Chuck swung open the door.

The sight of Father Paul Sterner and Father Kenneth Wasowski on his front porch sent the Lieutenant's spirit soaring. The flight only lasted a moment, stalled by the sight of Father Paul's constant companion, Frankie the toy poodle. The priest had Frankie tucked in his arm, a ball of white against the folds of priestly black. The pet was never far from the pastor of St. Joseph's Church.

"Come in, come in," invited Chuck, as he eyed the dog suspiciously and stepped aside gesturing for the guests to enter.

"Father Paul, so good to see my old friend and confessor," said Chuck. He threw his arms around Father Paul and hugged him, causing Frankie to yelp.

"I haven't seen you at confession in a while, Chuck," said Father Paul solemnly. "Don't keep God waiting if you want a clear conscience. But, enough of spiritual matters for a moment, let me introduce you to my new associate, Father Kenneth Wasowski."

The pastor led the young priest forward by the elbow.

"Father Ken is fresh out of the seminary and all of twenty-six, but I know in time he'll be a big asset to my parishioners," said the priest.

"Father Ken, welcome to Vineyard Beach and my home," announced Chuck, shaking his hand with authority. "It's an honor."

Chuck released his grip and took a step back. "That's some handshake you got there, fella." He admired the broad shoulders of the new priest. "And I know something about handshakes."

"Hey Dad, remember us?" chimed Sean.

"Of course, of course," said Chuck. "This is my wife, Lorraine. And this smart guy is my son, Bus...er...Sean. This is Sean."

Chuck patted the boy on the head as he motioned for the priests to follow him into the den.

"Let's have a drink while Lorraine puts the final touches to dinner," said Chuck cheerfully. "Father Paul, may I put your dog in the garage or backyard?"

Father Paul waved him off.

"Frankie's fine, he's no trouble at," replied the priest, settling into a chair in the den. "I'll have my usual libation, Chuck."

"I'll just have a pop, please," said Father Ken.

Chuck exited to the kitchen to fix martinis, leaving Sean with the two priests. Frankie bolted from Father Paul's arms and dashed behind Chuck into the kitchen, yipping peevishly at his heels.

Lorraine looked on in amusement as the dog sniffed around her ankles.

Sean was deep into a conversation with Father Ken about the upcoming season of the Cleveland Browns when Chuck returned with a tray of drinks and distributed them to his guests. He was about to take his first sip, when Frankie suddenly dashed back into the den, his nails clicking on the hardwood floor. A white blur headed for Father Paul's lap. The impact of the five-pound missile sent the priest's drink sloshing across the glass-topped coffee table, extinguishing the priest's Marlboro that burned in a metal ashtray.

Chuck clenched his jaw, a sardonic smile locked on his face as beads of sweat formed a line across his forehead. Sean had witnessed this before—he knew his father was suppressing his quick temper.

Frankie's behavior was disrupting Chuck's sense of order. Pets were not allowed in Chuck Gerard's house. He had made an exception for the parish priest and now there was a puddle of gin pooling on the table and a smoldering cigarette in his favorite ashtray.

"Sean, come with me into the kitchen and help me refill the pastor's drink," commanded Chuck with a quick angry look at Frankie. "You can carry Father Paul's drink back for him. Anything more for you, Father Ken?"

Father Ken waved him off.

"I'm good for now," said the young priest.

Chuck draped an arm around Sean's shoulders as they turned the corner into the kitchen. When they cleared the doorway, the elder Gerard grabbed Sean by the hair and shook him.

"Do something about that stinking dog," he hissed into Sean's ear. "I want it out of my house."

Chuck pushed his son hard in the center of his back.

Sean spun around rubbing his scalp, eyes blazing. His father poked his chest with two stubby fingers.

"Don't give me that look, Buster," growled Chuck. "Remember, I'm your father and you will respect me."

"He's not my dog," whined Sean as he flung his arms in the air. "Can't you just relax so we can eat and get this meal over with?"

"Can you two please try and act like gentlemen," pleaded Lorraine. "The priests are going to hear you!"

"Stay out of this Lorraine," warned Chuck.

Lorraine leaned over the oak table that she had sat at as a child in her home in southern France, positioning the forks, knives and napkins in their right place, trying to ignore the brewing squabble.

"Are you trying to tell your father what to do?" demanded Chuck menacingly. "Don't push your luck, Buster. When I want to hear from you I'll let you know."

"Dad, why don't you talk with Father Paul about his dog?" said Sean, trying to mat down his hair. "Maybe he'll put it outside."

"That's enough out of you, Buster," exclaimed Chuck heading for the collection of liquor bottles next to the breadbox. He refreshed his drink and poured another for Father Paul, handing it to Sean. He slapped a dishtowel over Sean's shoulder.

"Get back here when you're finished cleaning the coffee table," he ordered.

Frankie inched towards the kitchen door but retreated at the sound of Chuck's frustrated tone. He meekly curled up under Father Paul's chair.

Father Paul's poodle was a parish regular. From the schoolyard to the rectory, the priest always made his rounds carrying Frankie. On the mornings Father Paul said Mass, the dog waited outside the church doors for the stocky priest he could not live without. Father Paul's other passions were his Marlboros and his students. If Father Paul encountered a student in the school hallway or on the steps after church, he would smother his prey in a swirling mixture of cigarette smoke and Old Spice cologne. The boys hated the hugging the most. They even coined a name for it. To be 'Sternered' was not a good thing. Most boys picked up the pace when they saw Father Paul coming.

Sean quickly cleaned the coffee table, glancing at Father Paul as he gulped his new martini.

Lorraine appeared at the door.

"Dinner is ready," she announced, gesturing towards the kitchen.

Lorraine escorted the two priests to their seats as Frankie dived under the chairs. Chuck made another martini, downing half of its contents before heading for his place at the head of the table. Sean was under the direct gaze of his father, wedged between Father Paul on his right and the new priest and his mother on the left.

Father Paul made the sign of the cross, clearing his throat of smoke and gin. Heads bowed. The casserole pan in the middle of the table filled the kitchen with the aroma of tuna fish and melted cheese. A steaming loaf of homemade bread rested nearby.

"Father will you please mention my boys in your blessing tonight?" asked Lorraine. "I say a rosary every night for their safety because I'm afraid they're headed to Vietnam."

Chuck leaned forward, glaring at his wife with eyes aflame with blood and alcohol. Even with guests, he liked his meals to be quiet affairs, where he controlled the conversation.

"Certainly, Lorraine," said Father Paul, his cheeks growing redder with each sip of his drink. It was a color Sean recognized on days he had altar boy duty. The priest's face was occasionally the same shade before morning Mass and his hands trembled so violently sometimes that Sean had difficulty pouring wine into his communion chalice. That's when Father Paul hissed: "Pour it slower so you don't miss." It was the priest's responsibility to finish the leftover consecrated wine and he always did so with gusto.

"Heavenly Father, please watch over the Gerard family, especially the boys in the Army, and all the troops in Vietnam," said the priest. "Please guide President Johnson in these difficult times. And thank you for your bounty which we are about to receive."

Father Paul looked over at his associate.

"Father Ken, would you like to add a blessing?" he asked, picking up his martini glass.

"Yes, I would," replied the young priest. "It's been a long time since I've enjoyed a real family meal like this. No offense to our dinners at the rectory, Father Paul. Let's join hands."

The group followed the priest's instructions.

"Thank you Lord for this special evening and the sense of family in this kitchen tonight," said Father Ken. "May I count on your guidance and the help of the Gerards as I learn to help this parish? Amen."

Father Ken eyed the pan of hot tuna casserole bubbling in the middle of the table.

"I'm starved," he announced, taking off his jacket. His biceps strained the fabric of his short-sleeve priest's cassock.

"You're in great shape, Father," admired Chuck, studying the priest's physique. "Are you a weightlifter?"

"Yes, I work out all the time," he replied. "But I bulked up the old fashioned way, trimming frozen beef carcasses at my dad's butcher shop. These arms came in handy when I played football at Ohio State."

"Oh, sure. I should have recognized your last name sooner," exclaimed Chuck as he slapped Father Ken on the shoulder. "Wasowski and Sons butcher shop! My parents sent me there as a kid. Best cuts of meat in town. And you were some football player in high school too. I remember you making the Cleveland all-city team."

"I owe a lot to those days working with my parents," said the young priest. "Besides learning the value of hard work, I also had a front row seat on life. My dad liked to say that a butcher shop is the best place to experience human nature. Although I would have to argue with that point now that I'm a priest."

"I never heard of a priest who played college football," interjected Sean.

"I'd like to offer a toast," offered Father Paul, lifting his glass so quickly a small ice cube sloshed out and landed in the mound of casserole Lorraine had just spooned on his plate. "To Saint Joseph's parish and to the new high school that opens in the fall, with the grace of God and the charity of our fellow Catholics in town."

Everyone raised a glass.

"Remember, a church in a small town is for more than prayer, it's the mortar that holds the foundation of the community together," intoned Father Paul. "It's the place that provides meaning, identity and belonging."

"Here, here!" cheered Chuck, emptying his tumbler.

The pastor turned to Sean.

"All the things your parents hope you will become, Sean, were taught to you in my school," he said expansively.

Chuck beamed at Father Paul, whose legacy after building St. Joseph's into a thriving parish of 400 families over the course of twenty years would be the new high school. Father Ken had been selected as the pastor's successor, and he would be on duty for the next year to ensure a smooth transition.

"Listen to Father Paul," instructed Chuck. "If it wasn't for the nuns down at the Catholic school keeping you and your friends in line, God only knows what kind of future you might have, probably not a good one. And don't make a face at me, Buster."

"I didn't make a face," responded Sean sullenly.

"Don't argue with me! I saw what I saw," he snapped. "Are you calling your father a liar?"

Sean knew from experience to ignore his father's trademark challenge. Just once, Sean thought, he'd like to scream: "I'm not only calling you a liar but an idiot as well." But the image of his father's leather belt always proved more potent than his resolve.

Father Paul nodded his approval at Chuck.

"That's right, the nuns have straightened out more than one young man in this community," agreed Father Paul.

"Well, I think the mothers of this town had a few things to do with raising their sons to do the right thing," chimed in Lorraine. "At least that's how it is in this house."

"Lorraine makes a good point," said Father Ken. "I've seen the nuns work magic in the classroom with youngsters you wouldn't think had a chance. But the ones from good homes are always the easiest to reach." The young priest buttered a fresh slice of bread. "Chuck, Father Paul, the adults have been doing all the talking, let's hear from Sean," continued the priest. "Is there something you'd like to offer about the new high school? Go ahead, Sean, speak your mind."

Sean searched around the table for some sign of approval.

"Please go ahead young man," said his father, crossing his arms.

"Well, I've heard we're going to have to wear uniforms at the new school," moaned Sean. "Is it true? Can't we just wear regular clothes like last year? We're going to look a lot different than the kids at the public school."

Father Paul put down his fork. "Well, Sean, that's the point. You will look different and the reason is you are different. You are members of the one true faith. The uniforms will signal to the entire village our unity and commitment to our children, right down to the school monogram on every dress and tie. They will also underscore the code of discipline at the school."

Father Ken held up his hand. "Sean, don't get too worked up about the uniforms," said the priest, tossing his napkin on the table. "We are also going to field a football team in the Catholic Youth League for the first time. Just think of the recognition awaiting you and your friends when you represent your school. I am going to coach the freshman team."

"Well, at least there will be a reason for wearing a uniform at least on the football field," said Sean.

Chuck lurched forward in his seat.

"The youth of today are our future, Chuck. We must support them," Father Paul offered in Sean's defense, surreptitiously dropping a hand below the table with a morsel of bread for Frankie. "That's why I spend so much time with my students, meeting with them in the rectory, taking them on retreats. It's about letting them know someone in authority cares."

Chuck watched Father Paul dourly as he spoke, pushing a last bite of casserole onto a quarter piece of bread and popping it into his mouth. He rubbed his chin as he chewed.

"The problem with society today is its lack of structure," began Chuck. "Look at my boys in the Army. Hell, our family's been fighting this country's battles since the Civil War. There were Gerards at Gettysburg for God's sake. My boys are in the Army with a little war going on over in Southeast Asia. Heck, that's what you hope for, get in, do your duty, maybe come out with a commission. Do you think people in this town even care? Heck, no. All they see on TV are these college kids protesting. We're fighting a war to save them from communism! You'd think they'd be grateful. To hell with them all! Excuse me Father, but that's how I feel. The problem with today's youth is they have no patriotism. It's shameful. There will be revolution in the streets before it all ends. These kids today could never have done what my generation accomplished. We stopped Hitler and the Japs."

Several drops of sweat slid off Chuck's forehead, meandering down his cheeks to fall on his plate. He loosened his tie.

"Everything is changing," complained Chuck, opening his arms wide in frustration. "Look at our faith. No more Latin Mass, lay people giving communion, even talk of priests being allowed to marry and raise families. What has happened to the mystery, the tradition, the grandeur of our religious ceremonies? Who ever said "change is good' should have stayed away from my Catholic faith."

The monologue lost steam as Lorraine cleared the plates and the gurgling of a percolator on the gas stove distracted the guests. Lorraine served coffee with her signature cheesecake, baked square on a homemade crust of graham crackers.

"Chuck, I understand your feelings about the church," empathized Father Paul. "I've been a priest a long time. But the institution will survive. I'm more worried about society. We live in a post-Christian age in which the world of the flesh holds a strong attraction. Few, if any, of the people in this parish can say that they have not been seduced by materialism and sensual pleasures. Based on what I hear in the confessional, few, if any, can say they have not given into its siren call."

"In the confessional booth, Father!" exclaimed Lorraine.

"Not to worry Lorraine, I'm talking in general terms," instructed the elder priest. "What is said in the confessional stays in the confessional. But the trends are revealed there and in my counseling. I'm not going to sugar-coat this, members of our parish are succumbing in greater numbers—outside the sanctity of marriage and with partners who are not their spouses."

"That's as old as the Bible, Father, you can't stop human nature," said Lorraine, patting Chuck's arm. "We are programmed to have sex and some are more inclined that way than others."

"Yes, Lorraine, but I'm talking about a moral code that is not being followed, I'm talking about monogamy, I'm talking about upholding wedding vows with the same commitment as a priest upholds his vow of celibacy," he said with finality.

"But we're not helplessly at the mercy of our inclination to sin," suggested Lorraine. "We should not underestimate the power of prayer."

"Your devotion to your daily rosary is well known throughout the parish, Lorraine," smiled Father Paul. "You are a role model."

Sean coughed nervously.

"Can you please bring up a different subject to talk about?" pleaded Sean.

"Stay out of it, Sean," barked Chuck.

"I want to get back to Chuck's point about today's young people," interrupted Father Ken. "I think every generation finds a way to test the establishment. Man's nature is to cling to his beliefs. Whenever we confront something that contradicts a conclusion we cherish, we reject it, often not even comprehending the messenger. Blaming these complex issues on today's youth because they are being vocal is far too simplistic."

Chuck threw his fork on his dessert plate, putting his face in his hands, only the top of his crew cut visible to guests at the table. "I cannot believe what is happening to this country I fought to serve," he groaned. "Look at the role models of today's young people, long-hair, pot-smoking, free-loving pains-in-the-ass, if you ask me. Hell, their music is just one big celebration about getting high. On top of that, you got people burning their draft cards, Martin Luther King agitating the Negroes. Where is it all going to end?"

"Chuck, we can't control what's happening in society," soothed the young priest. "Look to your family, young Sean here, and Lorraine, protect them. Ask God for guidance. He has an answer for those who seek his help."

Chuck sat up straight to look directly at Sean.

"I've raised all my sons to do the right thing, to live by a code of conduct," said Chuck. "My rules are simple ones. Never lie, respect others, always stick together and above all, never give up." Chuck paused for effect. "Oh, there's one more thing that the Gerard boys know well. A Gerard never dies from a hit in the head—our skulls are just too thick."

Chuck's gentle laughter about the last family rule lightened the mood in the kitchen. Even Sean smiled at his father. Lorraine used the moment to begin clearing the table. Father Ken pitched in to speed up the work.

"Father Ken, what are your thoughts about our parish?" asked Lorraine.

"Lorraine, it's only been a few months since my new assignment," answered the priest as he returned to the table. "But there are so many demands that some days I don't even have time to read a newspaper."

"I'll add you to my prayer list when I say my rosary tonight," offered Lorraine.

"That's wonderful," said the priest. "I'm adjusting to the loneliness of being a parish priest, something Father Paul counseled me about, but I take solace in a wonderful night like tonight."

"What about the football team?" blurted Sean.

"That's my first big challenge," replied Father Ken. "It will be difficult to build a team from the ground up, but I'm confident we can succeed. Sean, I want you and your friends to know that everyone has an equal chance. I hope you'll consider trying out."

"You can count on Sean being there," boasted Chuck.

As the conversation waned and darkness thickened outside, Chuck slouched in his chair and stroked his stomach.

"This has been an great evening and I want to thank both our visitors and my wife," effused Chuck, clapping his hands in approval. "Father Ken, as president of the Knights of Columbus, you can count on our full support to help get the football team off to a good start."

Frankie stirred under the table, coughing loudly as he moved away from Father Paul's chair. His little body suddenly started to convulse, his breath coming in rapid bursts as he fought to clear his throat. Father Paul bent over to check on his dog just as Frankie retched a runny mass of partially decomposed bread and dog food all over Chuck's shiny wingtips.

"Your dog just puked on my shoes," marveled a disbelieving Chuck. The corner of Sean's mouth curved up, which he quickly hid with his napkin. The head of the Gerard household was momentarily frozen in his seat, his shoes dripping in dog vomit. Chuck tried to salvage the situation by sliding his feet out of his shoes, pretending to be unruffled by the conduct of the canine intruder.

"Please forgive my precious little one," apologized Father Paul. "He's not been feeling well lately and this is of great concern to me. Frankie is all I have in the way of a family or best friend."

"Don't forget all those children at the school you've helped over the years, Father Paul," reassured Chuck. "They look up to you."

Father Paul started to say something, and then shook his head in silence, a painful sadness crossing his face.

"I have the early Mass tomorrow," announced Father Paul, scooping his dog into his arms. "I should get Frankie to bed."

The priestly entourage headed out of the kitchen with Chuck, Sean, and Lorraine in tow.

Father Paul and Ken stopped in the foyer.

"Sean, I'm taking all the new altar boys to Cedar Point amusement park for a long weekend, you are welcome to come along," offered the priest.

"I can't, Father," said Sean quickly. "I promised my friends I'd go fishing with them tomorrow."

"Sean, if you ever need my help, come to the rectory, I'll always hear you out," said the priest, raising his right hand. The Gerards bowed their heads. "May the blessing of almighty God, Father, Son and Holy Ghost descend upon you and remain with you forever." By the time the Gerards finished making the sign of the cross, the priests were out the door.

"Chuck, I hope to see you in confession soon," reminded Father Paul as stepped out on the porch.

Chuck guided the priests out to their car in the driveway. Sean headed to the kitchen to help his mother finish the last of the dishes, drying them with a towel after the rinsing. Soon, Chuck swayed into the kitchen, still in his stocking feet.

"Sean, clean off my shoes after you're finished with those dishes," commanded Chuck. "That's a direct order. And stay away from the power plant tomorrow. Fish down by the park. It's a lot safer there. Mark my words, Buster."

Chuck abruptly walked out of the kitchen.

Sean looked at his mother and shook his head. "He treats me like one of his employees at the truck factory," moaned Sean.

Lorraine threw her arms around her son, pressing her cheek against his face and kissing him softly on the forehead. "Sean, my little one, you have such an aura of goodness," comforted Lorraine. "Don't waste your precious energy trying to understand your father. You will always have my support and love."

"Yes, but what about my dad's love?" countered Sean.

"Sean, your father is a wonderful provider for this family," said Lorraine. "That's how he shows he cares about you."

"Sometimes that's not enough for me," said Sean, pulling away from his mother.

"Enjoy your summer while you can, the time will go fast," said Lorraine, pointing her finger at Sean. "Remember this from your mother: the friends you grow up with are your friends for life, everyone else you meet later in your journey will only be acquaintances. Never take them for granted. Now, Monsieur Sean, go to bed."

CHAPTER SIX

The sound of rifle fire cracked the early morning quiet. Three short bursts: *Blam! Blam! Blam!* could be heard over the gulls squawking near the shoreline.

"Crazy Dell must be shooting rats again," observed Sean to the other Caper Brothers as they pedaled their bikes toward the tackle and boat rental business named for the legendary rodent hunter of Vineyard Beach.

Dell Pilot liked nothing better than to stand in the doorway of his one-room tackle shop and squeeze off rounds from his .22 automatic rifle. There never seemed to be any end to the rats that scurried around his place looking for fish scraps. The rats were so abundant that Dell was accused of breeding the vermin under his pier simply for target practice. Dell had invented so many ways to foil his prey, Jimmy Moran declared him the Leonardo da Vinci of rat killers. His latest invention was arsenic-laced dough balls. He made these lethal pellets by hand and strategically planted them around his property. He especially enjoyed luring rats with the laced wads he placed on top of pilings that held his pier off the water. That way, when he shot a rat, the dead varmint would tumble backwards and splash dramatically into the lake. Dell delighted in the sound of the enemy hitting the water. It was his way of connecting with his watery surroundings.

Dell shoved his baseball hat back on his gray head and held up his hand as the boys approached down his rickety pier.

"Quiet, you! I'm about to dispatch another bastard into the hereafter," gloated Dell as he sighted down the barrel of his rifle in the direction of the lake.

Blam. Blam. Dell's two shots launched a large brown rat off the end of the pier.

"Mother Erie, please embrace another one of God's creatures to your bosom," cheered Dell, closing one nostril with his free hand to blow a load of snot onto the deck. "That was a fine shot if I do say so myself."

Dell set his gaze on Sean.

"You boys stay away from my dough balls if you know what's good for ya," warned Dell. "If you get any arsenic on your skin, it might get into your blood stream and make you sick as hell."

The Caper Brothers piled their bikes and fishing gear near the side of Dell's shack. They scampered past the fisherman to get a good look at the rat carcass bobbing on the surface.

The trick to tolerating Dell Pilot was to stand upwind of him. His body reeked of rotting fish and old sweat. Dell filleted fish daily and his idea of a bath was dipping his hands into a bucket of lake water and splashing some on his face. His trademark green work pants and shirt were encrusted with dried fish blood and guts. He rubbed his whiskers when he talked, occasionally smearing in the remnants of the day's catch into his gray stubble.

"You boys fixing on renting a boat or are you sneaking behind the power plant on the cheap as usual?" prodded Dell, nodding in the direction of the Vineyard Beach landmark looming next door. "I've seen the security guard this morning walking the perimeter. He doesn't often do that. You better watch yourself if you're going through the fence."

Dell started hopping from foot to foot.

"Maybe one of you will get lucky and land the first Coho salmon around here," he said excitedly. "No one's claimed the $500 prize yet. Of course, every nibble you get on your line today you'll be yelling, Coho, Coho, Coho! Hell, you'll be lucky to pull up a measly carp."

Dell did a brisk business nine months of the year renting boats to customers trying to take advantage of schooling fish drawn by the coal-burning plant's discharge. Every day, the power complex sucked thousands of gallons of prime Lake Erie water to cool its turbines. The warm water pumped back attracted white bass and yellow perch from miles around.

"Hey, Dell! Look over there on the power line to your motor wench," shouted Buddy Trotz, his voice carrying across the small cove protecting the boat launch. "See that big rat crawling down near the motor?"

"Yeah, I see it, you dumb bastard," fumed Dell, spinning in the direction of Buddy's pointed finger. "Why are you yelling at the top of your lungs? I'm standing right here for Christ's sake."

He raised his rifle and fired a single bullet through the rat's head. As the target fell into the lake, Dell held his gun aloft in victory.

"You boys ought to hang around longer, you're natural rat bait," teased Dell. "I might hire you four to sit on my pier. You might attract more rats than my special dough balls."

Dell put another round into the chamber and slammed the bolt home.

"Wouldn't you boys have more fun hanging out at the counter at the Vineyard Beach Pharmacy talking with Veronica Maggione?" challenged Dell, pausing to wipe his nose on his sleeve. "You'll have better luck ogling the best tits this side of Cleveland with the rest of the horny toads around here than trying to catch a Coho."

"That's a fine idea, old man!" exclaimed Jimmy. "I can see Veronica leaning over that counter...what a sight. That pharmacist knew what he was doing when he married that she devil."

"Sorry, gang, but we've got other business," declared Sean. "I've heard Dell say it a dozen times, the time to go fishing is any day that ends in 'y' and this is one of those days."

"Then git off my pier before I decide I don't like you four any more," ordered Dell. "You can pick your bikes up on your way back, if I don't decide to sell them to the first passerby."

The boys collected their fishing gear and moved out, the four big stacks of the power plant belching columns of smoke off in the distance, providing a good wind gauge for the fishermen. Gray fly-ash as fine as baby powder painted almost an acre on the edge of the property, the gritty residue from the coal-fired furnaces pushed into large dunes. Brick storage buildings lined the perimeter, blocking a clear view of the poisoned landscape, the patch of ground as barren as the lunar surface.

"Just like Sean to be leading the way," snapped Jimmy. "Leader Boy to the rescue!"

"I'm not taking the bait this morning," retorted Sean. "It's too nice of a day for your bull."

The friends fell in behind Sean as he picked up the pace down a rutted path from Dell's, blades of tall grass along the route licking their bare knees as they hiked. They came to a stop in a small grove of oak trees about twenty feet from the plant's security fence. On the other side of the six-foot barrier, a warehouse shielded their approach. The boys could see a dump truck raised off the ground on blocks through large windows running to the building's roofline, panes missing here and there like teeth that had rotted and fallen away.

"Okay, here we go," whispered Sean. "Remember, once we get inside, stay low and move fast down to the beach. If the security guard sees us, start running and don't stop for nothing."

The troupe stepped out from the shelter of the trees and moved quickly to the fence.

Johnny Pasquale reached the fence first, grabbing a section of the wire mesh near an anchor post. He peeled back a four-foot section, allowing the group enough space to wiggle on their stomachs onto the property. Once released, the section of fence flapped back neatly against the pole as if never disturbed.

"If my dad could only have seen his heavy wire cutters in action," claimed Johnny.

"If he found out, you'd probably get your ass kicked," warned Jimmy, dusting off his legs.

They rounded the corner of the warehouse, ready to navigate the fly-ash pit down to the beach.

Buddy Trotz ran ahead. Enough rain had fallen recently to pack the surface of the ash field, making it possible to climb the mountains of gray dust. Buddy dropped his fishing pole to scoot up the nearest heap, his high-top, canvas sneakers leaving a trail of corrugated tracks.

"Hey, watch this," Buddy yelled to the boys from his perch fifty feet above. Buddy leaped head first off the top, doing a forward somersault as he flew through the air, landing on his feet halfway down.

"I didn't know Polish pigs could fly," bellowed Jimmy.

Buddy raced down the slope until he collapsed in a sunken spot where the powder was a deeper shade of gray.

"This feels like walking on Jell-O," Trotz exclaimed to his friends, bouncing up and down on the ash. "This is cool. You guys should try this."

As the boys approached the lip of the small pit, Buddy began to sink. His bouncing had worked water to the surface, turning the ground into a thick soup. They froze at the sight of their friend slowly disappearing into the muck.

"Stop moving around," instructed Sean.

Buddy tried to lift his legs out of the ooze, only to see the ash inching up over his knees.

"You guys better do something fast," screamed Buddy, his voice breaking. "I'm doing down fast. Go for help!"

"We won't have to go for help if you don't lower your voice," hissed Sean. "Your big mouth will alert the security guard and then he'll drag your fat ass to jail."

Sean took a few tentative steps into the pit, extending a hand to Buddy. Johnny yanked Sean clear by the back of his shorts just as he started to slip into the watery mush.

"Help me for God's sake," cried Buddy, his eyes red with tears. "I'm still sinking!"

The boys held out their fishing poles in desperation. Clutching a rod in each hand, Buddy stopped his descent at mid-thigh.

"Jimmy, run back to that storage building with the broken windows and see if there's something inside we can use to pull Buddy out of this muck," commanded Sean. "Kick the side door in if you have to. Johnny and I'll stay here with Trotz."

"Hurry, Jimmy! Hurry. My grip is starting to slip," howled Buddy. "Do something, damn it."

"Stay calm Buddy, we'll get you out," instructed Sean. "Stop yelling and moving around, you're just making it worse. Jimmy will be back in a few minutes, hang in there."

Buddy's head drooped in resignation.

"I don't want to die in this shit," he moaned.

Suddenly, the pole in Buddy's right hand snapped, sending him another inch deeper. Johnny scrambled for another pole and extended it to his terrified friend.

"I'm almost up to my balls in this stuff," whimpered Buddy. "If I sink to my waist, I'll never get out. I can't even feel my feet anymore. Please go to the security shack for help! Now!"

"Don't give up," comforted Sean. "Here comes Moran!"

Jimmy arrived panting, a two-by-four in one hand and a length of oily rope in the other. He tied the rope in the middle of the plank and threw it to Buddy, who clutched it tightly to his chest.

Sean, Johnny and Jimmy lined up, pulling the rope over their shoulders.

"On the count of three," ordered Sean.

They leaned hard against the rope, digging the heels of their sneakers into the dirt for traction. With a yell, the boys yanked in unison, fighting the suction power of the wet goop entrapping their friend.

"Don't stop! Don't stop! Don't stop!" yelled Trotz. "I'm breaking free."

Buddy launched out of the muck with the power of an exploding champagne cork, clearing the pit and slamming into his friends. All four boys tumbled into a heap.

The whooping and hollering at Buddy's deliverance echoed across the field.

"You did it. You did it," whispered Buddy. "You saved my life. Thank you, thank you, thank you."

The sharp blast of a whistle ended the celebration.

A uniformed security guard with a black billy club secured to his belt raced through an obstacle path of fly-ash moguls in their direction.

"Freeze right there you idiots," he shouted, still 20 yards away.

"That fat guy can't catch us," hissed Jimmy. "Grab the fishing gear and let's get out of here. I know a place where we can hide."

They broke into a run, retracing their steps to the warehouse. The side door hung open.

"In here quick and shut the door," instructed Jimmy. "That guard's not gonna spend all day looking for us. Hey, there's something inside you have to see, too."

Jimmy put his finger to his mouth and then scooted under the dump truck in the center of the building, motioning for his friends to join him.

"Now, everybody quiet," coached Jimmy.

The heavy breathing and footsteps of the security guard could be heard through the open windows as he paced the length of the storage shed. After a few minutes, he gave up, heading back towards the power plant.

"The coast is clear," said Jimmy gleefully. "You won't believe what I found when I was in here looking for something to save Trotz from the pig shit."

Jimmy strode to the wall under the windows and knelt to examine an elaborate heating coil that encircled the inside of the building. Using his pocketknife, he scraped off years of gritty rust from a small section.

"This old radiator is solid copper, just as I hoped," yipped Jimmy, jumping to his feet. "Do you have any idea what this is worth? We can get forty cents a pound for this stuff. I know a salvage place in Lorain where no questions are asked. We just pull up, dump our haul on a scale, weigh it and get our cash. I went there with my dad a couple of times."

"What a great caper this would be," Jimmy said, running his hand through his mop of red hair. "We can chop up this copper with an ax, throw it over the fence, load it in the trunk of a car and make one hundred bucks just like that."

"There's one big hole in your plan, Master Thief," interrupted Sean. "Are you forgetting that we have learning permits but no car?"

Jimmy approached Buddy.

"What about your sister's old Fairlane?" he asked. "It's still just sitting on your street getting plastered by bird shit."

"The reason it's parked out front is because the transmission is screwed up," said Buddy, scraping mud from his shin. "It only goes in drive. No reverse at all. If you're willing to get out and push if we have to back up, it's a deal."

Later that afternoon, after retrieving their bikes from Dell's and changing clothes, the boys returned in the Fairlane, Sean steering the car off the road and into the field, stopping near the hole in the security fence. Jimmy popped the trunk and unloaded an ax and two weathered Army blankets.

"Are you sure you want to go back in there after what happened to Trotz today?" demanded Sean, pointing to the warehouse on the other side. "If this doesn't work it's going down as your idea. Not that blaming you would help us any if we get caught."

"Relax, Leader Boy, it's time for The Caper Brothers to make their mark," said Jimmy. "We'll finish this job before any one sees us. Just don't chicken out now, we need all of us to make this work."

"Let's get this over with so you'll stop yakking about another caper this summer," sighed Sean.

Jimmy outlined the scheme. He and Sean would go into the warehouse to chop up the radiator, haul the pieces to the edge of the property and throw them over the fence. Johnny and Buddy would use the blankets to catch the incoming chunks, packing them in the Fairlane's trunk.

In an hour, the boys had crammed ten sections of radiator into the Fairlane's trunk for the trip to the salvage yard. The rear end sagged under the weight as the vehicle approached the main road.

As the car slowed to go over the curb, Jimmy opened the passenger door, forcing Sean to brake quickly. Jimmy pulled a Zippo lighter from his pocket and started flicking the flint.

"Now what?" shouted Sean.

"Let's go back and start a little fire to cover our tracks," said Jimmy.

"Forget it, Moran," stated Sean. "Get in the car now! We're leaving."

Jimmy slammed the door and turned on the radio as the Fairlane emerged from the trees.

"Why's everybody so quiet?" crowed Jimmy, his face aglow. "I told you this would work."

"Maybe we're a little nervous," observed Johnny from his spot in the back seat. "We're not used to all this crap the way you are."

"Turn that song up," yelped Jimmy, bouncing on the front seat. "It's a good omen for our trip into Lorain."

"You know that it would be untrue, you know that I would be a liar, if I was to say to you, girl, we couldn't get much higher."

The group chimed in for the chorus to the Doors hit, filling the car with the sound of their young voices.

"Come on baby, light my fire, come on baby, light my fire, try to set the night on fire."

"We really set that place on fire didn't we, Caper Brothers?" declared Jimmy, turning to smile at Buddy and Johnny. "Just wait till we see those greenbacks in our hands, then we'll really light a fire."

The Fairlane crept along in traffic, the rear bumper just off the ground. Sean craned his neck to see out of the windshield, the nose of the car pointed in the air because of the weight in back.

The Lorain Metal Salvage Company was a one-man operation at the end of a short street near the steel mill district. The sign on the garage door read, "Honk for Service." The Fairlane swung around in the gravel parking lot, kicking up a cloud of dust. All four doors opened, disgorging the boys to push the car back to the loading dock.

"What you boys hauling in that jalopy?" challenged the salvage owner as he pulled up the garage door to reveal a large scale resting on the floor.

Jimmy turned to his friends as they ascended the steps.

"Let me do the talking," he whispered.

"We've got some copper we found in an old barn that belonged to my grandfather," said Jimmy, extending his hand. "We'd like to put it on your scale and find out how much it's worth."

"Come ahead then," said the man as he rubbed his enormous belly. "Be quick about it."

The scale easily accommodated the load. The boys caught their breath after unloading the trunk, studying the owner as he calculated the copper's weight.

"You got one hundred and eighty nine pounds here at twenty cents a pound," he said, shoving a pencil back behind his ear. "I'll give you thirty seven dollars and eight cents."

"I thought salvage copper went for forty cents a pound," said Jimmy, alarm spreading across his face. "Are you trying to gyp us?"

"Take it or leave it," said the owner with a shrug of his shoulders. "How'd you like me to call the police and you can explain this barn story to them when they get here? It's going to be fifteen cents a pound in another minute."

Jimmy's hand shook as he held it out.

"Okay, we'll take it," he said.

The owner counted out the money.

"Now get the hell out of here before I call the cops," he said, escorting the troupe out and slamming the garage door.

The boys retreated to the Fairlane for the ride to Vineyard Beach.

"All that work and risk for a measly thirty seven bucks," complained Sean as they pulled away. "We're out of our minds. That's some fire for our nine-dollar share. That is the last time we listen to your stupid Caper Brother ideas, Master Thief."

"We'll see about that, Leader Boy," said Jimmy.

CHAPTER SEVEN

Candy DeLane slipped on her bikini top and adjusted the little red triangles that cupped her firm breasts. She snapped the back of her suit bottom free from the space between her curvy cheeks. Her leather sandals flopped off her heels as she navigated the hallway outside her bedroom and moved down the spiral back staircase into the kitchen. Before heading outside, she checked to see if the maintenance man had skimmed the debris from the pool sunken into the stone patio.

The day beckoned clear and warm. Candy stretched out on a cushioned lounge chair, smoothing tanning cream over her freshly shaved legs. Her skin tingled as she rubbed in the oil, her hand lingering for a moment on her stomach, the sensation of moisture and sun enhancing her pleasure.

The smell of cigarette smoke announced the approach of her father.

"I hope you're going to put on a swimsuit before you start your sun bathing," teased Weldon, dragging on his unfiltered Pall Mall.

"Daddy, you are so stupid," replied Candy. "I have a bathing suit on. It's called a bikini, in case you've never seen one."

"There's not enough fabric in that bikini of yours to make a decent hand towel," said Weldon, bending his lean frame to kiss his daughter on the forehead. "It's a good thing your mother isn't here to see you parading around with barely enough covered to be respectable. This isn't a nudie beach, child."

"Maybe a nudie beach would be good for this boring little town," said Candy, looking at her dad over the top of her sunglasses. "When did you get so old-fashioned? I can remember when you and Mom liked to skinny dip in our pool in California."

"It was dark, darling, and you were supposed to be sleeping in your bedroom, not looking out the window at a couple of old lovers," said Weldon as he sat at the end of Candy's lounge chair. "I miss those days, seeing your mother gliding through the water in the moon light."

Candy patted her father's hand.

"Daddy, you're an old romantic," she said. "Just remember, I miss her too. And don't worry about anyone seeing me in my bikini. I haven't made any friends here yet and the nearest house is blocks from here. Don't be so uptight!"

"Uptight!" replied Weldon. "This isn't California, Candace DeLane. It's Ohio, for God's sake. Folks around here are a bit more conservative."

"And I guess wearing a bikini is going to keep me from becoming a decent woman," countered Candy, pulling her golden hair back into a ponytail. "If you really cared about me, you wouldn't have made this dumb move to Ohio."

"Candy, darling, I had the best intentions," pleaded Weldon, throwing his arms in the air. "California held nothing but bad, old memories. I thought we needed a fresh start. Please try to give Vineyard Beach a chance."

"Easy on the 'we' stuff, Dad," said Candy as she lathered more lotion on her arms. "It's hard being the new kid in such a small town. Just be happy you didn't raise a whiner. This sounds crazy, but I want school to start so at least I can meet some people."

Weldon inhaled the last of his cigarette.

"Keep your spirits up," said her father. "This too shall pass."

"Yeah, you're always saying that," said Candy, suddenly looking sad. "Can't it just pass a little faster?"

She rolled onto her stomach.

"Can you put some lotion on my back?" asked Candy.

Weldon picked up the bottle and squirted a healthy portion of white cream on his daughter's shoulders and worked it down to her waist.

"Why not try meeting some people at the club?" challenged Weldon. "Look what it's done for your dear old dad. I've got myself back in shape and even have a date lined up. Not too shabby for a guy pushing fifty."

"That would be gross, dad," said Candy, glancing back over her shoulder at her father. "You know me better than that. I have nothing in common with those stuck-up country club babes. I'm surprised you'd even say that. But thanks for letting me know that you'll be entering the dating scene. This should be interesting."

"Just trying to be a helpful father," said Weldon with a grin. He gave his daughter a pat on the back of her thigh.

"Don't you have someone else to bug this early in the morning?" taunted Candy.

"As a matter of fact I do, smarty pants," replied Weldon. "I'm headed for the office. At least there my advice is followed. By the way, I heard from one of the locals that a big wedding is planned this morning over at Saint Joe's. My helicopter is finally fixed so I want to get going before I cause a commotion during the bride and groom's big moment."

"So, are you going to tell me who your date is with?" asked Candy, propping herself up on her elbows. "A daughter deserves to know these things in advance."

"I met her on the practice range at the club," Weldon said, standing up. "Man, can she hit a golf ball. But that's all I saying for now."

"And how old is this new woman?"

"She's in her mid thirties and a real go-getter," Weldon said. "She does a lot of business at the club with all the hotshot doctors."

"Couldn't you at least date someone a little closer to your age?"

"Well, I didn't ask to see her birth certificate," Weldon said, walking off the patio.

"And if it gets serious, you'll be the first to know."

"You could at least share her name with me."

"Not yet, I'm going real slow."

"Well, if you're starting to keep secrets, then so will I," huffed Candy.

Weldon turned on the bottom step. "I'm just protecting her privacy. Don't go sensitive on me. You'll know everything in good time. Are you going to light a candle over at the church today?"

"Yes, Daddy," Candy said, looking directly at her father. "I go every week, just like mom requested on that last night in the hospital. It's a way to honor her life."

Candy tossed a towel at her father.

"You wouldn't be hurt by a visit to the church," she said in mock anger. "God might answer your prayers too, once he gets over the shock of seeing you in His house."

Weldon looked down for a moment.

"After all that's happened in my life, I've really questioned my faith," he said. "I guess I'll stay a CEO for now, my daughter."

"What's a CEO?" asked Candy.

"I'll go to church with you on *Christmas* and *Easter only*," Weldon said with a laugh. "That's my promise."

Candy watched her father march towards the helicopter pad. She loved the man, even more since her mother died. The sound of her father sobbing in his room for days after the funeral had touched her as deeply as her mother's death.

"I hope he finds some peace again," whispered Candy, waving to the helicopter as it lifted off. "Heck, I hope I find some peace soon."

Candy languished in the padded chaise, turning slowly from her back, to her sides, to her front, working for the perfect skin tone. She took energy from the sun. It helped to ease her moodiness, something that had plagued her more since the death of her mother. She didn't hurry. The wedding would not be over till noon.

When the sun moved overhead, Candy tied her long braids into a knot, and slipped a T-shirt and shorts over her bikini. She moved slowly down the long driveway to Lake Boulevard, whistling softly in the light breeze. The last of the wedding guests headed to their cars as she crossed onto the church property. She paused at the side doors, knowing that the candle stand was just inside.

Candy surveyed the interior, the scent of roses and smoldering wax hung in the air. White pedals dotted the carpet up the center aisle, a trail of floral love leading to the front doors. The leather cushion felt warm as she eased onto the kneeler in front of the burning candles.

She gazed up at the statue of the Blessed Virgin, her arms open to receive the prayers of the suffering. Lifting a long wooden match from the box on the side of the stand, she held it over a flame. Slowly, she moved the smoldering tip to the wick of a candle.

"Oh, Blessed Mary, I miss Mom so much," she prayed. "Please guide me and my father in the days ahead."

Suddenly she sensed the presence of someone behind her. She jerked around as a powerful hand engulfed her wrist.

"You're shaking a bit, my child," said a kind voice. "Here, let me be of assistance."

He held the match steady, causing the wick to burst into flame.

Candy stood up to face of the pastor of St. Joseph's parish, Father Paul Sterner, holding his poodle, Frankie.

"You seem startled," said the priest with a smile. "Didn't you hear me walking up the aisle?"

"You surprised me. I didn't know you were near until the last moment. I was focused on trying to light my candle."

"There, it's done and your prayers are on their way," the priest said studying Candy intently. "I know just about every child in this parish, but I'm afraid I've never laid eyes on you, young lady."

The priest grasped Candy gently by the elbow.

"What brings you to church on such a pretty day?" wondered the priest. "I hope your need for the Blessed Lady isn't a dire one."

The priest caressed Candy's cheek. "But enough of my interruption," he said bowing at the waist. "I ask only one indulgence, please tell me your name."

"My name is Candace DeLane," she said extending her hand. "I just moved to Vineyard Beach from California with my dad. I'll be starting school at Saint Joseph's in the fall."

The priest pumped her hand vigorously.

"I'm Father Paul Sterner, the pastor of this parish," he said. "You can call me Father Paul. This fluff ball in my arms is my friend, Frankie. And your mother, where is your mother?"

"She died in a car accident exactly five years ago this summer," Candy said eyeing the sturdy, gray-haired priest. "I'm here keeping a promise to my mom so her soul rests in peace."

"My poor child, to lose a parent at such a young age, especially your mother," lamented the priest, shaking his head. "And to see how you've recovered by making this pilgrimage to the church. How good of you. It must be difficult being in a new town and not having a mother to help you get settled."

Father Paul flicked a strand of Candy's hair off her shoulder. "God bestowed many gifts upon you. I didn't know your mother, but I can see from her daughter that she was a beautiful woman."

Candy blushed at the compliment and dropped her head in embarrassment.

"We've only just met, but please know that I care about all the children of Saint Joseph's parish," Father Paul said, placing his hand under Candy's chin. "I will do anything within my power to help, like the father of any family. You can confide in me, my dear. I'll never break your confidence."

The priest draped his arm around Candy's shoulders.

"Please, follow me into the sanctuary," instructed Father Paul. "I want to show you something that will inspire you and we can take a moment to pray together in private."

Father Paul kept his arm around Candy as he led her up the stairs past the altar and through the main entrance into the sanctuary. Once inside, he closed the door and set the dead bolt, the load click of the lock startling Candy. The priest guided the young woman to a single kneeler in front of a framed likeness of St. Joseph. Candy knelt, seduced by the attention being paid to her by the holy man.

Frankie jumped from the Father Paul's grasp and scooted onto a cushioned wicker bed pushed against the wall under a small gold crucifix. He curled into a ball and fell asleep.

"This oil painting was a gift from his Holiness himself, given to the parish to celebrate the opening of the church," Father Paul said, standing behind Candy as he caressed the back of her neck. "The Vatican commissioned one of Rome's best painters to create this image of our patron saint, Joseph, Mary's husband. The faithful have received many blessings in this setting. You should feel comforted being here today, Candace."

She bowed her head.

"Take a few moments to make your offering," ordered Father Paul. As Candy prayed, the priest stepped to the back door of the sanctuary that led to the altar boys room on the far side of the church. He checked the hallway, and then quietly locked the door. He returned to stand over Candy, straddling her legs from behind as she knelt. He slid his black coat off. It fell to the floor next to Frankie.

"Concentrate now on your prayer," he commanded. "Keep your eyes on the painting of St. Joseph. He will hear you."

Father Paul inched closer, laying his hands on Candy's shoulders. She glanced at the priest's ordination ring, a symbol of his bond with God. She could smell the sweet red wine from the wedding Mass on his breath.

"You seem tense, little one," whispered Father Paul into her ear. "Don't worry, God is watching over you and so am I. We will protect you."

The priest gently massaged Candy's shoulders.

"Father, you're making me uncomfortable," cried Candy, attempting to rise off the kneeler.

"You haven't stayed long enough to say your prayers," insisted the priest, his voice suddenly loud. He pushed her back down on her knees.

His tone made Candy shiver. She tried to get up again. The priest held her on the kneeler.

"Keep your eyes on the painting," the priest ordered. "St. Joseph is looking directly at you."

His hands encircled her neck.

"There, there, my little one," he cooed softly. "No need to worry, you are safe with me."

The priest kissed the top of Candy's head, breathing in the scent of her tanning lotion and freshly shampooed hair. He released his grip to untie her ponytail.

Candy wanted to scream, to run, but fear froze her to the kneeler. Father Paul clamped his legs together, binding Candy's knees. He

57

tightened his grip around her throat and pressed his groin into the back of her head, sliding his crotch up and down.

"Yes, my child, yes," moaned the priest. "That's it. Don't move."

Candy shook her head to ward off a finger the priest tried to plunge between her lips. She attempted to scream, but no sound came out of her mouth.

"That's it, that's it … that's," groaned the priest, his breath catapulting out of his lungs.

The priest continued rubbing his pelvis against Candy's head until she felt the jerking motion of the priest's erection as he ejaculated in his trousers.

The priest's utterances woke Frankie. He let out a low howl.

"You have been a great help to me, more than you'll ever know," sighed Father Paul. "Thank you, my child."

The sound of footsteps echoing down the back hallway caused the priest to drop his hands from Candy's neck and step away from the kneeler.

"Father Paul, Father Paul," said a voice from the other side of the door. "It's me, Sean Gerard. I've cleaned up the altar boy's room after the wedding like you ordered. Are you in there? Why is the door locked?"

Sean banged on the door.

Frankie rose from his little bed and raced to the door, barking loudly.

"You need to see how much the wedding party tipped me for the service," yelled Sean.

He rattled the door handle.

"Open up, Father. You have to see this. Are you in there?"

Father Paul leaned over and licked the inside of Candy's ear.

"You'll go to hell if you tell a lie about me," he hissed. "I have complete control of this parish and its members. No one will take your word over mine. Remember that."

Father Paul moved away from Candy towards the door.

"Hold on a second Sean, I'm with someone," advised the priest. "Give us a minute."

"Stand up," commanded the priest, pointing at Candy as she staggered to her feet.

"Every member of this parish is beholden to me," he said in a low voice. "And now, so are you. Don't make a peep about today or you'll regret it the rest of your life."

"Now, compose yourself," he said soothingly. "Nothing happened here."

Father Paul threw open the door.

"Sean, come in young man," said Father Paul, spreading his arms wide. "What's all the screaming about? Okay, this better be good. Let's see what you have."

Sean held up a crisp twenty-dollar bill.

"Check this out, Father Paul," announced Sean. "Pretty generous, wouldn't you say?"

"Congratulations young man, I would have to agree with you, Master Sean," said the priest, admiring the bill. "As I always tell the new recruits, it pays to be an altar boy at a wedding."

Father Paul stepped aside, allowing Sean to enter the sanctuary. His face filled with light seeing Candy DeLane.

"What are you doing here?" blurted Sean.

"Let me make the formal introductions," said the priest.

"No need to Father, I know Candy DeLane," Sean declared, walking with his hand extended in her direction.

Candy stood silently, her arms crossed over her chest.

"What's wrong, you don't recognize me?" demanded Sean, looking intently at Candy. He dropped his hand.

Sean shot a bewildered glance at Father Paul.

"Uh, are you alright?" inquired Sean. "We have met before you know. I hope you haven't forgotten me already."

Candy inched towards the front door to the sanctuary, her eyes locked on Sean.

"Sean, since you have already been introduced, I can count on you to escort Candace out of the church," said Father Paul. "She was just leaving after a short visit to learn about our school and admire our famous painting of St. Joseph. The Ladies Auxiliary has invited me to lunch over in the church hall so I don't have time for chit chat. A priest must always serve his flock. I can't keep the ladies waiting. They hate it when I'm late."

Father Paul gestured for the two teenagers to wait, picking up his suit coat and Frankie off the floor.

"Here it is," declared the priest after rummaging through the coat's pockets. "Candace, I want you to have this holy card of St. Joseph so you'll have a memento of your visit. I hope to see you again soon."

Candy didn't move.

"Here, I'll hang on to it for you," said Sean, reaching for the holy card. It fluttered out of the priest's hand. As Sean snatched the card in mid-air, Candy dashed past the priest, running down the center aisle of the church, not stopping until she burst through the big wooden doors into the afternoon light.

"Don't just stand there, Sean, go after her," ordered Father Paul. "Report back to me if anything is amiss with that young lady."

Sean stuck the holy card in the pocket of his dress slacks and raced after Candy.

By the time Sean cleared the building, Candy had reached the far edge of the property. She leaned a shoulder against a tree, her head in her hands. As Sean pulled closer, she pushed off and hopped a ditch near the shoulder of Lake Boulevard. Sean reached Candy as she started to bolt into the street. He dragged her back by the top of her shorts.

"Hey, don't you believe in looking both ways before crossing a street!" exclaimed Sean, hanging onto one of Candy's belt loops. "You need to be more careful. Cars haul around that curve."

Candy spun around.

"Let me go! Just let me go!" she shrieked.

She smacked Sean's hand several times.

"Why are you hanging on to me?" she cried.

"I was just trying to keep you from getting hit by a car for God's sake," replied Sean. "I'm not trying to hurt you."

"Oh, Sean, I'm sorry," moaned Candy. "Here, just let go of me, please. I'm not going across the street without looking."

"Okay, but if you try to run into traffic again, I'm going to tackle you right here," said Sean, letting go of the belt loop.

Candy fell into the grass next to the ditch, dropped her head between her knees and wailed.

"Oh, why, why?" she said between sobs.

Sean looked alarmed, he had never witnessed anyone cry this hard in his life. Sean moved down next to Candy, wrapping his arms around the young girl and pulling her against his chest. The thought that Candy had been hurt made the anger rise in his throat.

"I'll be okay, just give me some time to calm down," sighed Candy, easing her head onto Sean's shoulder.

"What's happened?" inquired Sean gently. "You can tell me."

She looked up at Sean, her eyes red. "I need a friend now, Sean."

"I want to be your friend," said Sean.

Candy dropped her head.

She muttered something so softly Sean didn't understand.

"I'm sorry, I didn't hear you."

"If I told you something, something bad and evil, would you believe me no matter what?"

"Yes I would."

"Would you tell anyone else?" she pleaded.

"No, I'll keep your secret."

Candy rose out of the ditch, brushing grass from her legs.

"I can't talk anymore now, Sean," whispered Candy.

"I'll help you," said Sean, tears brimming in his eyes.

"I'm really messed up and need to be alone," she wailed. "I want to go home and lie down. I need to take a nap and forget this day."

CHAPTER EIGHT

"Dell, have you ever had a friend in trouble, but you weren't sure what to do to help?" asked Sean, perched on a rocker inside the old fisherman's cabin.

Dell jerked his bottle of Old Crow off an overhead shelf and poured a long draft into his coffee mug.

"It's awful early in the morning to be asking deep questions, Mister Gerard. I've not had my eye-opener yet," complained Dell. He twirled his finger in his cup, plopping the grimy digit in his mouth when he finished.

"Never take a cup of coffee with natural sweetener for granted," Dell chuckled, gulping deeply. "It's one of life's simple pleasures. And there aren't enough of them in this crazy world! So what important matter made you to ride all the way down here and knock on my door? Is this a philosophical question, or is trouble actually brewing? Let's get down to the nit and the grit."

"I'm not sure," said Sean. "But I do know we need some fresh air in here."

Sean cranked open the lone window in Dell's tackle shack.

"If you think there's trouble a coming, there's usually something bad about to happen," advised Dell. "That's been my experience. Not enough people trust their intuition. Everybody's trying so hard to be civilized and letting the so-called experts tell them how to live. It's they say this, and they advise that. Hell, if I ever find out who they are, I'm gonna ring their necks."

Dell's left eye suddenly fluttered uncontrollably. He smacked the side of his face in frustration.

"I'm not winking at you Mr. Gerard," growled Dell. "This damn tic just has a life of its own. I'm in for a long day if it's going this fast already. Maybe another sip of my coffee might settle things down."

"You drink too much of that special coffee," teased Sean, his head propped against the window screen to take advantage of a gust of fresh air.

"Sean, here's a tip from an old guy," Dell instructed, draining his mug. "Trouble is like rats. They both try to sneak up on you. You better start preparing yourself, my boy."

Dell lifted his .22 rifle from the rack over the door to his hut.

"Hell, look at this conflict," continued Dell, pointing the weapon out the window. "I know the rat bastards are out there and they know I'm in here. I don't even count causalities in this war. It's not important. The only thing that matters is executing my battle plan. If I do that, the furry bastards don't have a chance of getting the upper hand. Remember this, dealing with adversity boils down to personal initiative. When all else fails, you gotta count on yourself."

"Dell, I didn't know you were such a philosopher," Sean said with a wink.

"Well, are you going to share your thoughts on this matter or do I have to read your little mind?" asked Dell. "Hurry it up. It's a dog-eat-dog world out there, Sean. And right now, you're wearing the dog-food underwear. If you don't want your ass chewed on you better think of something."

"It's about a girl," revealed Sean.

"It's always about a girl," Dell interrupted, pouring another mug of coffee and bourbon. "Start at the beginning."

"I met this new girl," said Sean. "She's from California. Her name's Candy DeLane and I really like her."

"Do you mean the flying DeLanes? The rich folks buzzing the town all the time in that fancy helicopter?"

"Yup, Dell, those DeLanes," answered Sean.

"Sean, what are you doing getting friendly with a rich girl?" asked Dell, the coffee and bourbon making him perspire heavily. "There's no future in that. Rich people are different than you and me."

"What do you mean?" responded Sean.

"They rich!" steamed Dell. "They have money! You don't! See the difference? Jesus Christ, Gerard, if bullshit was money, you'd be the John D. Rockefeller of Vineyard Beach."

"Hey, I think this girl likes me."

"For God's sake, you not playing 'hide the pepperoni' and now she's missed her time of the month?" challenged Dell. "Lad, you're too young for such mischief."

"Dell, calm down," cautioned Sean. "I haven't even kissed her yet, but she's special that's for sure. But something upset her the other day when I saw her at Saint Joe's. I've got a bad feeling."

Dell leaned his rifle against the door jam and paced the floor of his cabin.

"Listen to your gut, boy," Dell advised, waving his arms in the air. "There's all kinds of evil in the world. There's natural evil and moral evil. A storm comes up off the lake and drowns a bunch of drunk fishermen, that's just plain old natural evil. Then there's the other kind, the conniving and thieving kind. That's just plain wickedness. That's when you see the real suffering of the innocent."

"I just hope to God that Candy wasn't hurt," said Sean, worry creeping into his voice.

"Those nuns over at that Catholic school of yours want you to believe an all-knowing God sees everything that happens," lectured Dell. "I don't accept an all-perfect God. He's a force for good but there's also a force for evil. But God doesn't know the future any better than us—so evil surprises him too. And if that can happen to the Big Guy, than you, wee man, are just shit leaking out of a dead rat."

Dell stopped pacing and perched on the edge of a metal folding chair to fill his coffee cup with Old Crow.

Sean started to edge towards the door. "Dell, did you ever care enough about someone to help them out of trouble?"

"Sure, there's my niece out in Michigan, who will inherit my boat operation one day," Dell admitted, slurping from his mug. "She's all the family I have. I care enough about her to sleep with my hands folded over my chest every night like I'm praying."

"Huh?" smirked Sean.

"That way if I die in my sleep, the mortician won't bill her for straightening my arms when rigor mortis freezes up my body," laughed Dell, slapping his knee. "I want to look like an angel resting in my casket."

"You are so caring, Dell."

"Well, I try to look on the bright side, cause life has a way of beating you down sometimes," said Dell, suddenly turning serious. "I know what you're feeling right now about this young lady. There was a special girl in my life once, my high school sweetheart. We were together fifteen years, then she ran off, said she needed freedom. She didn't have the courage to tell me there was someone else, but I found out in time. There's no worse betrayal in the world than to have a wife cheat on you. That's when I chucked everything and moved down here to this pier."

"Gosh, Dell that must have been terrible," moaned Sean.

"I've never told that to anyone and neither will you, if you want to stay my friend," Dell said, looking down at the floor. "Like my momma used to say, sadness comes in like a mouse, grief arrives like a rat. Maybe that's why shooting the furry bastards is so much fun."

Dell slammed his mug on a pine crate and crossed the room to stand in front of Sean.

"Before you go running out of here, mark my words, Sean," warned Dell, placing his hand on Sean's shoulder. "Understand that rats come in all sizes and varieties. The two-legged ones, if you catch my drift, are the hardest to stop. But never show mercy to a rat, they're only out to cause harm. Just be careful when you corner the two-legged kind. That's when there's real trouble."

"Dell, I'll never forget your advice," gushed Sean. "You're a big help. I know what I need to do next."

Sean slapped the bill of Dell's baseball cap as he stepped out onto the pier, and then slid onto the seat of his bicycle.

In a short time, Sean's earnest pedaling down Lake Boulevard pulled him within sight of the DeLane estate. Turning into the long driveway, he spotted Weldon behind the wheel of his Corvette convertible driving towards him, his wavy hair swaying in the breeze.

Sean hopped off as the car braked.

"Hello, young man," said Weldon, taking off his sunglasses and placing them on the dashboard. "You're probably here to see Candy, I'll bet."

Sean nodded.

"She's out back by the pool, but be careful," cautioned Weldon, flicking his Pall Mall butt into the grass. "That girl has not been herself in days. I don't exactly know what's wrong with Candy but I know her well enough to see she's struggling. Maybe your visit will do her some good."

"I hope so," replied Sean. "I'm here on a mission."

"What mission? Sean, do you have any idea what's bothering her?" asked Weldon, his voice oozing frustration.

"Not really." Sean stepped closer to the car. "I saw her last Saturday coming out of Saint Joe's Church and she was upset. That's all I can tell you."

"Well, that's more than I know," complained Weldon. "I'm counting on you, Sean, to be a gentleman and I'd appreciate hearing about anything I can do to help my daughter."

"I'll do my best, sir," assured Sean.

"Candy needs a good friend, Sean," said Weldon.

"I'm going to try," answered Sean.

"I'm heading to the store for some provisions for dinner," said Weldon, putting the car in gear. "You know where the pool is. Just don't sneak up on her, she's a bit jumpy."

Candy, in brown corduroy shorts and a long-sleeve yellow blouse, dangled her toes in the water from the end of the diving board.

"Hey you," announced Sean, rounding the corner of the main house.

"Hey you, yourself," replied Candy, looking back over her shoulder.

Sean climbed the patio steps, halting at the chrome ladder to the pool.

"You just gonna sit out there all day?" teased Sean.

Candy stood, put her hands on her hips, and slowly jumped up and down on the board.

She turned to give Sean a soft smile. "Pushy Vineyard Beach boy," she taunted. "Come on out and get me if you think you've got the courage."

Candy turned her back to Sean, shot her legs out, falling smoothly until her buttocks hit the end of the board, the force propelling her back to a standing position.

"I didn't know you were raised in a circus," laughed Sean, a good deep one rolling out of his throat. "Nice trick!"

"Any fool can do that," pointed out Candy. "Are you fool enough to try?"

"I surrender to your superior talents, your highness," replied Sean, bowing with a flourish.

"Okay, then here I come," she conceded.

Sean waited at the steps, watching Candy with an appraising look as she came towards him. He held out his arms.

"My lady, may I help you down?" he offered.

"Yes, you may, my good man."

Sean put his hands around Candy's waist and lifted her gently in the air, spinning her until she came to rest on the deck, her face inches away.

"I guess kissing you is out of the question?" whispered Sean, pulling Candy closer.

"One light one, if you must," she said, leaning in and putting her lips on Sean's mouth.

The smooch lasted only a few seconds.

When Sean pulled back, a tear fell from the corner of Candy's right eye.

"You okay?" he said, suddenly startled.

"I hope to be one day," she proclaimed. "But today is not that day."

"What can I do?"

"Don't quiz me," she shot back. "Just go slow until I feel normal again."

"Sure thing," said Sean. "I'll do as I'm told."

"That's reassuring actually," said Candy, placing a hand on Sean's cheek. "There may come a day when I really need your help."

Sean straightened up and threw his shoulders back.
"When that day comes, I won't let you down," assured Sean.
He hugged Candy tightly.

CHAPTER NINE

The rockets slashed the muggy darkness, trailing a line of embers that danced like fireflies high above Lake Erie. Overhead, the missiles exploded into bursts of crimson and gold. The light illuminated the faces of The Caper Brothers, smiles bent towards the heavens.

"I love that smell," Buddy Trotz announced, wiping beads of sweat off his face with the bottom of his white t-shirt. "That's the best part of watching fireworks, the smell of burning gunpowder."

"Yeah, it reminds you of those greasy Polish farts you like to rip," snapped Jimmy Moran. "Thank God there's a breeze tonight or there would be more than just the smell of gunpowder in the air."

"Always the wise guy, Moran," said Trotz, glaring at Jimmy. "I haven't farted once today."

"Good thing, cause that would be the end of the fresh air on this July Fourth," laughed Jimmy. "Just be sure to keep your fat butt cheeks pinched tight."

Jimmy turned to look at Johnny Pasquale. "Hey, Pasquale, why don't you at least grunt over there so we know you're alive."

Pasquale spit hard through the gap in his front teeth.

The Caper Brothers had spread their blanket near the edge of the cliff overlooking the water. Below, they had a clear view of Weldon DeLane parked on a small barge attached to his pier. He waved a smoldering flare to signal another round of rockets. Whoosh! Off the corner of the barge they launched skyward to erupt in a roar of green and blue.

"This beats lighting firecrackers in the street back at my house," marveled Sean. "That Mister DeLane knows how to throw a party. Man, are we lucky Candy asked us to come tonight."

Sean studied Vineyard Beach's most prominent residents from a short distance off by the side of the pool. The gathering included Father Paul Sterner, the pastor of St. Joseph's parish and the new priest, Father Ken, mingling in the DeLane's manicured backyard. The crowd buzzed the two bartenders at the long table temporarily set up near the diving board, which burned bright from an armada of floating outdoor candles. The coolers of iced beer had needed replenishing every thirty minutes, testimony to the thirst of the guests and the heat of the evening. Even Sean and his friends were lucky enough to plunge an arm below the surface of the frosty water to scoop out cans of Stroh's. The alcohol did little to stop Sean from rocking on the blanket. He rubbed a St. Christopher medal in his pocket, a good-luck memento his father had worn thin during his days as a bomber pilot.

"Stop your damn shaking, it's driving me nuts," snapped Jimmy, putting his hand on Sean's shoulder. "I guess you were hoping your little firecracker would get lit by your California beauty. But no such luck, Leader Boy, she's nowhere around. Concentrate on drinking the free beer."

"It's your turn Pasquale," ordered Jimmy. "Crawl over there and get us another round like a good putz. The adults are already toasted."

Johnny flipped onto his stomach, his sleek body melding into the lawn. He moved with the stealth of a large reptile towards the tubs of beer resting on the edge of the light sprayed around the pool. He crawled slowly in the dark, hiding his face in the cool grass at the sound of someone approaching. Johnny held his breath until the footsteps faded. When it drew quiet, he plunged his arm into the nearest bucket, plucking another round for The Caper Brothers. He wrapped the beers in his t-shirt and retreated, the laughter of the adults in the backyard hanging in the air as he slid away.

"Stroh's beer all around," announced Johnny. "Let's pop these suckers, you losers."

Johnny pushed a can of beer against his face. "Ah, this feels better than drinking 'em."

"You jerk, just pass out the beers," barked Jimmy. "Our stomachs need cooling off more than your mug. This is the best chance we'll have this summer to knock some down."

One by one, the four friends tilted their heads back, opening their throats to let the beer slide to its destination.

Sean finished first. He picked up another can and studied the lake.

"He's waving two flares in the air, this must be the grand finale," shouted Sean.

The boys stopped drinking to watch Weldon whirl two flares over his head, creating circles of burning embers in the night sky.

"Hey, look, he's making big O's for the great state of Ohio," exclaimed Buddy.

"Easy moron, it's more like a big O for your brain capacity," responded Moran.

"And stop talking or we won't hear the damn fireworks going off."

Weldon touched the flares to fuses running the length of the barge, sparks flying as the flames raced towards the rockets. He jumped for the pier, running for the stairs, his long legs taking the steps three at a time. He spun around at the top of the cliff in time to see the missiles rise in unison.

"Alright," exalted Weldon, pumping both fists into the air. "This is gonna work. Get ready!"

Several dozen spheres of red, white, and blue painted the sky, the accompanying booms echoing down on the partygoers.

Weldon sprinted towards the pool, the joy of his work lifting his spirits. As the last of the ashes fell overhead, he weaved through the yard with the agility of a halfback nearing the goal line. He slowed at the edge of the gathering to scan the faces of his guests.

"Has anyone seen my daughter?" asked Weldon, shaking hands with Father Paul and a couple he didn't recognize. "She loves this holiday, especially the big ending. She would never miss this."

"Don't be upset, teenagers go through many stages, especially girls," said the pastor, shifting Frankie in his arms. "You should anticipate some moodiness at her age." The priest drank deeply from his gin and tonic.

"Something's up with Candy and it's killing me because she won't confide in me," declared Weldon. "That's never happened before."

"Take my word for it," advised Father Paul. "I've been around children all my life. Give her time and this will all blow over. Just don't press her. That would be a mistake."

A bartender approached with a tray of chilled shrimp. Weldon waved him off.

"Maybe those boys know something," wondered Weldon, pointing at The Caper Brothers. "Candy invited Sean and his friends because she wanted to get to know the Gerard boy better."

Father Paul fell silent for a moment at the mention of Sean.

"Is there something wrong?" inquired Weldon.

"I know the Gerard family," said the priest, ending the awkward silence. "Sean is one of my altar boys and I've been to their home for dinner with his parents, Chuck and Lorraine."

"So he is a good kid?" asked Weldon.

"As far as I know, he is," said the priest.

"Then you will excuse me for a moment?" Weldon said, walking off the patio.

The boys spotted Weldon heading in their direction. Sean rose off the blanket, swaying slightly. He slipped his last can of beer under his shirt.

Weldon stuck his hand out as he approached, gripping Sean tightly.

"Sean, glad you're here," said Weldon. "Sorry about infringing on your night of fun but I'm sick about Candy. She should be here enjoying the party."

"I'm surprised she's passing all this up," said Sean, waving his arm at the crowd. "Something is bothering her, that's for sure but …"

"She hasn't said hardly a word in a week," interrupted Weldon, "and she didn't even come down for the fireworks. I even sent food up to her bedroom and she didn't eat a bite. She's usually good for three hotdogs on the Fourth."

"I'll go see her if you think it would help," said Sean.

"Please, Sean, go up to her room and check on her," pleaded Weldon. "Her door is the first one on the right when you come up the back stairs. Your friends are welcome to stay. Let me know how she is, please."

"I need to get back to my guests," he said, turning and heading back to the party.

"We'll be right here waiting for you, Leader Boy," Jimmy said, draining his can of beer. "Hurry along, your dream girl needs to be rescued. Oh, my knight in shining armor, where are you?" Jimmy pointed at the DeLane mansion. "There's the castle, get going."

"Piss on you, jerk," replied Sean.

Sean tossed his beer can on the grass and marched towards the main house, pausing at the kitchen's big bay window to watch the revelers inside snacking on warm crab cakes. The memory of Candy's breakdown outside the church washed over him. Sean rubbed his throbbing forehead. No one noticed as he slid the door open. He glided around the far side of the room, to climb the back stairs.

At the top landing, a small stream of light from the hall bathroom illuminated the cover of the Beatles Sgt. Pepper's Lonely Heart Club Band album taped to the bedroom door.

"This must be her room," said Sean, knocking softly. "Hey, Candy. You in there? It's me, Sean."

He slowly turned the handle. As the door opened, Candy nearly bowled Sean over.

"Get in here and shut the door," she whispered, burying her head into his chest. She started to sob, her body shaking violently. Candy broke free of Sean's grasp and crawled to her open window. She braced her back against the wall and pulled her oversized t-shirt over her bare legs to peer over the windowsill.

"Come over here and look down there at the pool," cried Candy. "Do you see that man?"

Her hand trembled as she pointed out the window.

"There, the one in black! He's holding that dog!"

"Can I turn a light on, it's awful dark in here?" asked Sean.

"Don't you dare."

Sean inched across the room in the direction of Candy's voice. She reached up and pulled him to the floor.

"Hey, what are you doing?" demanded Sean, looking into Candy's blood-shot eyes shining in the faint light streaming through the window. "What are you so afraid of?"

"Be quiet and look down there," hissed Candy.

Sean stared out the window at the party by the pool.

"What man in black?" asked Sean. "Do you mean the priest? Why it's just Father Paul."

Candy fought to catch her breath. "So it is Father Paul," she gasped. "Oh, God, why did he come here!"

"Hey, what's got you so upset?" asked Sean. "Maybe you should just tell me what's..."

Sean stopped talking at the sound of water splashing onto the oak floor. Candy pushed her head hard against her knees. Urine had soaked through her panties, forming a small pool encircling her feet.

"Oh, Sean, I'm so scared and embarrassed," moaned Candy. "Run to the bathroom and get some towels. Please hurry, I don't want to be alone."

Sean lurched out of the room and into the hallway.

"What a mess," mused Sean. He was finally in Candy's bedroom, it was the Fourth of July, she was wearing only a t-shirt and now this—a big pool of urine. Sean peered inside the bathroom, pulling two towels off the nearest rack and retracing his steps. He thought about what his dad said about men of character—they always try to do the right thing, even in the face of adversity. What's the right thing now, he wondered.

As he entered Candy's room, Sean tried to readjust his eyes to the darkness. Over by the window, Candy's panties and shirt lay bunched next to the large wet spot. She had crawled across the room and lay balled up under a sheet in her double bed. Sean wiped the floor dry and rolled the soiled clothes in a towel when he finished.

"Hide that stuff, please," whispered Candy. "I'll worry about *that* in the morning."

Sean slid the bundle under the bed with his foot and then perched next to Candy.

"I don't know what to say or how to help you, but I'll be your friend, no matter what," Sean said, stroking Candy's jumbled mass of golden hair.

Her body stiffened.

"You have no idea what I've been through," she blurted. "I'm not even sure how this happened to me. I just know it was bad. And he's a priest!"

"I don't understand…what are you blaming on Father Paul?"

"If I tell you what happened, you must believe me. You *have* to believe me. The only way I can handle this is to know that someone, you, knows the truth. Promise me you won't think I'm lying."

"I promise."

"Okay. I'm taking a chance."

Candy sat up in bed, making sure the sheet covered her naked body. She pulled her hair back off her face and tied it in a loop on top of her head.

She motioned for Sean to come closer.

"Don't you let me down," she said.

Candy moved her mouth within inches of Sean's ear.

"Look straight ahead," she whispered. "I don't want you staring at me when I tell you my story. This will make it a little easier. Even better, close your eyes."

Candy slid her hand over Sean's eyelids to make sure they were shut.

"Okay, here goes," she started, "that priest out by my pool is the devil. He lured me into the sanctuary and then he…" Candy's voice broke. "The priest is a filthy creature. He's a bastard. He took advantage of me. I was in the church to light a candle for my mother and he tricked me. He made me kneel down and then he pumped his…his…his dick against the back of my head. I was so scared. I just froze. I knelt there like a little baby and didn't move. I couldn't even scream. It was gross."

She pulled her face back from Sean's ear. "There, I said it. Now you're in this with me. You have to believe me."

Sean folded his arms across his chest and rocked, "Oh, Jesus Christ."

Candy placed her head on Sean's shoulder.

"Don't get sick, Sean. I've cried enough already for both of us."

"But I always thought that Father Paul was a good man. I believe you. But how do we get anyone else to believe us! This is a big problem."

Sean looked down at Candy. Their lips were just inches apart. She smelled of fresh soap and tangerine shampoo.

"I want to kiss you right now to show you how much I care about you but I know the timing is all wrong," said Sean. "You've been through so much."

Candy pulled Sean's face closer, holding his cheeks in her hands. She gently kissed him on the lips.

"Life is all screwed up right now," cried Candy, lowering her head back on his shoulder. "And I didn't do anything wrong. I'm a good girl."

He rocked Candy in his arms. As her breathing deepened, Sean eased her down to the bed, pulling up a quilt up from the foot of the bed.

"Just put the blanket over my feet, it's still warm in here tonight," said Candy softly.

Light snoring soon filled the room. Sean slid off the bed. At the door, he looked back to check on Candy one last time. He made sure the door would lock before walking quickly into the hallway.

"Now what?" wondered Sean as he headed outside.

Weldon stood at the far side of the stone patio near the pool, talking with Father Paul. Sean maneuvered through the guests parked on the steps leading down into the grass. He walked slowly to the dark perimeter outside the arc of floodlights. Once in the shadows, he raced for the blanket and his friends.

Sean plowed into Jimmy, knocking him down.

"Calm down, Leader Boy, you're gonna get somebody hurt," howled Jimmy. "You Gerards might have the thickest skulls around but the rest of us feel pain when we get hit on the noggin. What's the matter? Did that pretty girl send you packing?"

"All three of you gather round on this blanket," ordered Sean. "I need The Caper Brothers tonight. We need to stick together on this. Trust me."

The tone of Sean's voice startled the boys.

"Are you in trouble cause of that girl?" taunted Jimmy. "You sure were up in her bedroom a long time. We were about to go off and leave you, Mister Leader Boy."

"Mister DeLane is going to be looking for me," warned Sean. "But I can't talk to him tonight. I have to sneak out of here so he doesn't see me."

"Then we need a distraction to cover us," said Jimmy. "I'm an expert on creating trouble. Just give me a minute to think of something."

Sean, Buddy and Johnny crouched while Jimmy paced around their blanket. Jimmy stopped to face his friends.

"We need to toss something into the pool," announced Jimmy. "That'll get the adults all riled up trying to figure out what happened and we'll just walk on up the driveway to freedom."

"Better yet we need to toss someone into the pool," countered Sean, pounding his fists together. "I know just the guy."

"Hey, I'm not causing any trouble," said Buddy. "Why don't we just run around the side of the house and get going?"

"Did you forget the wrought-iron security fence?" said Sean. "We'd never get over it, especially you, fat boy. Besides, everybody will see us go by the pool. It's as bright as day over there. Then Mister DeLane will stop me for sure. Besides someone over there needs a good dunking."

"Now, who is the crazy one?" laughed Jimmy.

Buddy moved off the blanket. "I want no part of this," he said.

"Then just stay back till this goes down," said Sean. "How 'bout you, Pasquale? I know you'd rather just sit there but it would be good for your friends if you said something."

Johnny ran his hands through his dark hair. He smiled and shook his head. "I'm no chicken," he said, his voice rising. "Once a Caper Brother, always a Caper Brother. Count me in."

Sean gestured to his friends to come closer. He lowered his voice.

"Then here's the plan," said Sean "Me and Johnny will crawl back to the pool using the hedge by the patio for cover. We can get right behind that group of adults with their backs to us. See the long-handled pool skimmer on top of the hedge? We're gonna use that. Jimmy, I need you to work your way over to the garage. Take Buddy with you. Look for the outdoor light switch. When you see the pool skimmer disappear, hit the lights."

"So, who's going in the water tonight, Leader Boy?" demanded Jimmy.

"Father Paul," said Sean.

"You really are nuts, Gerard," said Jimmy. "Damn you. You sure you know what you're doing?"

"Yup, my mind's made up," announced Sean, pulling Johnny by the arm. "Let's get going."

Jimmy threw the blanket over his shoulder, pushing Buddy towards the garage. Once inside, Jimmy found the outdoor floods clearly marked on the wall panel. He focused on the pool skimmer.

Down went the pool equipment. Out went the lights.

Fifteen minutes later, when the lights came back, the partygoers were gathered around Father Paul and Frankie. The little dog shook the water off his shaggy white coat. Someone had draped a towel over the priest's shoulders.

"Someone jabbed me in the back with this," howled the priest, holding the pool skimmer aloft. Water dripped off the end of his nose. He slammed the pole down, cracking one of the marble tiles.

The pastor shook both his fists at the people encircling him. "I *will* find out who pulled this stunt." His voice echoed across the back of the DeLane property. "No one should ever do something like to this to me, a priest, the pastor of Saint Joseph's. This was more than a practical joke. This was an assault on the sacred priesthood."

Father Paul looked for a chair, his energy suddenly drained by the night of gin and the plunge into the pool. Frankie jumped into his arms.

The boys raced down the driveway, their laughter interrupted by the sound of Father Paul's booming tirade.

"Go home and don't tell anyone," whispered Sean, slapping all three friends on the back.

The Caper Brothers split up near the main road.

Sean crept into his room, relieved that his parents were already asleep. He stretched his small frame on his bed, pulling the extra pillow over his head. He prayed that sleep would ease the memory of the day's events. Exhaustion swept over him.

Sunrise came too soon, filtering through the wooden shutters like beams from miniature flashlights. Sean kept his eyes shut, trying to hold off the day as long as possible. He plunged his feet deep into the corner of the bed, searching for cool spots on the top sheet.

Sean bolted up, remembering the duty that awaited him at St. Joseph's Church. He made his way down to the kitchen, quietly sliding into his chair at the side of the big oak table.

"You could at least say good morning," said Lorraine limping over to her son. She scooped the last of the potato wedges browned in butter and spices from her cast-iron skillet and piled them next to the cheese omelet.

"My little one, I put a drop of my love in your breakfast this morning," said Lorraine warmly. "I hope you appreciate your mother's affection. And in my country, it's impolite to leave food on your plate."

Lorraine pulled the black curls back off Sean's face and kissed his forehead. "Mothers always worry. Now eat."

Sean stabbed at his food, finally harpooning a large piece of omelet and potato. He spun the fork in his hand, examining the morsel from every angle. He slowly placed the food into his mouth, chewing deliberately as if the act of swallowing would hurt.

"Why is it so important to eat breakfast anyway?" Sean said, looking down at his omelet.

"Because you are still growing, your stomach is empty and you have an important duty awaiting you," Lorraine said, sliding the skillet into the soapy water in the sink. She wiped her hands on her apron before turning around.

"I'm also your mother and I'm entitled to tell you what to do. Now stop complaining and finish your meal. Be quick about it. You're needed down at the church. Father Paul will be angry if you're not on time for the early Mass."

"Mom, I don't feel so good, can't I just go back up to bed?" whined Sean.

"Non. Absolument non," instructed Lorraine "You're an altar boy and it's your duty."

Lorraine snatched Sean's plate off the table.

"Enough, get out of my kitchen before I forget my good nature and report you to your father," said Lorraine, wagging her finger in her son's face.

The mention of his father got Sean out of his chair and moving for the door. Lorraine blocked her son's path, pulling him into her arms.

"You are so anxious this morning," said Lorraine soothingly. "Why my son?"

Sean jerked free of his mother's embrace.

"Mom, are you sure I have to go?" I don't want to be an altar boy this morning."

"What are you saying?" demanded Lorraine. "You've been doing the Saturday morning mass with Father Paul all year. He is counting on you. What has upset you?"

"It's just not the same," said Sean, sliding his hands into the front pockets of his jeans. "Can't you just believe me and let me stay home?"

"Believe what? Look at me when you're talking."

"I don't know how to say…" stammered Sean, staring at his mother.

"Young man, serving on the altar with Father Paul is a sacred honor," scolded Lorraine. "He is the pastor of our parish and a good friend to our family. You are talking about a man of God. Out with it or hold your tongue. Lorraine straightened the front of her apron, eyeing her son suspiciously.

"You'll never understand," complained Sean. "Just because he's a priest doesn't mean he's always right."

Lorraine pointed grabbed Sean's arm.

"You are duty bound," she said. "Do I have to get your father to make the point better."

"That's not fair, Mom," said Sean. "He never listens to me."

"I'm tired of your little whining," she concluded, walking back to the sink. "Be sure to comb your hair and put on your black slacks before you leave. And don't forget your good shoes. Your cassock won't cover your tennis shoes."

Sean changed his clothes, then made his way to the garage for his bike. He raced the short block to the church, ignoring the "Keep Off The Grass" sign in the freshly cut front lawn. His tires left tracks in the grass still moist from a light overnight rain. He didn't mind upsetting the groundskeeper; he just didn't want to be late for Mass.

By the time Sean changed into his vestments, the usual small turnout for the Saturday Mass was sprinkled around the church. He peeked out from the altar boys' room. No sign of Father Paul.

Sean hauled the brass candle lighter, with accompanying snuffer, onto the altar. His hands shook as he raised the burning wick to the four large candles at the front of the church. He headed for the sanctuary to retrieve the unconsecrated wine. Sean knew from experience to fill the wine pitcher to the top. Father Paul always ordered extra wine. Sean breathed deeply, his heart thumping. He eyed the wall clock. Only ten minutes until the service began. Father Paul was usually dressed in his vestments by now.

The outside door to the sanctuary flew open. Sean backpedaled, the pitchers of wine and water sliding across the glass tray in his hands.

"Whoa there Sean," boomed Father Ken, ensnarling Sean's shoulders in his grip. "Balance that tray or we'll have a mess to clean up before Mass. I hope I didn't give you too much of a jolt when I came through the door."

Sean sighed in relief at the sight of Father Ken.

The young priest took the tray from Sean.

"Let me walk this out," he said. "You look like you've just seen a ghost, or at least, the Holy Spirit. I'll be back in a jiff."

Sean leaned back against the far wall.

"The clock is running and this Mass is going off on time," said Father Ken, striding back into the sanctuary. "Hop to it now, Sean. We must be on time. Catholics hate to be kept waiting."

The priest began to put on his vestments.

"You're probably wondering where Father Paul is," offered the priest as he kissed his stole and placed it over his shoulders. "He's not feeling well enough this morning to say Mass so he asked me to step in. Let's do God's work and we'll talk after the service. I want to know about that worried look on your face."

Sean shuffled out to the altar, relieved that he would not have to deal with the pastor. His mind wandered as Father Ken led the faithful through the service. He felt there might be trouble after the Mass, but for now he was safe.

It wasn't long before he heard the refrain of freedom.

"May almighty God bless you, in the name of the Father, Son and Holy Spirit. The mass is ended, go in peace. Have faith in Jesus Christ. Love the Lord."

"Thanks be to God," said Sean with the congregation.

Father Ken smiled down at Sean.

"Another Mass done well, my young friend," he said, draping his arm around Sean as they walked back to the sanctuary. Sean could feel the priest's bulging forearms under his vestments.

Father Ken's easy grace disarmed Sean. He was so unlike the stern Father Paul. The young priest laughed easily and often, his manner attracting supporters like Catholics to the Friday fish fry put on by the Knights of Columbus.

"It's a good thing you didn't have to say Mass this morning with Father Paul," said the priest, winking at Sean. "There's plenty of pressure for the pastor of a parish. He was angry or sick, or both, but he wasn't in the right mind to connect with God. Now protect me with that story. Don't share it with anyone."

"I've been asked to keep a lot of secrets lately," said Sean. "What's one more."

"Well, Sean, at the core of a friendship is the sacred duty of protecting a confidence," he counseled. "That's a lesson I hope will stick with you for life."

The priest folded the last of his vestments, placing them carefully in the long dresser running the length of the wall. He turned and leaned back on the counter top, supporting himself on his elbows.

"But I think I know one story you may not be able to control," said Father Ken.

"I don't understand," stammered Sean, shaking his head.

"Were you planning on starting a career as a lifeguard last night at the DeLane's party?" demanded the priest, reaching out to thump Sean on the chest.

Sean backed away from the priest.

"Look, it doesn't take Sherlock Holmes to figure out the good pastor was pushed into the pool," said the priest. "You and your friends were at the big party when the lights went out, and when they came back on, Father Paul was soaking wet and you guys were long gone."

"What does that prove?" muttered Sean.

"Nothing exactly, but gossip spreads fast in Vineyard Beach and once it starts it never dies," said the priest. "Plenty of people were milling about the DeLane's party. There were many eyes on you and your gang. It's only logical that your name would come up."

"Father, I don't know what you're talking about," said Sean.

"Hush," replied the priest. "Don't dig a deeper hole. Character is your destiny. Learn to lie now and you'll never stop."

Priest and altar boy watched the last of the parishioners depart through the side doors.

"My advice is to stay clear of Father Paul and pray this blows over," said the young priest. "In the meantime, I expect to see you in the confessional later today. You might feel better once you cleanse your soul."

"Father I need to get on my bike," whispered Sean. "Please, let me go home."

The priest placed his hand on Sean's forehead, squeezing until his knuckles turned white.

"You go with my blessing. But stay out of trouble or I'll make it hurt more next time."

"You made your point Father," said Sean, massaging his scalp.

Sean ran for his bike resting next to the side door of the church. He jumped onto the seat, not noticing the blinds in the adjacent rectory office slowly rising.

Father Paul put down his glass of gin. He picked up Frankie off the floor, cradling him in his left arm. With his free hand, he took a pair of handcuffs out of his desk drawer. He twirled them around his finger as he watched Sean glide away.

CHAPTER TEN

The breeze crept down from Canada, kicking up white caps across Lake Erie. By mid-morning, waves ran up the beach, crashing off the foot of the shale cliffs that snaked along the shoreline. The low growl of the wind and surf carried several blocks inland, forcing the Vineyard Beach lifeguards to haul out the "no swimming" signs at the park; no reason to challenge the lake's reputation for turning deadly. The onslaught yanked leaves from the town's ancient canopy of oak trees, creating a blanket of green over the main road by the water.

The gusts kissed Sean's face, announcing that the cool days of autumn would soon arrive. The weather change also signaled that the start of school wasn't far off.

"Don't move from that porch, Buster, if you know what's good for you," Chuck Gerard barked, stepping out of the garage with a shovel over his right shoulder. "That load of top soil out back isn't getting any smaller. I told you to spread it out in your mother's flowerbed two days ago. And don't tell me you forgot, because forgot don't count."

"Dad, I've got something important to do today," said Sean. "Can't I come back later and finish the job? Please, cut me a break, it is Saturday."

"Please cut me a break," Chuck mimicked in a squeaky voice. "You whine like a little girl. A break? You want a break? That's not happening and when I want your opinion, I'll send you a telegram, special delivery."

Chuck swung the shovel off his shoulder and propped it under his arm.

"Front and center, Buster," he ordered.

Sean stood at attention, his arms pressed to his side.

The elder Gerard pointed a crooked finger at his son's forehead.

"When the job is done you'll be free for the rest of the day," said Chuck. "But don't push your luck. Complete this mission or pay the price."

"But—" said Sean.

"But nothing, Buster," Chuck snapped, cutting off his son.

Chuck swung the shovel and pointed it at the flagpole in the middle of the front yard.

"See Old Glory snapping in the wind?" instructed Chuck. "Stay away from the lake. It'll be a crazy soup with this storm front. The undertow could pull down a horse."

"Dad, there's someone I have to go see today," said Sean. "Do you ever think that maybe just talking to me would be better than ordering me around all the time? Just once."

"Talking is for women."

Chuck threw the shovel at his son. Sean ducked, grabbing the wooden handle in midair with both hands just inches from his head.

"I'm in charge here. Now get going."

"Yes sir, Lieutenant," said Sean. He shouldered the shovel like a rifle and snapped a crisp salute. His father returned the gesture, spun on his heel and marched towards the house.

"That man is a pain in the ass, that's all there's to it," whispered Sean.

The pile of topsoil was keeping him from Candy. He walked to the backyard and started to spread the black dirt. He plunged the shovel into the mound, imagining the blade digging into his father's back with each stroke. The image made Sean smile.

"Take that you old bastard," hollered Sean.

Sweat soon trickled down his spine, forming a large wet circle across the back of his t-shirt. By the time he finished, the tops of the tall oak trees creaked in the whipping wind. The lake is gonna be wild, imagined Sean. He took off his shirt and held it aloft, letting the gusts of wind dry his body. The damp spot on his shirt quickly disappeared. He sniffed his arms pits. Not too smelly. Skipping a shower would save some time.

Sean pulled on his shirt and started out up Maple Street in the direction of the DeLane estate. Keeping Candy's secret about Father Paul, and the priest's plunge into the DeLane's pool, was never far from his thoughts. Moving the topsoil was a break from his worries; using his body and concentrating on the task at least had eased his anxiety. He remembered the nightmare that jerked him awake in the early morning hours. Father Paul had him cornered inside the church, the big front doors clanging shut just as he reached for freedom. Sean hated that dream; it invaded his sleep now weekly.

At the top of the driveway to the mansion, Sean could see all three garage doors hung open. Dust was blowing in on Mr. DeLane's prized Corvette. Sean scanned the inside of the garage. His eyes bulged. The surfboards The Caper Brothers had hauled from the DeLane helicopter the day it was forced to land were not in their usual spot. Sean raced through the building making sure he had not overlooked anything. He stopped to catch his breath. As he exhaled, the blood suddenly rushed from his face.

Sean sprinted to the edge of the cliff overlooking the DeLane beach. He shielded his eyes against the wind, trying to scan the lake through the sheets of biting spray hurled up by the eight-foot waves crashing at the base of the crag. He focused on a spot several hundred yards from shore. The mist cleared enough for Sean to glimpse a surfboard and its passenger, Candy DeLane.

"Oh my God!" screamed Sean. His body started to shake.

Candy headed straight out into the lake, her golden hair and bikini clearly outlined against the blue board. She struggled against the walls of surging water, pumping her arms and legs with determination. Her board slowly crept further from land.

Sean ran for the wooden steps winding down the rock face, quickly covering the distance to the end of the cement pier. Out in the surf, Candy kept kicking, her head lowered tight against her board. Sean frantically waved his arms.

"Come back, come back." The wind swallowed his plea. Sean knelt next to a surfboard and a pile of towels left near the ladder leading into the water. He rocked on his knees, trying to comprehend his predicament. Sean stood up and made the sign of the cross.

The waves cruised in with the power of an unstoppable armada of grey barges. Each new assault slammed into Candy. Sean strained to see through the spray. He glimpsed her again for a moment breaching the top of another monster wave. Suddenly, she stopped kicking. Her board froze for an instant at the apex of the wall of water, and then slowly flipped backward. The surge sent its passenger reeling. Candy bobbed on the surface, treading water as the waves rolled over her. She made no attempt to reach for her board before the next rush of water sent it towards shore.

"Christ, why did she stop kicking?" moaned Sean. He stripped to his shorts, knotted a towel around his waist, then lifted the surfboard off the pier and carried it down the ladder. Sean straddled the board, grasping the ladder firmly for protection from the undertow. He gained his balance as Candy's board rushed by the pier. Sean pushed off and moved out into the lake, squeezing the board against his chest, kicking hard in the direction of Candy.

A faint scream drifted over the roar of the waves. Sean aimed his board in the direction of the cry. He raised his head off the board, scanning the water. Candy turned towards Sean and waved her arms just as another wave broke over her, pulling her under. Sean pumped his arms and legs in a fury, cruising to the spot where Candy disappeared. He stared frantically at the surface for what felt like several minutes, pouring over every inch, hoping for some sign of Candy. Sean angled his board alongside a mass of jumbled blonde hair just below the water line. He reached down, grabbed a handful of locks and jerked Candy's head above water. He swung the towel off his waist and looped it under the girl's shoulders. Water oozed from Candy's mouth and nose as Sean lifted her onto his board.

After several attempts, Sean managed to turn the board towards shore. Candy's body felt cold against his skin and her breathing came in short, panicked gulps. Her eyes were closed as she started to moan.

"Hang on, we're not out of this yet!" roared Sean. "Don't give up. Just hold on tight!"

With the wind and pounding waves now to his back, Sean soon had his board and its passenger swooping into shallow water.

Sean lifted Candy onto his shoulder and slowly tottered up the beach, his legs aching on the climb up to the high ground. At the top of the stairs, he lowered Candy onto the lawn, dislodging her bikini top in the process. Sean blushed at the sight of the soft, white skin of her left breast. He leaned over and adjusted her top to cover her exposed nipple, then turned Candy on her stomach. Sean sat on Candy's hips and pushed hard between her shoulder blades. She vomited a bucket of Lake Erie.

Candy's eyes were still closed but her breathing improved. Sean stretched out on the grass next to her, wrapping his arms and legs around her thin frame to generate some heat. She coughed several times as she turned towards Sean. She was only inches from Sean's face, close enough to see the tears in his eyes.

"Can you please tell me what you were doing out on the lake in this wind?" sighed Sean. "You scared the hell out of me."

"Oh, Sean, I'm so messed up," muttered Candy as she wiped a tear from Sean's cheek.

"Listen to me," said Sean standing up. "What you did today was crazy, just plain crazy."

Candy pushed her face into the grass.

"Talk to me damn it!" shouted Sean.

"I'm having a hard time dealing with myself," cried Candy, turning on her side. "I don't want to face my problems any more. I just want to crawl in a hole and die."

"Hush, you just hush for a minute," said Sean. "I didn't risk my neck today for you to say such crap. If you went out there to hurt yourself on purpose, I'm telling your dad everything."

"Don't do it," Candy said, sitting up. "Don't make this any worse," she said softly. "My dad would go nuts. You promised not to tell anyone about what happened. It's our secret, remember? I thought I could count on you."

Sean held out his hand and pulled Candy to her feet.

"Look, I'm your friend and I'll keep your secret but you must never pull any more shit like you did today," ordered Sean. "Tell me you won't try to hurt yourself again."

"I promise," said Candy, leaning over to kiss Sean's cheek. "Thanks for being my guardian angel."

"You're welcome," said Sean, shaking his head. "But we've got another problem. Father Paul knows I pushed him into your pool on the Fourth."

"I heard all that commotion that night," asserted Candy.

"It's a long story but he knows, and we have to be careful," said Sean.

Candy started to cry. "What are we going to do?" she pleaded.

"I'm not sure, but for now, will you take it easy, please?" Can I at least trust you to be alone the rest of the afternoon?"

Candy nodded.

Sean moved towards Candy, wrapping her in his arms. He held her till she stopped crying.

"I'll try and make it," said Candy. "My dad is due back from his golf game soon, so I won't be alone. You go on, you've done enough today already."

"I'll walk you to your door," offered Sean. "Just promise me you won't do anything foolish. Promise me."

On the porch, Sean gave Candy a quick hug.

"I'll check on you in the next couple of days," he whispered. Candy patted his shoulder as she opened the kitchen door. Sean watched through the window as Candy made her way up the back stairs to her room.

Sean returned the surfboards and grabbed his clothes before heading down the driveway, knowing that The Caper Brothers would be at their weekly gathering at the Vineyard Beach pharmacy. He stepped behind a tree at the sight of Mr. DeLane's car rounding the corner at the far end of the driveway. When the car passed, he ran off the property, not stopping until he crossed the main road.

Sean glanced at the slowing clouds as he neared the pharmacy. He stopped at the entrance to make sure his shorts were dry, then ducked inside, a brass bell at the top of the door announcing his entrance.

"Man, look at your face, Gerard," said Buddy Trotz, pointing at Sean. "That grumpy look is a sure sign we need to have some fun. School's gonna start soon, then the nuns will make our lives miserable."

The Caper Brothers

Buddy spun on his stool at the small soda fountain in the back of the store. He stopped to suck the red barbeque salt dusting his chubby fingers before launching an empty bag of potato chips for the trash can near the sink. It bounced off the back wall, falling silently near two others he had already dispatched.

The other Caper Brothers—Jimmy Moran and Johnny Pasquale—shot worried glances at Sean as he took his place on the last stool at the cramped counter. The store was empty except for Veronica, the pharmacist's wife, who slowly wiped the Formica with a damp hand towel.

"You boys can talk about the last days of summer till your drinks go flat, but for now, you are hurting my business," teased Veronica, throwing her towel over her shoulder. She adjusted her breasts under her white cashmere sweater, slowly pushing up her bosom to expose her ample cleavage through the plunging V-neck. "I believe my regulars are scared to come inside once they see you desperados camped out. Can't you fellas find another place to hang out?"

"But, Veronica, we come here because we like your company," said Jimmy.

"Don't think about giving me any lip, you Irish troublemaker," chided Veronica. "I don't put up with any crap. Besides, I haven't seen such a sorry bunch, since, well, your last visit."

Veronica's throaty laugh echoed off the walls as she patted the strands of black curls piled high on her head, pursing her lips for a moment to be sure the boys were paying attention. Her tongue painted a glaze of moisture across her full bottom lip, the saliva lingering like early morning dew on a rose petal. She arched her back to point her bosom towards the ceiling.

The boys stared at Veronica's every move.

"Sean, let me get you something to get your smile back," Veronica said, sliding a glass of ginger ale in front of him. "How about the rest of you? All full up for the afternoon?"

For The Caper Brothers, Veronica Maggione was *the* reason for their weekly trek to the pharmacy. The boys loved the mounds of wonder under her signature thin cashmere tops. The boys assumed the dark-haired beauty, who never discussed her age, was several years younger than her husband, the fifty-ish pharmacist she called "Daddy."

Veronica strutted behind the counter like a lioness in heat stalking a mate through tall grass. Throughout the day, a steady stream of the town's most respected men paraded into her den buying toothpaste or a comb or nail clippers, anything to get a better look at her impressive chest.

The Caper Brothers speculated, like everyone else in town, that Veronica lived with the balding pharmacist because of his lucrative business. As the only supplier of the town's drug needs, the pharmacy generated steady cash flow, which Veronica loved to spend on clothes, especially her expensive sweaters. But the owner did marvel to his friends that for all her spending, Veronica was good for better than any form of advertising.

For weeks, Jimmy had kept a close watch on Veronica when she dispensed her wares from behind the cash register. He wondered about the strange ritual he witnessed. With a discreet gesture from a male customer, Veronica would slide a small package across the counter that was quickly palmed. No words were exchanged, just a nod to Veronica. Jimmy stared from his stool as another one of Veronica's customers left the pharmacy.

"Hey, Veronica, where's that jealous husband of yours?" challenged Jimmy. "He's usually around making sure you don't bust out of your sweater. And if that day ever comes, please God, let me be here."

"Now you calm down, Jimmy Moran!" chastised Veronica. "I declare you are a bold one. The good priests of Saint Joe's wouldn't approve of their charges acting in such an ungodly way. You Catholic boys better be careful."

Sean lowered his head at the mention of the priests. He pushed his empty glass to the edge of the counter.

"Why so quiet, Sean?" inquired Veronica.

Before he could answer, Veronica leaned over to scoop up the change the boys had left to pay their bill. All four heads turned to focus on Veronica's breasts as she bent over, their eyes lost in the folds of pale bosom held in place by a black lace bra.

"I swear, you boys could stare a hole through a wall," claimed Veronica, counting the coins in her hand. "If I didn't know better, I'd think you were trying to undress me with your beady eyes. Don't you know it's impolite to look at a lady for more than a few seconds? Unless, of course, you're looking directly into her eyes. And boys, my eyes are up here."

Veronica stood back from the counter, fluttering her dark lashes for emphasis.

"You need to work on your gentlemanly manners if you ever want to get close to a girl," advised Veronica. "And you Sean, sure aren't your usual self. Did a nun get your tongue?"

"Forget Leader Boy over there," said Jimmy. "Just tell me, what are you selling to those old guys coming in here all day? I mean, it's kinda of obvious there's something they need from you besides that cheap junk they're buying."

"You are an impetuous one, Jimmy Moran," said Veronica. "I should shake your head until some of that red hair falls out."

"Come on Veronica," assailed Jimmy. "You can trust us."

"Why should I tell you anything?" replied Veronica. "It's up to those nuns over at Saint Joe's to explain life to you. Don't you boys get any sex education in that Catholic prison?"

"Yippee, sex!" yipped Buddy, rising off his stool. "Did you say sex? I heard it. Sex. Sex. Sex. Maybe we will have some fun this summer."

"You just woke up some Canadians on the other side of Lake Erie," said Johnny. His quick slap to the side of Buddy's head knocked him back off his stool. Buddy crashed to the floor still holding his glass of ginger ale.

"Hey, look, I didn't spill a drop."

"That's cause your ass is the world's largest emergency cushion," growled Johnny. "If you want to yell something at the top of your lungs, try screaming 'I'm an asshole.' Now, get back up on your stool."

Veronica whistled through her fingers.

"Boys, now pay attention," she said. "If you four think you're ready to learn something, I just might oblige."

"Hey, before you start telling us any secrets, the nuns did show us a movie last year about puberty," offered Buddy. "We know all about wet dreams and body odor and hair under our arm pits and stuff."

"Trotz, your middle name is body odor, now just shut up for a minute," said Jimmy. "Let Veronica talk. So you gonna explain the big mystery behind those visits from your men customers?"

Veronica raised her right hand.

"Get 'em up boys and take an oath," she said. "If anyone talks about what you are about to see, may Pope John show up at your front door. Do we have a deal?"

The Caper Brothers nodded in agreement, shooting their right hands into the air.

Veronica reached under the cash register and held up a shoebox. She placed the box on the counter, sliding off the lid to reveal neat rows of small, square packets. She lifted one, ripped the plastic seal and pulled out its contents.

"This, my little brothers is a condom, also known as a rubber, or a raincoat, or a tool wrap," coached Veronica, holding the condom by its ring. With a light shake, the thin skin fell away to its full length. "My customers use these to have sex with their wives or girlfriends without creating any babies. You understand how that works?"

"That wasn't in the movie the nuns showed us last year," said Buddy.

The laughter ricocheted off the walls, smothering the sound of the pharmacist striding through the back door.

Veronica stretched the condom to its limits.

"Now boys, when the moment is right and your penis is..." Veronica's mouth fell open at the sight of her husband.

"You crazy bitch!"

The pharmacist grabbed the condom from Veronica, swinging his free hand high over his head. The blow he struck to the side of Veronica's jaw rocked her on her heels.

The pharmacist wheeled to face the boys, his hands trembling by his side. The sight of Veronica's bleeding mouth, and the condom vibrating in the pharmacist's clenched fist, sent the boys scrambling for the front door.

They tumbled outside onto the sidewalk.

"Run you bastards before the old man gets after us," yelled Sean.

After several blocks, the pack slowed.

Jimmy's laughter broke the tension.

"I thought the pharmacist's face was gonna explode," chuckled Jimmy. "I've never seen a shade of red like that. I just hope Veronica will be okay."

"What do you care about Veronica, you were looking out for yourself, as usual," hissed Sean. "I saw what you scooped up going out the door."

"Right again, Leader Boy," Jimmy answered, holding up an unopened condom. "This little guy might come in handy one day."

"Do you even know how to use that thing?" taunted Sean.

"I'll figure it out," said Jimmy. "Maybe that cutie from California can give me a few pointers. Candy baby, here I come!"

Sean stuck his middle finger in Jimmy's face. "Screw you."

Jimmy gently slid the condom inside his wallet.

"No, screw you, Leader Boy," said Jimmy. "We'll see who gets to use this condom first."

Sean pushed Jimmy in the back.

"Yes, we will Jimmy Moran," shouted Sean. "Put the damn thing on the end of your nose. It'll improve your looks."

CHAPTER ELEVEN

The manila envelope arrived in the Gerard mailbox with the rest of the day's deliveries just after lunch. Sean's name blazed across its cover in bold, capital letters. On the next line in smaller handwriting were the words, "Prospective Football Player." The St. Joseph's school emblem, a black cross stamped with the letters STJ, dominated the upper left corner.

Chuck Gerard lifted the envelope off a small table next to his recliner when Sean entered the den. An opened letter postmarked "Republic of South Vietnam" rested in his lap.

"Well, Buster, I think you might be expecting this," said Chuck, holding out the package.

Sean's heart thumped as he ripped open the envelope.

"Gosh, I think I know what this is!" exclaimed Sean.

Chuck leaned forward at the exuberance in Sean's voice. He put down his newspaper and took off his reading glasses.

"Well smarty pants, are you going to share your discovery or do I have to get all the way out of my chair and walk over there," said Chuck, smiling at his son. "Come on, Buster, give it up."

Sean studied the letter for a moment then pumped his fist into the air.

"Listen to this, Dad," said Sean, holding the letter with both hands. "Dear student, you have been invited to try out for the freshman football team at St. Joseph's High School. This letter contains the information you need to attend the first practice two weeks before school officially opens.

"Yippee, it's really gonna happen," shouted Sean as he danced in a circle.

Chuck clapped his hands while his son did a jig in his den.

"Why would they even want a little runt like you?" taunted Chuck. "Then again, you are a Gerard. Maybe they can use your head in practice for a kicking T. Your skull is just about indestructible."

"Funny, Dad," retorted Sean. "You can't even hurt me today. I feel that good. I can't wait to tell my buddies the news."

The mention of Sean's friends sank Chuck's mood.

"Slow down there, Buster. Hand me that letter so I can read it for myself. And watch your tone when you're talking to me. I'm your father."

"*Yes sir*, I always remember that."

Chuck motioned Sean over to the adjacent chair, holding out his hand for the letter. Sean watched his father review the paper. When he finished, Chuck folded the letter in half.

"You and I need to have a talk," he said.

Chuck rubbed both hands through his crew cut, fixing his gaze out the window facing the street.

"Sean, right now I'm worried about your older brothers," started Chuck, dropping his hands to his lap. "There's 200 Americans dying every week in Southeast Asia. The Mekong Delta, where Michael and Terry are stationed, is turning into a rat's nest."

Chuck pounded his fist on the cushioned arm of his chair.

"Three weeks ago some gook bastards snuck through the perimeter wire at Terry's base and made it right up to the barracks," he said. "Your oldest brother said in his letter that eight of his comrades died that night before they killed those sneaky shits. Next week, Terry takes his turn guarding the perimeter. Hell, he's supposed to be a damn helicopter pilot by now but they're still ordering everyone to take a turn protecting the base. God help him."

Chuck made the sign of the cross. "Nothing better happen to my boys," he said, his voice trailing off. "Nothing."

The concern in his father's voice surprised Sean. Chuck watched the news every night, turning off the TV with the same confident prayer: "Dear God, please help the faithful stomp the shit out of those atheist Commies."

"I thought you said that the United States of America was undefeated in war and the Viet Cong were just the next losers on the list," said Sean.

"Lower your voice," said Chuck, turning to his son. "Your mother is upstairs resting. Her arthritis has flared, a sure sign she's upset. I don't want her to hear us. She can't worry all the time."

Chuck slammed his fists together.

"I heard you say it many times that an enlisted man hopes for a little war somewhere," said Sean. "It's a chance to get promoted. Isn't that how you got your commission to lieutenant?"

"Hush up, Buster," snapped Chuck. "I was in the Big One. This thing is crazy. The Viet Cong use all kinds of dirty tactics, including booby-trapped bicycles, for Christ sake. We need old Harry S. Truman in the White House. He'd nuke Hanoi and toast that slant-eyed Ho Chi Minh."

"That's a pleasant thought," chided Sean.

"Enough about Vietnam," said Chuck. "Your mother will be up soon."

Chuck rose from his chair and loomed over Sean.

"Did you hear the phone ring early this morning?" inquired Chuck.

Sean nodded.

"It was the good pastor of Saint Joseph's, Father Paul," said Chuck, staring intently at his son. "How exactly did you piss him off? Speak up before your mother gets down here and comes to your rescue."

Sean took a deep breath.

"Father Paul accused me of not doing enough to keep you in line. He was foaming at the mouth. Hell, I could almost feel his saliva over the phone line. When I pressed him for details, he said I should question you."

Chuck wagged his reading glasses at Sean. "Right now, I don't need you causing any more grief in my life, especially with the pastor," he said. "So give it up."

Sean dropped his head.

"I'm not going to wait all day, young man," said Chuck, stepping closer to his son.

"I want to know what's going on. That's an order."

"Dad, I didn't mean any disrespect to Father Paul," said Sean. "I've been late getting to church to help with Mass, that's all. Just twice, I promise. You know how Father Paul is about being on time. I'll do better in the future."

"If that's the problem, fix it fast," ordered Chuck, returning to his chair. "But you better not be lying or you can forget trying out for the football team. You got that, Buster?"

"Yes, sir!"

The sight of Lorraine trying to maneuver down the stairs interrupted the conversation.

"Go over and help your mother," directed Chuck.

Lorraine had paused at the first landing, holding the railing with both hands.

"Sean, get my cane out of the front closet," she said. "I need it for the rest of the trip."

When he returned, Lorraine caressed her son's cheek. Sean could tell from the redness around her eyes that his mother had been crying.

"My dear one, a pleasure to see you," said Lorraine. "It makes my day as you know. But why no sparkle in those blue eyes? Your light usually beams for all to see."

"Ah, mom, why do you say things like that," lamented Sean.

"Sean, my darling, because you are my life," said Lorraine, pushing a black curl off Sean's forehead. "Don't tell me you have worries. You're too young to take life so seriously."

Sean offered a weak smile and guided his mother down the rest of the staircase and into a chair next to his father. Lorraine placed her hand on Chuck's arm as she settled into her place.

"I have something very important to share with you both," said Lorraine, pulling a lace handkerchief from the pocket of her pink housecoat.

"A Marine chaplain visited the Doyles this morning," she said, her chin quivering. "That's the family that runs the dry cleaners in town. Marie opened her door before breakfast and there was Father Paul and the chaplain on her front porch."

Lorraine paused to dab her nose.

"They told Marie that her son is missing in action somewhere north of Saigon," she couldn't contain her sobs. "Marie fainted right there in her foyer."

Chuck leaned over to hug his wife.

"What can we do?" he asked.

"All the mothers in town with sons in the military are going to hold a vigil at church," she said. "We're going to say the rosary. You and Sean are welcome to join us."

Lorraine's deep moans brought tears to Chuck's eyes.

"Such trouble," she muttered. "All we can do now is put our faith in God and seek his blessing."

Sean looked away at the sight of his parents crying.

CHAPTER TWELVE

"How well do you know Sean Gerard and his friends, especially that Moran boy?"

Father Paul posed the question while finishing a ham sandwich inside the rectory kitchen. He placed the last bite in his mouth, wiping a small spot of mustard off his chin with a linen napkin. A platter in the center of the white table brimmed with luncheon meats and fresh breads. The pastor rolled a slice of salami up in a piece of Swiss cheese and held it up to the light streaming through the bay window.

"Do you see this piece of salted meat inside the cheese?" asked the priest, glaring at Father Ken across the table. "This is the Gerard and Moran boys—wrapped up in each other's lives, inseparable. When you see one, you see the other. I'm so angry with those boys right now that I could spit. They embarrassed me and nobody gets away with that."

Father Paul ripped the salami and cheese in half with his teeth.

The hands of the young priest began to tremble. He made two tight fists to quell the shaking, and then lowered his hands onto his lap. His shoulders slumped and his eyes, normally intensely green, seemed to fade under the stare from Father Paul.

"Why the stunned look?" asked Father Paul.

"I don't know Sean or Jimmy that well," answered Father Ken. "But I can't see any reason for you to have such malice towards them or any other child at our school."

"Is that right?" Father Paul demanded, piling rare roast beef onto his plate. "I've got it on good authority that the Gerard and Moran boys were behind the dunking incident at the DeLane party. That rumor is all over town."

Father Paul tapped his ring finger on the kitchen table. "What do you have to say about that?"

Father Ken cleared his throat, suddenly finding it thick with mucous. "Father, I'm just learning the complexities of being a priest in Vineyard Beach. I can't comprehend yet how much stress you've endured being the man in charge all these years."

"You're not answering my question," challenged the pastor.

"I think those boys, and all the children in our care, deserve the benefit of the doubt," offered the priest. "They are only children."

"Father Ken, once you've been a pastor as long as I have you'll understand how to treat the students," said the elder priest.

Father Paul folded a piece of beef and plopped it into his mouth. "Hell, there's been so many children go through this school over the years, I can't even remember most of their names," he said, chewing the morsel. "It's all a blur."

Father Ken watched a moth fluttering near a crucifix that dominated the far wall of the kitchen. The moth bumped against the body of Christ nailed to the cross, as Father Paul continued, "The important thing to know is that the success of the school is built on discipline and control," he said. "Forget nurturing. Keep the boot on their neck, if you want to keep the place running right."

Father Paul's Adam's apple plunged up and down.

"That's why what happened on the Fourth has to be dealt with," said the priest. "I don't want the word spreading through the school that Gerard and his gang put one over on me. It will encourage more mischief until the guilty are punished."

"That sounds like revenge," said Father Ken. "You can't find someone guilty based on gossip?"

Father Paul pushed his empty plate to the center of the table, wiping his face with his napkin.

"How do I know?" hissed the pastor, throwing his napkin on the table. "Gossip is one of this town's leading currencies. Secrets have a way of making the rounds and the incident at the DeLane's has tongues wagging. That one won't go away."

"But where's your evidence?" asked the young priest, the agitation in his voice causing Father Paul to scoot forward in his chair.

"You ask stupid questions. Proof. I don't need proof. I'm the pastor of Saint Joseph's and the folks in this parish have trusted me for over twenty years. All I need is my word. That's good enough."

Father Paul slammed his hand on arm of his chair. "Sean Gerard and his friends are not going to run wild from one end of Vineyard Beach to the other. Not on my watch. No way. No how. There will be an end to this incident soon, believe you, me."

"That sounds like a threat," said Father Ken, spreading his arms out. "What ever happened to forgiveness? That's what we teach. Shouldn't you ask for God's help to rid yourself of this poison?"

"That's easy for you to say, you weren't the injured party," lamented Father Paul.

"No I wasn't," replied Father Ken.

"I'm not asking you to forgive simply because we are supposed to forgive," said Father Ken, rising from his chair to place a hand on the pastor's shoulder. "I'm asking you to forgive so that you can find some peace. If it makes it any easier, I also heard the rumors about the DeLane party."

"See there, I told you so," said the pastor, brushing aside Father Ken's hand. "You didn't need to put up such a defense for the culprits."

"Father, I sought Sean out to let him know directly that what he did was wrong," said the young priest. "He followed my instructions, went to confession and made his penance."

"You warned Sean Gerard," barked the pastor. "You have much to learn about being a priest in this town."

Father Ken strode towards the door leading to the second-floor private quarters. He grabbed the handle and turned to the pastor. "Surely, you could be a role model to Sean and his friends instead of spending so much energy being angry."

"I'll take your advice under consideration," said the pastor, looking down at the table. "However, restitution needs to be made first. I'm sorry but that is how I feel."

"I'll pray tonight Father Paul that you find some peace and put this behind you," said the priest.

Father Paul reached for the lunchmeat as the kitchen door closed.

Ken Wasowski sprinted up the back stairs to his bedroom above the rectory office. He was behind schedule for the afternoon practice and he needed to arrive at the football field before his prospective players.

As he took off his dark shirt and collar, he felt his body come alive, taunt and muscular, snapping loose like an uncoiling spring. He dressed in a sweatshirt with cut-off sleeves, gray cotton shorts, white crew socks, and black athletic shoes with rippled soles.

The priest looked down to make sure his shorts covered the large panther tattooed on his upper thigh, a reminder of a drunken night in Montreal during a wild college road trip in the days before he devoted his life to Christ. His bulky thighs twitched at the start of his deep knee bends. He stretched his thick torso from side to side, finishing his routine by pumping his arms with hand weights until the blood gorged his biceps into tight balloons.

Father Ken picked up his coach's whistle off the dresser and looped the cord around his neck, then glanced at the clock above his bed. Time to go. He grabbed his clipboard and an equipment bag full of footballs as he darted out the door.

The priest ended his short jog to the field at the fifty-yard line. He walked slowly to the center, slipped off his shoes and folded his socks neatly. He dumped out the footballs, picked up the nearest one and held it out in front of his body.

Thump.

The football sailed off his foot high into the air and landed in the end zone at the far end of field.

Thump.

The priest did not acknowledge the gaggle of boys assembling on the sideline. He concentrated on his task

Thump.

The skin on his instep started to turn pink.

Thump.

The feel of the ball leaving his foot produced a deep laugh from the priest. Several of the boys started to cheer, all eyes on their coach with the magic foot smacking the ball higher and farther than they had ever seen.

Father Ken launched the last of the dozen footballs, squatting to don his socks and lace up his shoes.

He checked his watch, precisely four p.m. He leaped from the ground, sounding a long wail on his whistle.

"So what do we do now?" jabbed Jimmy Moran. "Come on Leader Boy, think of something."

"To hell if I know, this is all new to me too, smart-ass," replied Sean.

Another blast pierced the air.

"Gather round if you want to be part of this team," shouted the coach.

Sean and Jimmy ran with the pack to the middle of the field.

"Spread out around me," Father Ken ordered, drawing a big loop in the air with his finger. "Come on now fellas, get into a circle. It can't be that difficult. Hurry it up."

The boys jostled for position around their coach, who stood with his hands on his hips. It took several minutes for them to form up to the coach's satisfaction.

"Now, everybody shut up," announced the coach, holding up his hand. The group fell silent, fear sealing their lips.

Father Ken paced inside the circle, pausing in front of each player. Several flinched at the intensity of his gaze.

"Hey, Leader Boy, just what is this guy up to?" hissed Jimmy out of the corner of his mouth. "This is no priest we've ever seen before. Let's hope he doesn't join the tackling drills. Maybe Trotz and Pasquale were right not to try out."

Sean stared at the approaching coach, a slight smile crossing Father Ken's face. He winked at Sean and moved on. When he finished his inspection, the coach exploded into a sprint, racing inside the circle pointing his finger at the players.

The coach came to a sudden stop.

"Pay attention," he roared. "This is the first piece of business today. There are exactly sixty players here today but we have only forty uniforms."

Father Ken paused, watching the reaction from the assembly.

"I will be awarding gear to the players with heart and grit, starting with this first practice," he stated. "I'm looking for players who can compete. That means more to me then any amount of natural ability."

Sean and Jimmy exchanged worried looks.

"Now, turn to the teammate on your left, then to the one on your right," ordered the young priest, tapping his foot in the soft grass. "One of the players you just looked at won't be part of this team when the season starts. Those that do make the roster will have a sense of accomplishment that will stay with you the rest of your life."

He marched around the circle, studying his new recruits.

"No excuses! That's our motto this season. No excuses! Let me hear you say that. Right now. On the count of three."

The boys shouted in unison as ordered.

"I have one rule that can never be broken. Here on the field, I am Coach Ken. Off this practice field, I am Father Ken. It is important to remember that what happens on this field, stays on this field."

"Now, we are going to spend the next two hours running."

A collective groan floated over the field.

"Those who do well will go home with their helmets, the first step to being awarded a uniform," he said. "Eight laps around the field and back here. Last guy picks up all the footballs. Get going."

The players peeled away. After a lap, several boys, including Sean, pulled ahead of the pack. The coach studied the leaders. By the time practice ended, Sean's body oozed sweat. Even his sneakers were wet from the water running off his body.

Coach Ken stood at midfield, holding his clipboard and flanked by five silver helmets in a neat row at his feet. The St. Joseph's burgundy insignia glistened in the afternoon light.

The coach started to read off a list names. As each recruit approached, he tossed a helmet to them. Sean was the last one called.

"Keep working hard young man and you'll make this team," he said, nodding in approval. "Just don't pull any more stunts around town."

"Am I still in trouble with Father Paul?" blurted Sean.

"Let's just say you should steer clear of him for a while," answered the coach. "We'll find another time to talk. Go get some rest."

"Nice going, Leader Boy," said Jimmy, patting Sean on the head. "I didn't figure on you getting a helmet the first day. I need to step it up if I'm gonna get a uniform. See you at the next practice."

As Sean shuffled off carrying his prize, Candy DeLane glided through the trees at the far end of the field. She had watched the practice from the second-floor balcony of her estate across Lake Road.

Sean spotted Candy and waved his arm high in the air. He dropped to his right knee, propping his arm on his helmet he had placed on the ground.

Candy moved with the grace of a young deer, all sleek and nimble, her body covered only by white shorts and a red bathing suit top. She slowed at the edge of the field to flick her golden hair over her shoulders. She picked up her pace, her bare feet just clearing the tall grass. She stopped directly in front of Sean.

"You run pretty good for a little rich girl," offered Sean. "Are you sure you weren't raised by a bunch of wild dogs or something?"

"Stop being such a teaser, Sean," replied Candy. "I saw you hauling around here at a pretty fast clip. Maybe you're the one raised by wild animals. Certainly, you act like one sometimes."

Candy stuck her hands in her back pockets, swaying lightly as her breathing slowed. "You know, you could improve some on your manners, especially around young ladies," she said.

"Touchy, touchy," said Sean, standing and putting his helmet under his arm. "Are all rich girls this sensitive or is it only you?"

Candy waved her hand in front of her nose.

"My god, what is that smell?" challenged Candy. "That must be you Sean Gerard. Why you even smell like a wild animal! You could use a dip in my pool. Come along now."

"That sounds more like an order," responded Sean. "Do rich girls always get what they want? How do you know I'm going to follow you home?"

Candy held out her hand. "Because I have something important to show you. And I am a rich girl. Here, let me carry your helmet. I'd give you a quick hug but too many of your teammates are still around."

"What I really need is something to drink," pleaded Sean.

"I can fix you up with something to cool your insides too," she said, slipping on Sean's helmet and trotting off in the direction of her home.

"Hey, who said you could put on my helmet, you crazy rich girl!" yipped Sean. "Wait up. I'm not running any more today, not even for you."

Candy giggled as Sean caught up to her.

"That thing is way too hot!" she said, pulling off the helmet.

"Good to see you again, Sean Gerard," Candy said, sliding her hand into Sean's palm. They strolled across Lake Boulevard and up the driveway to the DeLane mansion.

At the top of the driveway, Candy handed Sean his helmet.

"I'll make some iced tea, you go ahead and hit the pool," she said. "Don't worry about a suit, you can go in your shorts or go in without them if you want."

"Is that a dare?" wondered Sean.

"Sean, I was only kidding. Do what makes you feel comfortable but leave your boxers on. I'll meet you around at the pool."

Candy smiled over her shoulder as she headed inside the main house.

The pool beckoned, calling to Sean like the shade of a tall oak tree beckoning an old dog.

Sean stripped to his boxers and dove off the board. He swam to the far end and crouched on the bottom step, the water soaking away the tightness in his legs.

Candy appeared carrying a silver tray adorned with a glass pitcher and two frosted mugs. She placed the tray on the edge of the pool.

"Are you ready for your tea, smelly boy?" she laughed.

Sean smiled.

"Watch me take off my shorts," she teased, filling both mugs. "I want to see the look on your face when you see all of me in my bikini. I've really been working on my tan."

Candy wiggled out of her shorts, kicking them towards Sean.

He caught them in midair.

Candy placed her hands on her hips and spun around revealing her white bikini, her brown sleekness causing Sean to exhale slowly.

"Gosh, you are a vision," gushed Sean. "Well, show-off, you look a lot better than the last time I saw you out on the lake."

"Don't be a smarty pants," cooed Candy as she slipped in the pool behind Sean. "I'm feeling like my old self again so don't bring up bad memories and ruin the moment." She wrapped her arms around Sean's shoulders, pressing her firm breasts tightly against his back. Sean took several deep breaths.

Candy scooped up a handful of water and sprinkled it over Sean's head, stroking his dark hair with her free hand.

"That feels so good," he moaned. "No one's ever massaged my head before. Don't stop. The pain of that practice might go away."

"I'll only quit to give you a chance to kiss me," announced Candy.

Sean spun around to look at the girl from California, her brilliant blue eyes dancing.

"Are you just going to sit there and stare at me all day?"

"I'm sorry," giggled Sean. "My brain locked up."

Sean pulled Candy onto this lap.

"I always feel better when I'm with you," pronounced Sean. "Everything about you, the sound of your voice, your touch, everything, makes my spirit soar."

Sean engulfed Candy in his arms, running his fingers over her back, her shoulders and finally her neck. His hands tingled at the feel of the cool water dripping off her soft skin.

Candy leaned in and pulled Sean's lips tight against hers, flicking her tongue inside his mouth.

"Open your mouth a little bit more," instructed Candy.

Candy parted her lips and Sean pushed his tongue deep inside her mouth. They stayed locked tightly together, Candy returning Sean's passion, her breathing growing deeper. She gently guided his hand under her bathing suit top.

"I want your hand there but don't squeeze too hard," she whispered. "They're not cantaloupes."

"Yes, I will do as I am told," said Sean excitedly.

"Finally, some manners from you."

Sean gently caressed her breast as their kissing intensified. Candy could feel Sean's hardness pushed against her buttocks. She slowly began to slide up and down in his lap, using her body to increase Sean's excitement. She took off her top and moved Sean's hands to cup her breasts. His face turned bright pink as Candy continued to push against his body. After several minutes, Sean yanked his mouth away and arched his back.

"Oh God, oh God!" moaned Sean.

His body shook. Ecstasy.

"Don't say anything for a minute or two 'til you catch your breath," she whispered.

Candy moved off Sean's lap, threw a towel down and stretched out on the side of the pool.

Sean drained his mug of iced tea, staring at the half-naked goddess resting in the sun.

He waded through the water to Candy, bending over to kiss her breasts. Candy held the back of his head as he took each nipple in his mouth.

"Be gentle, gentle, gentle," she purred.

Sean filled the mug with pool water, slowing pouring it over Candy's stomach.

"Candy DeLane. Candy DeLane," mused Sean. "That was an amazing feeling. I've never had that happen before. You are …."

Candy put her finger over Sean's mouth. "Hush, Sean Gerard. I'm the lucky one to have a friend like you. Kiss me again."

CHAPTER THIRTEEN

Sean gently rolled his head from side to side, stretching the muscles at the base of his neck. He pushed his chin hard over until the vertebrae separated at the top of his spine, the sound of his joints cracking spooking an old seagull at the end of the pier. The bird flapped away into the sunlight leaking over the Lake Erie horizon. He leaned against the weathered oak door to Dell's shack, the intoxication of his poolside rendezvous with Candy still lingering at a level he couldn't fully comprehend. He thought back to his shower before bed, the cold water doing little to quell his excitement. He'd hung the washcloth on his erection as he stepped out of the porcelain tub, unable to abate his arousal.

The gentle hum of waves lapping against the pier's barnacle-laced pilings mingled with heavy snoring as it filtered through an open window. Sean paused for a moment on the threshold, inhaling the cool morning air deep into his lungs.

"Time to raise the dead," he whispered. He lifted the rusty hammer off the door that Dell had rigged as a knocker and banged three times.

"Wake up, Sleeping Beauty!" shouted Sean. "The sun is starting to come up. You need to get moving."

A loud thump sent a shudder through the pier's hand-hewn planks, the force of the gyrating boards running up Sean's legs.

"What was that noise, one of your famous farts," yelled Sean, his voice echoing across the cove. Sean stifled a laugh, the notion of Dell stumbling around in his darkened cabin an image worth savoring.

"Who goes there this early in my day?" roared Dell. "Friend or foe."

"It's one of Snow White's dwarfs, open the door and take a look," teased Sean.

"You better be careful or I might come out shooting. And it ain't gonna be the same stuff I dish up for the rat bastards piloting around here. It'll be something much worse for two-legged varmint."

"Come on Dell, you wouldn't shoot me now, would ya?"

Sean closed his eyes and envisioned Dell on the floor groping for his glasses. From the power of the impact, Sean figured the old fisherman had probably fallen out of his hammock near the wood-burning stove in the middle of his cabin.

"Hurry up so I don't have to stand out here all morning," taunted Sean. "You'd be better off leaving your glasses on when you sleep. It would make your mornings a lot safer."

The unmistakable sound of bone hitting metal filled the air.

"Shit. Piss. Fuck."

Sean put his mouth up to the space between the door and its frame to ensure his voice carried into the cabin.

"Hey you old goat, why are you using up your favorite cuss words? I thought you saved those for special occasions. Your head must have bounced off that old stove of yours."

"Shut up, smart guy," moaned Dell. "My skull hurts."

"If you slept in a bed like normal people, you wouldn't have to worry about falling on the floor when you woke up."

Several minutes passed before the cabin door cracked open and Dell poked his face through the opening.

"You've heard of carpe diem, young man," grumbled Dell, staring at Sean. "That's seize the day. Well, buckaroo, there's also *crapo diem*, that's survive the day, which is what I'm doing right now looking at your sorry face. At least this morning I don't have to look up the word 'shit' in the dictionary, because it's piled up right in front of me in dawn's early light."

"You have such a way with words," said Sean in mock resignation. "I thought you liked me."

Dell slammed the door with such force the rope holding the hammer broke.

"You are not coming into my palace until I brew some coffee," said Dell from behind the door. "I can't stand your company before my wake-up juice oils my throat. And from the look on your face, I'll bet you've seen the rich girl again. A drop of my special coffee sweetener will make it easier to tolerate you, Sean Gerard."

"Heck, pour me a mug of that sweetener," said Sean. "Hate to see you drink alone."

"What's the point?" retorted Dell. "If I didn't drink alone, I'd never have a libation."

Smoke soon billowed out of the top of the small chimney jutting through the tin roof of the cabin. The aroma of brewing coffee mixed with the stench of a few rotting rats rolling in the surf near the shoreline.

When the door finally opened, the sight of Dell shocked Sean.

"I don't believe my eyes," stammered Sean. "To heck with my story, what the heck happened to you?"

Dell stepped out onto the pier carrying a steaming mug in his right hand, the scent of bourbon following him out the door.

Sean's eyes popped at the full vision of Dell Pilot. His gray hair was neatly trimmed and his usual five-day facial stubble was replaced by a light one-day dusting. His signature green overalls were recently laundered, not a fish gut or spot of blood in sight. Even his fingernails sparkled.

"Dell, you don't look right," said Sean, sliding around the fisherman for a full inspection. "Hell, you don't even smell right. What the hell is going on? Did Veronica Maggione come around and shake her big tits to get you to clean up?"

"No such luck, my little piece of fish bait," offered Dell with a wave of his hand. "My appendix blew up on me and I spent three days in the hospital. Just got out last night. Those crazy nurses scrubbed me from head to toe and a few places polite people don't talk about. Damn them, they shaved my pubic hairs for Christ sakes."

"Dell, does that mean you're not only a ball-less wonder, but a hair-less one as well?" laughed Sean.

"Not true," replied Dell, pausing to sip from his mug. "My two are still hanging around, they're just a bit lighter. And if you're not careful, I'll hang my package out right now just to prove my point."

Sean held up his hand.

"I give," he said. "Besides, with your luck, a seagull might swoop down and snack on your little worm for breakfast."

"Sean, why don't you take a bite out of one my arsenic dough balls and make the world a better place?" countered Dell. "This is a promise, give me a few days of fishing and I'll be back to my old self. Count on it, Mr. Gerard. Enjoy the fresh air while it lasts."

The old fisherman drained the last of his morning brew. "I've always done my best thinking out on the lake," he said. "Let's go wet a line. I'll grab the fishing gear."

"Maybe we'll get lucky and be the first in town to catch a Coho salmon," Sean said, slapping Dell on the shoulder. "The lake's been stocked since springtime. Sooner or later someone's gotta hook one, might as well be us."

Dell walked away shaking his head.

"You got fish eggs for brains," said Dell over his shoulder. "If you get lucky and snag a Coho, we're splitting the $500 prize the city put up. Get the boat ready."

Dell ducked inside his cabin.

The eighteen-foot aluminum two-seater, lashed to a piling and draped in a canvas tarp, bobbed on the water at the end of the pier. Sean pulled back the cover and folded it neatly before placing it under the backbench near the outboard motor. The twenty-horsepower Evinrude glistened in the sun, its dark green lid layered in a film of oil. Dell babied that old motor, pampering it after every fishing trip with gobs of lubrication. He liked to brag that his one prize possession never failed him unlike some of the people in his life. It purred with more consistency than any woman he ever loved and ran hard against approaching storms. And it always started on the first pull.

Dell returned carrying a bucket of live minnows and two fishing poles. "Get ready to push off, Ishmael."

"Ish-me-who?" asked Sean.

"Ishmael," said Dell, "you know, Moby Dick. The great white whale. God, you Catholic kids don't get to read anything. Were the nuns worried that the word 'dick' was in the title? Steady the boat, I'm getting in."

Before stepping on board, Dell tossed his head back and propelled a wad of saliva straight up. The spit spun in the wind over his head. He watched it closely, following it down until it smacked the pier.

"It's blowing down from the North," he said with authority. "It just might drive some fish our way. Push off, Matey."

Dell leaned over and gently kissed the top of his motor. "Come on, ole girl. It's Dell. Time to make love, my dear Mary."

When he pulled the starter cord, the engine sputtered for a moment, then jumped to life. The little boat crawled out of the cove trailing a thin of line smoke. Dell waited until they were out into the lake before opening the throttle, the surge of power lifting the bow towards the horizon.

"Hang on, Sean! Mary's an old girl but she's still got some kick left."

The dinghy plowed through the small waves, headed in the direction of the rock pilings that jetted out from the nearby electric plant. The smoke from the coal-burning facility hung in the air as Dell steered towards the biggest outcropping.

"Get ready Sean, we're dropping anchor," ordered Dell. The boat started to slow, giving Sean a chance to clear the anchor rope from under his bench. He stood with the weight in his right hand, the rope looped for a quick toss over the side.

"Say the word, Captain," said Sean.

Dell cut the engine and they glided towards the line of rocks.

"This is the spot, my good man," said Dell confidently. "Drop anchor!"

The weight quickly slid below the brownish water, bringing them to a stop.

Each fisherman pulled a live minnow from the bucket and carefully slid a hook through the soft skin just below the backbone. They made sure the bait wiggled with plenty of action before casting near the base of the stone jetty. The baitfish swam just below the surface, red topwater bobbers marking the spots.

Dell rested his fishing pole next to the motor.

"So, what's with the funny look on your face?" prodded Dell. "If life threw a wild card of love on the table, I hope you picked it up. Is that what happened?"

Sean worried what to tell Dell about his feelings for Candy and the secret about Father Paul bothered him even more.

"I'm not sure I can trust you," said Sean, sizing Dell up.

"Balderdash," replied Dell, spitting over the side into the lake. You'd better be careful if you're trying to get that girl hotter than a two-dollar pistol. Her Daddy is the biggest big shot in Vineyard Beach. I don't think he'd want a scallywag like you seducing his daughter."

"Dell, when did you become a preacher?" asked Sean. "Can't you just be my friend?"

"Sure, I'll be your friend," intoned Dell, pulling out a Camel. "Just don't make me have to read your mind."

Sean put down his fishing pole, leaned forward, and put his hands on his knees, watching Dell blow a series of perfect smoke rings.

"I'm waiting," Dell said, flicking his butt overboard.

"How much do you know about Father Paul, the pastor of Saint Joe's?" blurted Sean.

"Father Paul?" said Dell quizzically. "That's a surprise. I'm not the kind to go searching the priesthood for friends, if you know what I mean. But there's plenty of gossip around town about the pastor. Go real slow so I don't miss a thing."

"What's the rumors about Father Paul?" asked Sean.

"Well for starters, he likes his drink," said Dell. "At least that's what people say. It seems the pastor has a taste for Beefeater Gin, even before breakfast, which I don't have a problem with. But there's also talk that he steps out from time to time."

"What's that mean?" wondered Sean.

"It means Father Paul is down in the muck with the rest of the human race and likes to have sex," said Dell, wiping sweat off his forehead. "Why the surprised look? Priests are just like everybody else. You can forget that celibacy crap."

"I didn't know there was that much talk about Father Paul," said Sean innocently. "I never heard anything like that in my house. I guess I was raised to expect more from a priest."

"Heck, Sean, you're just a kid," lectured Dell. "You don't realize the struggle that comes with life. Most folks in the boondocks out here think there are only two kinds of people in the world, the God-fearing ones and those heading for hell. Sure the world is divided into two groups. There's one group who've had trouble in their lives. And there are the other ones who haven't lived long enough to have their turn."

The two fishermen stopped their discussion for a moment to check their poles.

"So which group do you belong to, Sean?" asked Dell.

"I'm definitely with the ones facing trouble," replied Sean.

"I gather from your questioning that you've got a problem with Father Paul, am I right?"

Sean nodded.

"You better be careful with Father Paul," warned Dell as he reached into the minnow bucket for fresh bait. "He's even a bigger shot than that Mister DeLane. You might want to get some more help before you make a move against the pastor. But you haven't said what the priest is up to, now did—Holy cow!" boomed Dell, "your bobber's disappeared and it's headed for frigging Toronto."

Sean jumped to his feet, grabbed his pole and jerked it hard overhead.

"Set the hook, set the hook, Captain Ahab," yelled Dell. "Keep your rod tip up. You don't want to lose *this* fish."

Sean stood in the bow, adjusting the drag on his reel to be sure the fish didn't snap the line that was streaming off into the distance.

"Jesus, that son of bitch is running for Canada!" hollered Dell. "Let that fish have all the line it wants, we'll tire him out."

"Dell, my line just went slack," cried Sean. "I think I lost him!"

"Holy saints in heaven, he's turned, he's turned," screamed Dell. "He's heading back towards us! Reel as fast as you can!"

Sean cranked the handle until his knuckles ached.

The line finally tightened. Sean's pole was bent in half and aimed directly under the boat.

"You still got him," coached Dell. "I'm gonna bring up the anchor so he doesn't rip the line clear on the chain. Get ready for another run!"

"Were drifting," said Sean.

"No were not," said Dell. "Your fish is pulling us!"

"When will this monster give up?" moaned Sean. "My arms are killing me."

"It won't be much longer now," said the old fisherman.

Sean sensed the fight was nearing an end. The fish stopped running and Sean could feel he had control now. He kept reeling, watching the water for any sign of his fish.

"What do I have on there, Dell?" exclaimed Sean. "Better get your net ready."

The fish broke the surface next to boat, the steel blue skin along its top clearly visible. The exhausted fish rolled on its side, revealing brilliant silver flanks.

"Dell, that doesn't look like any fish I've ever seen come out of this lake," said Sean gleefully. "Is it what I think it is?"

Dell scooped the fish into the boat and lifted it by the gills.

"Coho! Coho! Coho!" chanted Dell. "Sean Gerard, as God is our witness, you have hooked yourself a ten-pound Coho salmon, the first ever caught in Vineyard Beach."

Sean caressed the fish on his lap on the return trip, his heart pounding.

"Do you know what this means," yelled Sean over the wind

"Sure do," said Dell, gunning the throttle, "it means, Master Sean, that the beautiful fish you're squeezing so hard is gonna make you a legend in these parts and you owe me two-hundred fifty bucks."

"Right on both counts Dell, but it also means I'll get my picture in the Vineyard Beach Press," stated Sean proudly. "Right there on the front page holding my record fish. I think my old man might even be proud."

As the boat neared the pier, Sean jumped out carrying his prize under his arm.

Dell hurried off, trying to hunt up something to hold the fish. He returned from his cabin carrying a narrow wood box with a layer of fresh ice on the bottom.

"Drop that beauty in here, I believe it will fit," Dell said. The fish slid out of Sean's hands onto the ice. "Throw your bike in the back of my truck and I'll run you by your house on the way to the newspaper office."

"My dad's gonna go crazy when he sees this fish," chuckled Sean, his arm draped over the box on the front seat.

Dell massaged the gearshift guiding his truck towards the Gerard home.

"What's up with you?" asked Sean. "You've hardly said a word since we got off the water."

"Been thinking about what you were asking me out on the lake before Mister Coho came along," said Dell. "It's time you talked with your dad about Father Paul. He'll know what to do."

"I don't think I can do that!" erupted Sean. "No way."

The truck rounded the corner of Maple Avenue.

"Dell, look down the street at my house, what's all the commotion about?" demanded Sean, worry creeping over his face.

"Maybe it's a welcoming party?" offered Dell.

There were several cars parked in the Gerard driveway and more lined the street. One car in particular seemed out of place. The Ford sedan was parked next to the curb, its drab green in sharp contrast to the other cars nearby. Sean could read the words on the side door as the truck pulled up: "U.S. Army."

"What's that Army car doing here?" said Sean, his voice breaking. "This ain't right."

Sean jumped out of the truck before it came to a full stop, running for the house.

"Hey, what do you want me to do with this damn Coho?" shouted Dell.

Sean turned just before he reached the front porch.

"Do the right thing," said Sean. "Get your picture in the paper and hang onto my share of the money."

Sean studied the scene through the open front door, trying to comprehend what was happening. He recognized neighbors, and some of the other visitors inside, like his mom's bridge partners. But the house seemed jammed with strangers, including several service men in Army dress uniforms. The conversation in the foyer stopped when he crossed the threshold. The group stepped aside so Sean could make his way in. No one spoke as he headed for the back of the house.

The kitchen sink overflowed with plates, cups and dirty glasses. Several casserole dishes, a platter of cold cuts, and fresh bread adorned the counters. Baked goods of all kinds, cookies, cakes, and brownies, covered the big oak table in the middle of the room. A pot of coffee simmered on the gas stove. Sean stood in a corner, watching visitors trek past to refill their cups and sample the buffet.

Sean crept over to look through the shutter doors into the den. He needed desperately to see a familiar face. Lorraine would never allow this many guests into her home without constant attention to their needs.

"Where is my mom?" wondered Sean.

Sean felt relief to see Father Ken coming down the stairs but as he approached, the young priest's expression chased away any sense of well-being.

"Father Ken, where are my parents?" Sean inquired, his eyes brimming with tears.

"Sean, your folks are upstairs with Father Paul," the priest said, squeezing Sean's shoulder. "They'll be down in a little while to talk with you and the rest of the folks here. For now, they're praying with the pastor."

"Is it bad, Father? Please tell me," pleaded Sean. "Is it my brothers? Did something happen to my brothers in Vietnam? Is that why the Army is here?"

"Catch your breath Sean, and slow down on the questions," comforted the priest.

Father Ken put his arms around Sean. "This will be hard to hear, and harder for me to say but you need to know that your brother Terry died two days ago while on guard duty. His body will be shipped home for his funeral in a few days. Try and be strong, young man. Your parents will need your support."

Sean jerked away from the priest.

"What kind of God lets my brother die and still allows bad people to go unpunished?" wailed Sean.

"Sean, try and compose yourself," advised Father Ken. "The pastor would like to talk with you privately and offer his assistance in your time of sorrow."

Sean turned and ran out the back door, falling to his knees behind the garage. "Dear God, whatever has happened, give me the courage to face the rest of the day," cried Sean. He heaved the contents of his stomach onto the lawn.

The creaking of the rusty hinges on the back screen door announced the approach of someone from the house.

Sean felt two hands rest on his shoulders; he looked up into the face of Father Paul.

"My son, I'm so sorry," said the pastor. He took out his handkerchief and wiped Sean's chin clean. "Please get to your feet and let's walk around to the side of the house where we can talk and not be interrupted."

Sean began to turn the corner when the blow struck the back of his head. He fell forward, sticking his arms out at the last second to protect his face from smashing into the ground. The suddenness of the assault and its force knocked his breath away. He rolled to his side. The black Wingtip drove deep into his stomach, knocking the last of the air from his lungs. He closed his eyes and curled into a ball for protection. The attacker stomped his spine, spreading pain throughout his body. Sean's sobs came in short gasps. The kicking stopped. He lay motionless, fearing the assault would begin again.

"Open your eyes you little shit," ordered the priest, encircling Sean's neck with his hands. "I want you to see the next one coming."

Sean stared at Father Paul, his cheeks flushed, his mouth contorted in rage.

"My god, what are you doing to me," moaned Sean. "I think my ribs are broken."

"God can't help you now Sean Gerard," hissed the priest. "You made a fool out of me and nobody does that and gets away with it."

"Why are you hurting me, Father Paul?" cried Sean. "I'm sorry. I didn't mean any disrespect. Don't hit me again."

"Shut up with your whining," barked the priest. "I'm going to make your life a living hell. You'll wish you were the one killed by the Viet Cong."

The priest released his right hand, drew his arm back, and slammed his fist into Sean's side.

"Don't you shut your eyes on me," commanded the priest.

The priest tightened his grip around Sean's throat. "Keep them open. Look at me. Look at me. I'm the one in control, not you."

The priest poked his index finger into Sean's forehead, over and over again.

"Get it through that little skull of yours. I'm the boss, you understand, I'm the boss. I'd pound your pathetic face to a pulp right now but I don't want to leave any marks."

The priest leaned down to put his mouth next to Sean's ear.

"And if you mention a word about this, I'll tell everyone in town I caught you in the back of the church with Jimmy Moran's penis in your mouth," whispered the priest. "You got that, smart guy? And everyone, including your parents, will believe me."

The priest stood up, placing his foot on Sean's ankle and pressing his weight down. Sean screamed.

"Lower your voice or you'll get some more," said Father Paul, smoothing out his gray hair.

The priest stepped back, contemplating his next move.

The opening gave Sean enough space to roll free. He limped for the property line and didn't stop until he saw the Moran home ahead on the next street.

"Keep going you little creep," yelled Father Paul.

Father Ken met the pastor at the kitchen door.

"You look a bit flustered Father," said the young priest. "Everything okay with Sean?"

"He's fine, he's fine," replied the pastor, smiling. "He just wants to be alone right now."

CHAPTER FOURTEEN

The line of cars stretched for blocks behind the black hearse, slowing the procession of grief winding down Lake Road in Vineyard Beach. The obituary in the Cleveland *Plain Dealer* announced that the viewing for Terry Gerard, slain Vietnam War hero, would last two days at the Bryant Funeral Home, followed by a Mass of Christian Burial at St. Joseph's Catholic Church, Pastor Paul Sterner officiating. At the funeral home, an honor guard stood on each side of the fallen soldier resting in a mahogany casket covered in an American flag. People from all over town made the pilgrimage to sign the guest book in support of the troops and to show respect for Chuck and Lorraine.

Now, the same townsfolk dotted the street outside the church, the older men saluting as the hearse passed.

Sean perched next to Jimmy Moran in the back seat of the limousine creeping behind the hearse. He kept his eyes trained at the scene in the church parking lot. Watching the mourners was easier than looking at his parents facing him in the front seat of the car. His mom and dad stared at the floor mats. Lorraine's rosary was wrapped around her right hand, which trembled slightly as she adjusted the black veil covering her face. A high school graduation photo of his dead son rested on Chuck's lap. The patriarch slouched in his seat; little sleep and hours of crying had left his eyes puffy and red.

Sean held his left side, each breath rattling his rib cage. He thought back to last week when he showed up at Jimmy's side door, moaning in pain. He hid in the basement using an ice pack to help with the swelling

Tom Tozer

around his chest. In between sobs, he told Jimmy that Father Paul attacked him on the same day his older brother was reported killed in action in Vietnam.

"Hey putz, you gonna make it through the day?" whispered Jimmy.

"Dumb question, moron." replied Sean, shaking his head. "Why don't you just zip it?"

The limo turned the corner into the St. Joseph's parking lot.

"Who's the moron?" replied Jimmy. "I didn't get my ass stomped by an old priest."

"Bastard," snarled Sean under his breath.

"I'll shut up," said Jimmy.

The limousine stopped at the front of the church and was quickly surrounded by mourners who opened the doors to help the Gerards disembark. The boys ignored the outreached hands and slid to a small space in the crowd near the back of the vehicle. They watched two ushers escort Chuck and Lorraine up the marble steps.

"Hey, Leader Boy," said Jimmy. "I tried to talk you out of pushing the pastor into the DeLane pool. But you had to have your way as usual and now we're all screwed."

"I thought you were going to shut up for awhile," challenged Sean. "We shouldn't even be talking about that today. I'm scared enough about going into that church."

"Well, at least we don't have to be on the altar assisting Father Paul," asserted Jimmy. "Come on cry baby," he said, draping his arm around his friend and helping him up the steps with the last of the arrivals. "You're a mess. But I'm still your friend today, tomorrow and forever. Remember that. Now, get it together. We've got to make it through this funeral."

The boys stopped just inside the church foyer.

Jimmy pointed out Sean's parents near the front of the church in a pew adjacent to the casket.

"Buck up, Captain. Here we go," said Jimmy.

The boys crept up the center aisle, pausing at the pew behind Chuck and Lorraine. Before taking their seats, Sean leaned in and kissed his mother on the cheek. He squeezed his father's shoulder but Chuck made no sign of acknowledgement. Johnny and Buddy had arrived early to save space for their friends. The four boys only had time to exchange handshakes before the congregation stood up.

Pastor Paul Sterner, followed by his young protégée, emerged from the priests' quarters and stepped slowly to the front of the altar. Father Ken bowed his head to the parishioners before moving to a red velvet chair at the side of the altar. The pastor waited while his assistant took his seat. He then descended two steps to stand in front of his faithful.

The priest held his hands up. A fresh breeze pushed cool air through the small openings at the base of the stained-glass windows flanking the church.

"Before we begin this holy Mass, I want to address Chuck and Lorraine, and their son Sean," intoned the priest.

Sean startled at the mention of his name.

"On this day, I hope the Gerards feel the loving embrace of their Catholic brethren," said Father Paul.

Sean glared at the priest.

"Terry Gerard died defending his country, a noble cause that enables us to live in freedom," said Father Paul. "We know in our hearts that the life we honor here today was not lost in vain. This warrior rests with the angels in the tender care of Jesus Christ, our savior."

Father Paul's mention of heaven brought the anger inside Sean to a boil. How can this priest talk about such things? Sean fantasized about spitting in the priest's face. He slammed his fist into the prayer books stack at the end of the pew.

"Hey, you're coming back to life there," Jimmy said, tapping his friend on the knee. "Better tone it down, or the old fart up there might hear you."

Sean placed his clenched fists on his lap.

"Brethren, let me feel your hearts filled with the spirit of the Holy Ghost," said the pastor. "Pray with meaning, pray for peace, pray for Terry, pray for the Gerards, and pray for all of the sinners here today."

The priest moved towards the Gerards, stopping occasionally in the first few pews to bless a parishioner. He touched the casket and bowed towards Chuck. Lorraine pulled the priest's hand to her forehead.

"Thank you for your blessing," she uttered.

The priest smiled at Sean and his friends, his left eyebrow arching into a rigid peak, accenting the malice in his eyes. All four boys leaned back against the pew.

Father Paul closed the space to the boys, bending to speak privately to Sean. To the congregation, it was a priestly gesture from a man of God. Sean reeled at the hot breath against his ear. It smelled of gin.

"Be careful little boy," hissed the priest.

Father Paul blessed both sides of the church on his return to the altar.

"Man, this is crazy," moaned Sean.

"What did he say?" demanded Jimmy, pulling Sean's arm.

"You wouldn't believe it," replied Sean. "I'm not sure I believe it. We're all in deep shit with that guy."

The stress of the last few days flowed over Sean like a wave kicked up from a Lake Erie thunderstorm, the fatigue making his head spin. He closed his eyes and drifted off, his body slowly sliding down until his head rested on Jimmy's shoulder.

"You nap, my friend," murmured Jimmy, patting Sean's forehead. "I'll wake you if you miss anything."

Jimmy smiled at Sean's light snoring.

"Jeez, you are tired," he declared.

Throughout the service, Jimmy stayed in his seat. Buddy and Johnny moved to flank the two friends so other parishioners wouldn't notice Sean.

A mourner directly behind Jimmy touched his shoulder.

"I'm sure the young man's grief has drained him," observed the man.

Sean woke to hear part of the sermon, Father Paul expounding on living a good life based on the Ten Commandments.

"If God did not care for us, he would not have created this framework for living in his love, these commandments," lectured the priest. "Terry is with his heavenly Father today because he chose to take God's commandments seriously."

Near the end of the Mass, Jimmy nudged his friend, being careful not to touch his bruised ribs.

"Hey, you. Start coming around," he said softly.

Sean bolted straight up and heard Father Paul announce: "The Mass is ended, go in peace."

Jimmy helped Sean to his feet, holding him gingerly as he rose out of the pew. Sean wiped a small dab of drool from the corner of his mouth and tried to focus.

"This really is happening," admitted Sean, watching the two priests take their place at the head of the funeral procession.

The honor guard hoisted the casket of the dead soldier up to their shoulders with one clean jerk. As they passed in front of Chuck, his hand snapped to his forehead for a shaky salute. The old pilot stumbled out of the pew into the main aisle, grasping Lorraine's arm for support. Chuck took a minute to gain his balance before lurching towards the front doors. Sean, his friends, and the congregation fell in behind the Gerards for the trip to the cemetery on the edge of the church property.

In the back corner of the church, near the stand of candles, Candy studied the statue of the Virgin Mary hovering over the flames of the faithful, envious of the serene smile of the Madonna. The news of Sean's brother's death triggered another round of nightmares and bed-wetting. Standing inside the church for the first time since the attack, Candy fought the urge to run. She shut her eyes at the sight of Father Paul leading the funeral procession down the main aisle.

Candy tried to concentrate on finding Sean. She stood on her toes to scan the departing parishioners, spotting Sean with his head down walking slowly behind his parents. As the entourage passed, Candy slipped next to Sean and touched his arm.

"I can't believe you're here," he blurted. "I'm sorry I haven't seen you in a while. So much has happened in the last few days."

Sean stroked the side of Candy's face. "You're on fire," he said.

"It took all my courage to come here again," replied Candy. "But you should be worrying about yourself now."

"Yes, your highness. You know, looking at you is kinda comforting."

"Quiet with all the lovey, dovey stuff," remarked Candy.

Candy steered Sean towards the coat rack lining the back of the church foyer. Sean's friends acknowledged the couple but were careful not to approach. When the main body of the congregation had passed,

Candy ran her hands through Sean's dark hair and kissed him on the mouth.

"That was nice but I could really just use a hug," stated Sean.

"Don't be your usual difficult self. Come closer my wounded hero."

Sean stepped into Candy's open arms, drinking in her scent. The fullness of her small breasts and taunt frame pushed against his body made him feel safe. The couple held each other watching the last of the mourners exiting the church. They fell in behind the parishioners heading across the lawn for the internment service. Halfway across the front yard, Sean stopped and pulled Candy back into his arms.

"I'll need to lean on you now," admitted Sean. "Sorry about this serious stuff…"

Candy put her hand over Sean's mouth.

"*Shh!* Quiet down, I'll help you."

Sean returned a weak smile.

"I need your best friendship to get through this," he said.

"Oh, Sean, please be strong, I need you too. This has been a terrible summer."

"My mom says that in tough times, all we can do is stay true to God and not lose our faith," offered Sean.

"Are you sure there even is a God?"

Sean shrugged, swinging his arm around Candy's waist. "That is a good question with no good answer," he claimed. "Let's just get this next part of the day over with."

The procession slowed at the entrance to the cemetery, pausing for the honor guard to unlock the entrance. The wrought iron gates were bordered in a pattern of intricate grape vines. Woven into the design at the top of the arch were the words "May Ye Rest In Peace." The captain of the guard pulled open the double doors, the rusty hinges responding in a low growl.

The gravedigger had prepared the burial spot with surgical detail near an ancient maple tree, the green sod cut expertly with a spade and piled in clean rows next to a mound of dark Ohio soil. The air smelled of wet leaves and freshly cut grass. The parishioners pushed forward on the damp lawn, encircling the resting place in a tight embrace. The folks in the back rows craned their necks for a better view.

Chuck nodded at Father Paul. That morning, he had pressured the pastor to promise that the service wouldn't linger at the end. He wanted his son buried with military precision.

"Enough tears have fallen," he had said to the priest at breakfast.

Father Paul spread his arms over the congregation.

"Brethren, bow your heads in a moment of silence for Terry," he prayed. "Thank him for the life he led in Christ and for his great sacrifice. Remember, his soul rests with his savior, Jesus Christ and all the saints in heaven."

The only sound in the cemetery was the chirping of a cardinal perched on the fence as the priest shook holy water from a silver sprinkler over the casket. A few drops hit Chuck in the side of his face. He wiped the moisture off with his sleeve.

The captain of the honor guard slid the American flag off the casket and folded it into a tight triangle. Chuck rose off his chair to accept the memento, pulling it to his chest. He nodded to the soldier, then turned and placed the flag on Lorraine's lap. Chuck dropped into his seat, grasping his wife's hand as the honor guard lowered his son's body into the ground. When the ropes were pulled clear, Chuck and Lorraine tossed a handful of soil onto the lid of the casket.

Sean stood behind his parents, his hands shoved deep into his pockets. He kept his head down so no one could see the tears running in a stream off the end of his nose. He looked up at Candy. The pain on his face made her afraid.

"This is all unfair," he moaned. "Why did this have to happen? My brother didn't deserve to die."

Candy dug into her purse and held out a handful of tissues. Sean shook his head at the pile in her hand.

"Come on. Clean up fella."

Sean finally accepted the offer, wiping his eyes clear, then blowing his nose.

"I cannot believe my brother is being lowered into the cold, cold ground," he howled, the ache in his voice cutting to Candy's heart.

Candy motioned to Sean's friends, the three moving in to form a protective circle. Jimmy rested a hand on Sean's head, John and Buddy held a shoulder.

"All of us have to stick together," insisted Candy. "We have to look out for each other, especially Sean."

"Sean, are you going to ride with us?"

Sean stared at his mother, her face hidden behind her black veil. He marveled at her strength trying to hold the family together. Chuck had retreated to the basement where he sat for hours, his only movement the raising of his bourbon bottle to his lips.

"No mom. I'm gonna walk home with my friends. You go ahead."

Father Paul led the parishioners away from the gravesite. Several neighbors reached out to touch Chuck and Lorraine as they passed.

"Lorraine, let's go home. I can't stand to be here another minute," ordered Chuck.

Chuck steered Lorraine by the arm towards the parking lot. She looked back over her shoulder at her son and waved. Sean broke free of his friends to watch his parents walk off, not noticing the person approaching from behind. Suddenly his legs were off the ground, his body engulfed in a deep embrace.

"Hey, what the heck is going on?"

Father Ken's muscular arms squeezed tight as a vise. The priest bore down as Sean fought for freedom.

"Whoa there tiger," chided Father Ken. "I just wanted to give you a hug of encouragement on this dark day. I'm not trying to hurt you."

"You already have," cried Sean, trying to wriggle free. "Let go. My ribs are killing me."

The priest released his hold.

"Sean, what's wrong with you?" questioned Father Ken, patting him on the sides. "Why haven't you been coming to football practice? You were off to such a good start."

Sean motioned to his friends.

"They can't help you now," ordered Father Ken. "They best be heading out of here. I'm taking you home."

The priest waved off the boys.

"Get going you three."

"I'm not moving a inch unless my friend, Sean says it's okay," declared Jimmy.

"Don't worry about me," sighed Sean. "I'll see you guys soon."

His three friends walked away from the cemetery.

Candy froze.

"You can come with us on the way to the Gerards, but try and stay out of the conversation," advised Father Ken. "I need to hear from Sean."

Candy stuck out her tongue at Father Ken.

"Yes, and I respect you too little girl."

Candy blushed, her cheeks turning bright red.

"On that note, let's get going," ordered the priest.

The three headed off the church property in the direction of Maple Street.

"Are you going to be honest with me or do I have to tell you what I already suspect?" probed Father Ken.

Sean cleared his throat. "What does that mean?"

"Don't even try and fool with me, young man!"

The blast from a car horn distracted the priest. The last of the mourners leaving the church parking lot drove past. He returned the waves from a packed Chevrolet station wagon.

"I may be a priest, but I do have eyes and ears," he stated sternly. "In my neighborhood, where I grew up, you had to learn every day on the street or you didn't survive. You also had to have friends who protected your back. Now, if you're afraid of Father Paul, I understand that. Trust me. I've seen humanity's ugly side."

Sean and Candy stopped on the sidewalk.

Father Ken folded his arms across his chest, staring down at Sean.

"So do you fear Father Paul?"

Sean reached out and hugged Candy.

"I was in your kitchen the day your folks were told of your brother's death. I looked out the window and saw you running away. I picked up enough from the look on Father Paul's face when he came inside that something happened."

Sean shook his fist in the air. "I just want to be left alone!"

Father Ken thumped Sean's chest. "Life's not that easy. Obviously, Father Paul is not letting you off the hook. At least not in a way that I can see."

"Father, can we forget about this today? I just want to and go home and be with my parents."

"No Sean, I'm not accepting that," answered Father Ken. "I need to know, as your friend and as a priest responsible for the children of my church."

Sean let Candy go, putting his hands on his hips.

"Father Paul beat me up, okay?" screamed Sean. "He beat me, he beat me, he beat me!"

Candy staggered in the grass.

"Sean you never told me? Why?" cried Candy.

"I didn't want you to get upset, after all you've been through."

"Sean, you promised to never mention any of that."

"Candy, what secret are *you* keeping, my child?" wondered Father Ken, kneeling down next to the young girl. "Sean, what do you have to say about all this?"

Sean started running. He didn't look back.

"Believe Sean, Father, he's telling the truth," Candy said softly. "And I'm not saying any more. You just better help us."

"Go home Candy," instructed Father Ken. "I've got work to do now."

Father Ken whirled and raced back towards the church, picking up speed as the leather soles of his dress shoes clicked off the sidewalk. He pulled his jacket off and tied it around his waist so he could pump his muscular arms to propel his running.

As Father Ken approached the church parking lot, he spotted Father Paul's black Buick Riviera pulling away from the garage behind the rectory. Father Ken waved his arms in the middle of the road, gulping for air as the car braked. The driver's side electric window hummed as it lowered.

"Father Ken, why are you standing there covered in sweat?" demanded the pastor from the front seat. "You look crazed and not at all proper."

"I need to talk with you, Father Paul, immediately. It's urgent."

Father Paul turned off the ignition.

"This had better be important," droned the pastor. "I'm due downtown to have an early dinner with the bishop."

"The bishop can wait, this is about the safety of our students."

"What are you talking about?" challenged the pastor.

"Sean Gerard says you beat him up for the prank he pulled on the Fourth. In fact, I think his ribs are so bruised that he can't play football."

"Anything that liar claims is pure fabrication," said Father Paul, starting his car. "You should put that trash out of your mind. My life is not for you to judge. It is for my confessor, God Almighty."

"I understand there are two sides to a story but the boy claims…"

"Stop right there," ordered the pastor. "You are a young priest on your first assignment with a lot to learn. Sean Gerard is a degenerate under the influence of Satan. Why are you so gullible?"

"I asked you to offer forgiveness to Sean and friends, don't you remember?"

"Don't interrupt me again," said Father Paul. "Here's your first lesson, rookie. The pastor of the parish should not be challenged, especially not by the likes of that delinquent. My word is absolute, never forget that."

Father Ken tried to keep up with the Riveria as it pulled out of the parking lot.

"I'm going to talk with the bishop about my suspicions."

"You go right ahead, in fact, I'll let him know you want an audience. Bishop O'Connor and I are the best of friends. We go all the way back to our days in the seminary. He has complete trust in me and in the authority of the pastor of the church. I'll inform him of what has transpired here in Vineyard Beach. And your role in protecting the guilty."

The car picked up speed, leaving Father Ken struggling to stay abreast of the vehicle.

The driver's window started to slide up.

"And if you have a problem with anything I've said, I'll have you transferred to a coal town in West Virginia," yelled the pastor as his sedan sped away.

CHAPTER FIFTEEN

Jimmy rested his arms on the front of his desk and leaned forward in his chair to whisper to Sean.

"Penmanship," complained Jimmy Moran. "Are you kidding me? This is supposed to be high school. What a bunch of crap."

Jimmy's agitation grew with each new instruction from Sister Mary Martin Flanagan. This might be the start of freshman year at the new high school but the nuns weren't letting up. Jimmy steamed. Why else was he hunched over a tablet of blue-lined notebook paper with the ink cartridge in his Schaefer fountain pen running low.

"Sean, this is only the first day and they're killing us," yelped Jimmy.

Sister Mary Martin twirled the large black rosary that encircled her ample waist while striding through the rows of desks to check the work of her charges. The sister's stocky presence was a fixture at St. Joseph's for generations, her girth and advancing age slowing her gait but not her determination to keep order. The Irish nun was the commander in chief in her classroom, her rules or banishment, and now much to the alarm of her students, she had delayed her retirement to help teach the freshman class.

The nun raised a shiny brass bell off her desk and held it up before the class.

"It's time to change the assignment," she instructed.

Ding. Ding Ding.

"Let's work on our capital 'L's."

"How funny is this," fumed Jimmy to the back of Sean's head. "We all look alike in these silly uniforms, right down to the black shoes, and now we're still practicing how to write our letters. And the old bitch is ringing that new damn bell every time we have to do one!"

Sean confronted his father about the new dress code before leaving home. Chuck just pointed to the door and commanded, "March!" Sean soon joined a uniformed army in the playground, the boys all pressed out in short-sleeve white shirts, maroon ties with the school emblem, black trousers and matching shoes. The girls wore simple white blouses with rounded collars and blue-checked skirts that covered half the knee. White knee socks and black shoes completed the outfit. The boys also learned that they would be segregated from the girls for all classes, except lunch. Sean waved to Candy on the far side of the schoolyard just before the students were led into the building. The tiled hallways smelled of fresh paint.

"Watch out, here comes the bulldog in black," warned Sean.

Sister Mary Martin spun away from the slate blackboard, banging the chalk dust from her hands before heading down the aisle where Sean and Jimmy toiled.

"Mister Moran, if you don't sit back in your seat, I'll have you sent to the office for a little time with the principal," asserted Sister Mary Martin. "Sister Josephine would love to see you. And if that doesn't get your attention, I'll ship you to the rectory for a personal chat with Father Paul. His paddle doesn't discriminate, it's put many souls back on the road to redemption."

The nun loomed over Jimmy.

"Having a problem with your capital letters today, Mister Moran?" demanded the nun.

"Oh, no Sister Martin, I love repeating my letters over and over until they're perfect," snorted Jimmy. "It makes me so happy that …"

The smack to the back of Jimmy's head snapped him forward in his chair. The nun had made certain on the swing to dig her thick gold ring into his scalp.

"Mister Moran, it's not polite to talk to a nun like that," she insisted. "Not in Sister Mary Martin Flanagan's classroom."

Jimmy rubbed the knot bubbling up on his skull.

"You'll get more special treatment if you continue to be rude," threatened Sister Mary Martin.

The nun dropped her hands to her hips, a look of disgust covering her face. "There's nothing I dislike more than insubordination," she barked, swinging her rosary near Jimmy's face. "And you, Mister Moran, don't know what it means to follow orders."

When she turned her back, Jimmy raised his arm and shook his fountain pen with a quick jerk, the ink spitting out of the silver tip with the speed of snake venom. The bullets of blue ink danced up the length of the Sister Mary Martin's black silk habit. Jimmy raised his fist and smiled at his classmates. He angrily raked his pen again at her back, knowing the ink would go unnoticed in the dark garment.

The snickering spread like a wave across the classroom. Sister Mary Martin jerked her head at the sudden outburst, just as a row of ink dots darted up her starched white collar, over her nose, finally stopping along her forehead.

The sight of ink splattered across the front of Sister Mary Martin and her look of astonishment sucked the sound out of the room.

Jimmy crouched in his chair, his arm frozen in the air. The blood drained from his face.

"Put your damn pen down on your desk," whispered the nun.

Jimmy's hands shook so violently he couldn't screw the cap on his fountain pen. He placed both pieces in the pen trough edged into the top of his oak desk. He dropped his head.

"Mister Moran, what you just did is a sin," intoned Sister Mary Martin, her voice rising. "It's a sin against our school, a sin against the sisters, a sin against our faith, a sin against the Pope himself."

"Sister, I'm sorry, I didn't mean any harm, please don't..." pleaded Jimmy.

She put a finger to her lips.

"Be silent you miscreant," yelled Sister Mary Martin. "You're a disgrace to the Catholic Church. You don't belong with the rest of these fine students."

Her condemnation boomed off the walls and down the hallway.

"You are a human contaminant, a disease that must be expelled from our midst," she said, digging inside her deep pockets to fish out a handkerchief. She slowly dabbed the ink off her face, eyeing Jimmy with contempt.

"Mister Moran, right at this moment, I can't think of a punishment severe enough for your assault on the sisterhood," hissed Sister Mary Martin, the malice in her voice causing Jimmy to bite down on his right hand. "But the proper thing to do will come to me in time. While I'm calming down, get out of your seat and march over to the rectory. Confess your sin to Father Paul and pray he shows you the way to salvation."

"Sister, I don't want to confess to Father Paul," cried Jimmy. "Please give me another chance. I'll do anything, just don't send me to the rectory."

Jimmy's classmates looked away as he sobbed.

"Mister Moran, it's a little late now," chided the nun. "Your tears mean nothing compared to your dirty deed. Life is a test Mister Moran and you are failing miserably. God may show you some mercy, but I won't. Now is the time for atonement. Be sure to tell Father Paul the truth or your punishment will be worse."

The nun yanked Jimmy out of his chair by the collar of his white shirt, spinning him around and pushing him towards the door. Jimmy stopped just short of the hallway. Sister Mary Martin grabbed his arm.

"Don't make it worse," she barked, shoving him out of the classroom. "Go and receive your penance."

Jimmy shuffled away, shaking his head. Alerted by the shouting from Sister Mary Martin, several nuns stood in their doorways watching Jimmy inch towards the exit nearest the rectory.

Sister Mary Martin turned to address her class. "Mister Gerard, now you get out of your seat."

"Sister, I didn't do nothing, you can't...."

"Quiet. You may have escaped my wrath this time, Mister Gerard, but trouble is just around the corner for someone like you. Be careful or you'll join your friend."

"Sister, may I please say something in my defense," replied Sean, standing in the aisle.

"No you may not," she commanded, pointing to the door. "God has put us all here for a test, something you are too brazen to realize. And I don't intend to waste my precious time arguing with you. Now get out my sight. I'm putting you in charge of making sure that Mister Moran goes directly to the rectory. Follow him, be certain he goes inside and report back immediately to me."

Stepping into the hallway, Sean heard the exit doors click shut at the far side of the school. He sprinted, slowing by the door to the freshmen girl's classroom to wave at Candy, just catching up to Jimmy at the limestone steps leading to the rectory.

"Hey, wait up," hollered Sean. "Any clever last words?"

Jimmy had one foot on the bottom step.

"Not funny, Leader Boy," blurted Jimmy, exhaling deeply. "You here spying for the bitch nun?"

"She ordered me to check on you," insisted Sean. "Don't get upset, maybe it won't go so bad in there."

"Yeah, and maybe I'll fall over dead right here and buzzards will pick my bones clean to spare me from Father Paul," grumbled Jimmy. "After what he did to you, I'm screwed."

"Don't go chicken on me now, Caper Brother," advised. "The old bastard can't pull the same stuff he did in my backyard. You're in the rectory, for god's sake, there are witnesses."

"Leader Boy, I'm still scared, I don't want to go in there."

"Well, no one wants to go to the rectory," replied Sean. "Just think about it as part of the whole Catholic experience you're getting at this wonderful school."

"Not funny. Maybe I should run for it."

Run where? I don't think that's an option."

Sean reached out and took Jimmy's hand. "Look, the pastor can only spank you with his paddle, anything else is abuse," observed Sean. "If something happens, be sure to speak up and then maybe Father Ken or the authorities or someone will listen to us."

"It still just our word against the pastor's," whined Jimmy, shaking his head. "Without any proof, who's gonna believe us?"

"I made it through and so will you," reassured Sean.

"Go on back, Sean, I'm doing my duty," uttered Jimmy, his voice breaking.

"Is there *anything* you want me to do?" inquired Sean.

Jimmy stared at his friend for a moment. "Yeah, you can tell the good sister to kiss my ass and when class is done, I want you to sneak back and steal that miserable bell she rings."

He turned and climbed the stairs, pausing to knock on the screen door of the rectory. In minutes, the elderly housekeeper pulled the window curtain aside to peer out at the visitor on the stoop.

"I'm here to talk with Father Paul. It's okay to open the door."

The door slowly swung back and Jimmy moved into the foyer next to the kitchen. The aroma of turkey soup filled the air.

The housekeeper scrutinized Jimmy.

"Are you from the school, young man?" asked the housekeeper.

"Yes, I am and I don't want to be here."

"Then you are in trouble," she remarked. "Why else would someone your age come here in the middle of the day? The padre is up in his bedroom resting. He doesn't like to be disturbed but I will tell him he has a visitor. Go down the hall to his office. May God go with you."

Jimmy made his way to the back office, slumping into the chair facing Father Paul's ornate mahogany desk. The black marble surface glowed with an immaculate sheen, the only adornments on the top were a telephone and small desk calendar. Jimmy ran his hand over the stone. A red velvet cushion with "God Cares" embossed in gold, hand-stitched letters, rested in the pastor's high back chair.

The sound of someone pacing in the room above the office filtered down through the ceiling. Jimmy picked up the voice of Father Paul talking in a low tone. Suddenly the upstairs phone crashed to the floor, followed by booming footsteps echoing down the staircase. The office door flew back, banging off the dark paneling.

Jimmy covered his face with his hands.

"Open your eyes, Mister Moran, I'd like you to meet my little friend," ordered Father Paul smugly. "I call it the Board of Education."

The priest sauntered around his desk and dropped into his chair.

Jimmy peered through his fingers at Father Paul, decked out in a white t-shirt, dark dress slacks, his black loafers propped on his desk. Across his lap rested a three-foot piece of oak about four inches wide. At the base of the slab, the handle was covered in a red bicycle grip.

"No lies or excuses, young man," the priest said, caressing the paddle. "Sister Mary Martin called from the school office. You are a criminal and today is your day of reckoning."

The priest bent to unlock a drawer at the bottom of his desk out of Jimmy's sight. He retrieved a pair of handcuffs from under a hymnal and slid them into his pocket.

"See these holes drilled into this piece of wood?" observed the priest, the light from the office window filtering through the openings to create small white dots on the dark surface of the desk. "They're designed so there's no cushion of air slowing it down on the way to its target."

"How many swats do I have to get today?" pleaded Jimmy, lowering his trembling hands onto his lap.

"As many as I feel like, but don't worry, I know what I'm doing."

Father Paul rose from his chair and pointed the paddle directly at Jimmy's head.

"Get up. Get up now!" he shouted. "Come around to the side of my desk, pull down your pants and underwear and bend over. Let's get this over with."

Jimmy hesitated. Father Paul stepped to his office door, closing it with one clean jerk. He locked the deadbolt and put the key in his back pocket.

"Father, I just want to say…"

The priest grabbed the back of Jimmy's hair and pulled him out of the chair, swinging the paddle inches from his face.

"Get your pants down," commanded the priest, spinning the paddle in his right hand. The pastor backed off to give Jimmy room to step over by his desk. He studied Jimmy intently as he unbuckled his belt and slowly lowered his trousers.

"Father, can I leave my boxers on, please?" muttered Jimmy. "I don't want to stand here naked."

"Why should I give you a break today after what you did to Sister Mary Martin?" retorted the priest.

"Father, I'm a good boy, it was my first mistake."

"Who are you fooling?" challenged the priest, drawing back his hand.

The priest slapped Jimmy across the mouth.

"Enough of your whining," steamed the priest, his face flush. "You assaulted a nun, you little monster! That calls for the harshest treatment. Pull those boxers down now!"

"You can't hit me in the face, that's abuse!" cried Jimmy.

"Abuse? Abuse?" laughed the priest. "You're getting what you deserve. You are here to be punished for assaulting a nun. Whatever happens now will be up to me and only me. And the fine folks of this parish will thank me for punishing a nun-basher."

The priest pushed the boy down over the side of his desk.

"Now do as I say or it will get worse."

Jimmy slid his underwear down until they fell to his ankles.

"Step out of your boxers and grab both sides of the desk top."

The priest squared his body to the desk and planted his feet firmly on the Oriental rug.

"The only thing I want to hear from your lips is a decent Act of Contrition," growled the priest. "Say it slowly so I have time to turn your ass the color of that bright red hair of yours."

"Please, Father, don't hurt me!"

"Pray. You do remember how to say an Act of Contrition?"

"Yes, Father Paul," whispered Jimmy.

"O, my God, I am heartily sorry for offending Thee."

Whack!

"And I detest all my sins, because I dread the loss of heaven and the pains of hell."

Whack!

"But most of all because they offend Thee, my God."

Whack!

"Father, your blows are too hard."

"Shut up and keep praying. Your ass isn't red enough yet."

"Who are all good and deserving of all my love."

Whack!

"I firmly resolve with the help of Thy grace."

Whack!

"To confess my sins, to do penance and to amend my life. Amen."

Whack!

Jimmy reached back to rub the pain searing through his skin.

"Keep your hands off your ass," demanded Father Paul, wiping sweat off his forehead. "I'm not done with you yet."

He moved closer to Jimmy, positioning himself for one final swing. He kicked the boy's pants and underwear out of the way to get a better footing. The force sent Jimmy's wallet spinning across the lush carpet, the contents spilling out at the feet of Father Paul.

Something in the pile caught the priest's attention. He rested the paddle on his shoulder to reach down to the floor.

"What the hell?" shouted Father Paul, the surprise in his voice sending a wave of panic through Jimmy. He examined the small, square packet wrapped in blue plastic then placed it on the desk.

"Do you know what this is?" taunted the priest, dropping the paddle to the carpet. "Well, do you?"

He reached into his pocket and removed the set of handcuffs.

Jimmy stiffened at the sight of the forgotten condom package he had hidden in his wallet months ago.

Father Paul suddenly yanked Jimmy's right arm behind his back, quickly cuffing his wrist and then locking it to his other arm.

"What are you doing to me?" cried Jimmy, his face smashing into the desk.

"How does a Catholic school boy come into the possession of a condom?" he demanded.

"I got it at the Vineyard Beach Pharmacy. I found it on the floor near the counter. I liked the package, that's all I know, I swear."

"You're a liar."

"No, please Father Paul, you must believe me," pleaded Jimmy.

"Believe you. You're out of your mind. I'll bet you got the condom from the pharmacist's whore, that slut Veronica. I hear enough around town to know what she's up to. So, did she show you how a condom works?"

"I don't know what a condom is Father Paul," replied Jimmy, his knees starting to shake.

"You're lying again, Jimmy Moran."

"Father, you are making me uncomfortable. This isn't punishment anymore. It's torture. Your desk is cutting into my chest."

"You're uncomfortable? Too bad. How did you think I felt that night you helped shove me into the pool at the DeLanes."

"That wasn't my idea, you have no proof that..."

"To hell with proof," he said, lifting Jimmy off the desk by his arms. The priest released his grip, smiling as Jimmy fell hard onto the floor. He drove his knee into Jimmy's back and lowered his mouth to the boy's ear.

"Now I'm gonna show you how to use a condom," the priest hissed, unbuckling his trousers.

"What are you doing to me?" wailed Jimmy.

"Lower your voice," the priest ordered, stepping out of his pants.

"Help! Help!"

The priest balled his handkerchief, stuffing it deep into Jimmy's throat.

"There, choke on that a while."

Father Paul crouched behind the prone boy, using his knees to spread his legs apart.

"You will never forget this day my dear boy. And no one, and I mean no one, will ever take your word over mine. Remember that."

The priest pulled off his underwear and pushed Jimmy's face down into the carpet.

Jimmy passed out.

CHAPTER SIXTEEN

"Jimmy hasn't showed up yet," announced Johnny Pasquale, rubbing his dark eyebrows. The concern in his voice hung in the air over the lunch counter inside the Vineyard Beach Pharmacy. "I never thought he'd be this late to one of our meetings."

Johnny studied Veronica Maggione, the cleavage of her large bosom framed perfectly in her pink cashmere sweater. That morning before work, she had combed her black hair into a tight beehive, topping it off with a matching pink bow.

"He speaks," teased Veronica, a smile cracking open her face.

"You know something is wrong with Jimmy cause he's not here checking you out, Veronica," insisted Johnny. "He should have been here an hour ago."

He blew a kiss to Veronica.

"You can be a pig at times," she remarked. "I like you better when you're quiet." Johnny dropped his mouth to the straw in his glass and sucked up the last of his soda. Veronica winced at the slurping.

"Hand your glass over," she ordered.

Johnny drew in one more swig before sliding his glass across the counter. Veronica dunked it into the soapy water in the stainless steel sink, then slowly wiped it clean with her dishtowel.

"For you Veronica, I'll be a pig any time, just be sure to feed me. Maybe you can nurse me with those…"

Veronica threw her towel, smacking Johnny in the face.

"Hush you with the dirty mind," she fumed, her face turning dark.

Tom Tozer

"Oink, oink, sweetheart."

"I'm not your sweetheart, honeybunch," chided Veronica. "And you'll never get close to my big mamas. Better put your tongue back in your mouth."

Veronica picked up her towel and tossed it over her shoulder.

"So where is that devil Jimmy Moran?" wondered Veronica.

"Good question," observed Johnny, drumming his fingers on his biceps. "The village flooded the tennis courts days ago and we're suppose to go ice skating under the lights for the first time, and without Jimmy, it's just not the same. What the hell happened?"

Buddy Trotz perched on the next stool sucking on a large pretzel stick, his eyes locked on Veronica.

"You really are a vision, Veronica," marveled Buddy through a mouthful of pretzel. "I have to agree with my friend on that."

Veronica leaned over to pick up the change left by the boys on the gray Formica top. Buddy craned for a better view. Veronica stopped, feeling his steady gaze. She reached out and patted his hand.

"For all your bellowing, you are a sweet boy," she purred, running her hands over her breasts to smooth out the wrinkles running up her sweater.

Buddy's mouth fell open.

"Close your trap, Trotz," snapped Johnny. "Your idea of a vision is a dozen bratwursts with all the fixings."

"Hey Pasquale, I can't believe your yakking this much," cracked Buddy spinning on his stool. "You'll get a reputation as a chatter bug if you keep it up."

Johnny snatched the pretzel from Buddy's mouth and crushed it in the palm of his hand.

"Yeah, and you just woke up the Pope over in Rome," Johnny said, shaking the pretzel crumbs over Buddy's head. "If you give me crap again, I'll shove a hotdog down your Polish throat. I might even throw in a squirt of mustard."

Buddy moved past Sean to the stool at the end of the counter, remembering the last time Johnny unleashed his anger inside the pharmacy.

"Boys, let's have some decorum here," interrupted Veronica. "You know the rules, no swearing, fighting, and absolutely no spitting."

"Veronica, now you sound like one of the nuns," whined Buddy. "I need to spit all of sudden."

"Suck it back down," ordered Johnny.

"Excuse me, but I expect you to be gentlemen, at least around me," insisted Veronica. "After all, you're supposed to be jerking around those crazy nuns not causing trouble here."

Veronica moved around the cash register to check on Sean. His head rested in his folded arms on the counter. His eyes were closed.

"You've been the quiet one this afternoon," she gently prodded. "So what's happening with your pal, Jimmy? That boy used to have spunk."

Sean bolted up, rubbed his face and started to rock on his stool. He watched the second hand on the big wall clock over the counter tick all the way around.

"I'm not sure," said Sean finally. "But Jimmy hasn't been the same since Sister Mary Martin ordered him to the rectory to confess to Father Paul."

"When was that?" probed Veronica, her eyes narrowing.

"Back in September," offered Sean, recalling the day Jimmy sprayed Sister Mary Martin with ink. "I'll never forget the pain on his face when he came back to class. He kept his head down and squirmed in his seat like a wounded squirrel. That image is all I see at night when I close my eyes. It makes sleeping impossible."

"When's the last time you got a good night's sleep?" asked Veronica.

"I can't remember, I mean, heck last week sometime. I snuck down into the kitchen in the middle of the night and hit my dad's bourbon bottle. It's the only way my mind stops racing long enough to fall asleep. I may do it again tonight.

Veronica pulled a clean glass from the rack under the counter and poured a ginger ale from the fountain. She guided Sean's hand to the glass.

"Drink up young man," advised Veronica. "There's way too much sadness and worry here today. You are all too young for such things. And you Sean, should stay away from your dad's liquor collection."

"Jimmy's just plain not the same, he's flat out different," said Sean shaking his head. "He's real quiet at school and he does everything the nuns tell him. Something is really screwed up."

Veronica flicked the dust off her black silk skirt.

"What are you sitting here for then?" inquired Veronica. "Go find out why Jimmy didn't show up today. Go to his house, talk with his poor mother for God's sake?"

Buddy and Johnny nodded in approval.

"I ran into to Jimmy's mom at church," admitted Sean. "She wanted to know what was wrong with her son and I didn't have an answer. She says Jimmy only comes out of his room to eat. He spends most of his time staring out his bedroom window."

"Jesus, that does not sound right," replied Veronica. "Who else knows about this?"

"I approached Father Ken, but when I brought up Jimmy's name, he cut me off," said Sean. "Father Paul told him about the ink attack. I guess he's still upset at us for letting the nuns down and quitting the football team."

"What about your folks, Sean?" demanded Veronica.

"I'm not bringing this up at my house. My parents are barely talking to each other after my brother's death. I'd be afraid to even mention the word priest. I'd get the short end of that deal for sure."

Sean slammed his hands down on the counter. "It's all on Father Paul, he's to blame!" he yelled.

Veronica witnessed the fear flick across the faces of the three boys.

"I'm tired of this talk about Father Paul," Veronica blurted as she pumped a hand lotion dispenser next to the cash register. "He thinks he owns this town, but he's not God. Take away the collar and the fancy black clothes and he's just another man. He sure as hell can't tell me what to do."

Veronica stopped massaging cream into the cracked skin on her knuckles to refill Sean's glass.

"I'm gonna have a little chat one day with that old man, just him and me, I promise you," declared Veronica, her voice suddenly husky. "We'll see then what he's made of."

"You should just stay away from him," warned Sean.

"Do you know something that you're not sharing?" demanded Veronica.

"I'm not answering any more questions, I just want the old Jimmy back," said Sean, shaking his head.

"I thought you Caper Brothers took an oath to always stick together," said Veronica.

"I guess The Caper Brothers are slipping," said Sean. "I'm not sure we can hold together."

Johnny put his hand on Sean's shoulder. "Don't give up yet," he said. "Go over there and kick Jimmy in the ass. We need his company in our group."

Veronica reached out and put her hand under Sean's chin, raising his face up to look him in the eye. "You're the leader of the merry band," she said. "Seems like the only fitting thing to do."

"I'll go, but don't count on me finding anything out about what's bothering Jimmy," exclaimed Sean, moving away from the counter. "He's been quiet as a mouse." When he reached the pharmacy door, he turned to his friends. "Wish me luck brothers," Sean said, pulling on his coat and gloves. "I'd ask for your prayers but I don't think God is listening right now."

The wind whipped the pharmacy's steel door from Sean's hand, slamming it hard against the outside brick wall. Sean pushed it shut with his shoulder, pulling up the collar of his parka to cover his ears. Light snow blew in the early evening sky, the flakes swirling in the storm.

As Sean crunched through the snow, the squall grew in intensity, soon covering the sidewalks and roads in a thick blanket that added to the quiet spreading over Vineyard Beach. Turning off the main road, Sean inhaled deeply at the sight of the Moran residence framed in the streetlights at the end of the lane. He shuddered against the cold.

A few lights blinked in the windows of the small cottages lining the street. Sean stepped off the sidewalk into the middle of the road where passing cars had flattened the snow. He kept his head down until he reached the Moran's front porch. The main part of the house stood dark. Scanning the second floor, Sean made out someone silhouetted in faint light streaming from Jimmy's room.

"My poor friend," he whispered, waving his arms. The figure at the window didn't move. Sean knelt, scooped up a handful of fresh powder

Tom Tozer

and made a snowball. He glanced up to check his aim before launching his missile. The bedroom light went out.

Sean lowered his arm in defeat, the snowball falling to rest in a small drift by the front steps. He turned away from the house, tears starting to form.

"Oh, God this is too hard, way too hard," he wailed, spinning around at the sound of the upstairs window creaking open.

"Is that you up there, Jimmy Moran?" shouted Sean. "Why don't you come down?"

Jimmy put his mouth to the small slit created when he raised the window a few inches.

"You're crazy," Jimmy uttered, the cold rushing in against his face. "Why don't you leave me alone?"

"Jimmy, we missed you today," pleaded Sean. "Your friends missed you. Even Veronica asked about you. Turn on the light and pull up the blinds so I can see you."

"No thanks, worry boy."

"That's the Caper Brother I remember. Bring it on."

"Bring it on? Why don't you turn your ass full around and march out of here? And take your Caper Brothers shit with you. I quit!"

"What are you talking about?" lamented Sean. "You can't quit our gang. Will you please talk to me. I know how to listen and keep a secret that's for sure."

"Nice try, Leader Boy. I'm tired, really, really tired and I want to be left alone."

"It's Father Paul, isn't it?"

"Shut up," screamed Jimmy, the sound echoing down the street. "Don't mention that name to me!"

"I'm sorry," stammered Sean. He dropped his head in dejection.

The window slammed shut.

Sean waited, shuffling his feet in the snow. He went back up the porch, rang the doorbell and started knocking on the door.

Sweat slid down Jimmy's back while he stood in the dark watching his friend in the front yard.

"Why doesn't he just go away," complaining Jimmy, collapsing on the edge of his bed.

He laced on his boots over his pajama bottoms, grabbed a coat and stole another look down at Sean.

He opened the window.

"You stand right there, moron," hollered Jimmy.

He crept through the house to the back door, stepping out into the cold. He sprinted to the garage, going through the side door to get his bike resting inside on the far wall. Jimmy carried the bike out into the snow, pushing it down the driveway to pick up speed. He climbed aboard and started pumping his legs furiously.

Sean jumped at the sight of Jimmy flying past into the street.

"Hey, stop! Where are you going? Stop! Stop! Stop!"

Jimmy braked. He stood with his bike between his legs waiting for Sean to catch up.

"I'm just gonna go for a little spin in the snow, if it's okay with you," challenged Jimmy, his face flushed.

"Fine by me," replied Sean. "Mind if I tag along?"

"Yes I do mind," he asserted. "Where I want to go, I prefer to go alone."

"Hey wait a minute," answered Sean. "We're friends, right?"

"What I remember is my friend telling me not to worry about going to see the pastor at the rectory," muttered Jimmy. "And now my life will never be the same. I should have run away."

Sean stared at Jimmy.

"You don't look so good," declared Sean, taking a step towards his friend.

"You wouldn't look so good either if you couldn't sleep at night," moaned Jimmy. "I haven't slept in three days."

"My God, that's exactly the same for me!" cried out Sean..

"To hell with God," sighed Jimmy. "So you want to know what happened to me? Think you can handle it?"

Sean nodded.

"That bastard beat my bare ass till I couldn't stand up anymore," he whispered. "And then he found the condom I had hidden in my wallet."

"That must have gone bad on you."

"Bad!" hollered Jimmy. "He handcuffed me and used it on me!"

"I don't understand. What did he use? You mean the *condom*! How did he use it on a … Oh no, Jimmy! Oh no!"

Jimmy suddenly swung his leg out and slammed it into Sean's chest, knocking him down into the snow. He pulled away, racing up the road towards the lake.

"Jesus Christ, what now?" howled Sean, running after the tire tracks in the fresh snow.

Sean sprinted all out but Jimmy's skill with his bike, even in the snow, could not be matched. Jimmy disappeared into the storm. Sean kept his eyes on the tire tracks; they led straight to the city park.

On the far edge of the property, the security lights illuminated the village boat ramp that angled down to the shore. Sean spotted the tire tracks running down the middle of the concrete runway. At the end of the ramp there were footprints where Jimmy had dismounted and carried his bike over the short wall of frozen ice that had formed on the shoreline.

Sean peered out into the lake trying to glimpse his friend.

"Jimmy, come back, come back," yelled Sean, climbing to the top of the mound of ice near the shore. "Come back! Come back. Please come back." His screams drifted away, as loose as ashes blowing in a breeze.

Off in the distance, in the thin light from the moon, Sean spotted the outline of his friend against the night sky, peddling his bike at full speed straight out into the lake.

"Sweet Jesus, what is he doing?"

Sean cupped his hands.

"Jim-my! Jim-my!"

Jimmy Moran never slowed or looked back.

Then he vanished.

Sean collapsed.

Three days later, an obituary appeared in the weekly Vineyard Beach Press.

"James Elliott Moran, 15, beloved son of Thomas and Dana Moran, died suddenly November 10, 1967 as the result of an accident. He was born August 15, 1952 in Cleveland, Ohio and moved to Vineyard Beach the following year. He attended St. Joseph's Catholic School, where he was an altar boy. He is survived by his grandparents, Randolph and Betty Moran of Port Charlotte, Fla., and numerous aunts, uncles and cousins. A private Mass of Christian Burial will be held at St. Joseph's Catholic Church, Saturday, November 17 at 11 a.m., Father Paul Sterner and Father Kenneth Wasowski officiating. Internment will follow the ceremony in the St. Joseph's Church Cemetery. In lieu of flowers, the family is asking that donations be made to the James Elliot Moran scholarship fund, care of St. Joseph's Catholic Church, 800 Lake Boulevard, Vineyard Beach, Ohio, 44012."

CHAPTER SEVENTEEN

"Say that again Sean," coached the soft voice. "One more time."

"The pastor, he hurt Jimmy. He used a condom. He hurt Jimmy. He hurt Jimmy."

Sean's eyes flickered for a second before he slipped back into a deep sleep.

The caregiver by his side placed another light blanket over Sean and retreated to her chair to await sunrise.

Hours later, the steady chirp from a monitor slowly drifted down into Sean's consciousness.

"Where the hell am I?" Fear gripped his throat.

He blinked, straining to get his surroundings into focus. He felt the top of his throbbing skull, and ran his hand over a bandage that covered the entire crown of his head. The only light in the room leaked from a brass desk lap resting on a table near a large window. Sean could make out someone curled in a recliner and he picked up the hum of people talking in the distance.

The soft cotton sheets caressing his bare back and the overpowering aroma of Ivory soap sent a cold realization through Sean that his bruised body was in a bed, but not the one in his home on Maple Street. He kicked off his coverings and tried to sit up, the effort draining his energy. Sean rolled onto his side.

"Hey! Where are my clothes?" shouted Sean, pulling on the gown wrapping his body. "You there in the dark, what's going on?"

The person in the chair startled at the alarm in Sean's voice, sprang to the window to open the blinds. Rays of early morning sun streamed in, revealing Veronica Maggione.

"Oh, my aching skull," groaned Sean, shaking his head at the sight of Veronica by the window. "Why are you here and where the hell is *here*?"

"You're in Lorain County General Hospital," said Veronica, her ample frame covered in a gray sweat suit. "You've had a nasty fall and smacked your head real good."

Veronica pushed the recliner into the upright position and snapped off the lamp. "Your folks are down the hall in the waiting room stretched out on the sofas," she said softly. "Everybody in town is worried about you. Lots of your friends showed up to sit with you. It was my turn last night."

"What time is it?"

"The sun is just coming up," Veronica said, crossing the room to the side of the bed.

"How long have I been here?"

"The park custodian found you at the foot of the boat ramp Saturday around midnight on his last security check. You had fallen and hit your head on a jagged piece of ice."

Veronica gently squeezed Sean's hand.

"Today's Thursday, so you've been unconscious for about five days. You lost a lot of blood that night. The cold air and snow slowed down the flow, which probably saved your life. You were lucky too, no frostbite either."

Veronica raised a cup of ice water to Sean's lips.

He gulped feverishly.

"Whoa, slow down, take little sips till you get your bearings," ordered Veronica.

"My mouth feels like I've been chewing on an old sock," muttered Sean, tugging on a tube sticking out of his right arm. "What's this?"

"Intravenous fluids," said Veronica. "That's how you were hydrated while you were out cold. And those little pads on your chest are connected to that machine there that checks your vital signs."

"God, my whole body is sore," Sean said, lifting his arms over his head and stretching.

"Do you remember anything about last Saturday night?" inquired Veronica gently.

Sean fell silent, looking off through the open window.

"I'm sorry about my questions Sean," said Veronica, "It's just that everyone is mightily concerned. Your parents were so upset they asked Father Ken to perform the last rites on you just in case. That was Sunday. But you talked some in your sleep early this morning so I figured you were coming around."

"I'm not quite sure of anything right now," whispered Sean, taking another sip of water. "My memory is real foggy. What did I say in my sleep?"

"Let's not go there," advised Veronica, rubbing the back of Sean's neck. "There'll be a time to discuss all that, but for now, let me get your folks. Last night was the first time your parents left your side. I had to order them out so they could get some sleep. They need to know you're awake."

Sean's stomach suddenly released a loud growl.

"I'm starving," proclaimed Sean, patting his belly. "Please tell my folks to bring some food. One more thing, can you get someone to turn off that monitor, the sound is annoying."

"I'll tell the nurse," Veronica said, stepping away from the bed. "Now, just take it easy till I get back."

Veronica turned towards the door.

"Remember, food, food," yelled Sean. "I'll eat stale crackers. Just bring something back."

Minutes later, Lorraine and Chuck raced in, engulfing their son in a tight embrace.

"Hey, you're squeezing the heck out of me," chided Sean. "I love you guys too!"

Lorraine kissed her rosary. "The Blessed Virgin has answered my prayers," she said, caressing Sean's face. "Each night I said the rosary, asking Mary for a full recovery. And now, to see your face and that smile, well, this image I will take with me the rest of my days."

Chuck held onto his son, moving in to kiss him softly on the forehead. "You gave us a quite a shock, Buster," he muttered, tears spilling down his cheeks. "This is a day to cherish."

"I never thought I'd actually like hearing you call me Buster," chuckled Sean with a weak smile.

"Gerards never die from a hit to the head, but you had me worried there for a few days," admitted Chuck, scratching the little gray whiskers sprouting on the tip of his chin. "There's a bunch of people who want to see you. The whole town would file through if I'd let them, but you need your rest."

"I just want to go home," pleaded Sean.

"Yes, son, and that's where we want you too," said Lorraine. "From that drawn look on your face, you could use some of my home cooking."

"Just the mention of food has my mouth watering," gushed Sean.

"That's a good sign, son," said Chuck. "Now I know for sure you're going to make it."

The hospital door flew open and in marched Veronica.

"I ran into one of your doctors at the nursing station," Veronica said, placing a cafeteria tray on a side table. "It's okay for you to start eating and the doc will be in to see you soon. They're serving breakfast. Take a look! Eggs, bacon, hash browns, toast, and your treat for the day, a chocolate milkshake."

Veronica pulled the table over Sean's lap and raised the back of the hospital bed.

The room fell silent as Sean eyed the plate brimming with food.

He swung a piece of bacon under his nose, inhaling deeply. "There's nothing like the smell of fresh cooked bacon to get a guy's appetite going," he gushed, devouring the strip in a bite.

The milkshake was attacked next, Sean pulling on the straw as he shoved food into the other side of his mouth with his free hand. The entourage exchanged smiles, watching the young man clear his plate. Sean put down the empty cup and belched long and loud.

"That was the best meal ever," he declared, sitting up straight.

"Now that I see your appetite is improving, I'm leaving so you can spend time with your folks," said Veronica, blowing a kiss to Sean.

Sean smiled back at Veronica, pretending to catch her kiss with his right hand and placing it on his heart.

"Thanks for all you've done. See you soon Veronica," chimed Sean. She waved and left the room.

"There's someone special who wants to talk with you," said Chuck, taking Lorraine by the hand. "Your mom and I will step out for a few minutes."

Chuck leaned in close to Sean, pulling a pack of peppermint gum out of his pants pocket.

"Here, you don't want hospital breath for this visitor," he whispered.

"I need this bad," Sean said, tearing into the pack of gum. In short order, he had chewed three sticks into a fat wad, relishing the clean taste returning to his mouth. He stuck his feet off the side of the bed, enjoying the surge of energy running through his body. Wiggling his toes produced a smile.

Just then he noticed Candy DeLane at the foot of his bed, her hands folded in front of her. The light streaming through the blinds hit her golden hair just at the right angle, making it appear extra bright.

Sean was plainly startled at the vision of Candy decked out in blue jeans, a flannel shirt and brown leather work boots. He looked the visitor up and down intently, maybe too closely for someone just recovering from head trauma.

"So, you really are awake," stated Candy.

"Yes, and I'm feeling better by the minute just seeing you," said Sean, gesturing for Candy to sit next to him on the bed. "You are so cute."

The compliment sent blood rushing to Candy's neck, producing a bright shade of pink around her throat.

"Gosh, I'm sorry. Did I say something wrong?"

"Oh, it's just your timing," she said frowning. "I don't need you checking me out right now. I've been in these clothes for days praying with your family."

Sean spit his gum into a wastebasket next to his bed.

"I need to kiss you, right now. I must," said Sean urgently.

"Okay, but nothing fancy, I don't want to get you all excited. You're still in the hospital."

Sean threw her long locks over her shoulders, the feel of the silky braids making his skin tingle. He arched out of his hospital bed, pulling her closer to kiss her full on the lips.

"That's enough for now," demanded Candy, breaking free of his embrace. "You get better and we'll spend the afternoon smooching."

"If that's a promise, I'm ready to go home," claimed Sean.

"Did your folks talk to you about Jimmy?" asked Candy, lightly stroking Sean's cheek.

"How is my best friend, everything okay?"

"Oh, my goodness," Candy blurted, "I guess you don't…" She put her hand over her mouth.

"You guess what? What? Tell me what is going on," squealed Sean. "My folks didn't say anything."

Candy pushed Sean back on the bed and climbed in. She lowered her head to his shoulder, slowly stroking his dark hair. Sean put his arm around her as she sobbed.

"Oh Sean," cried Candy through her tears, "I can't say this out loud. It's too sad."

"My mind is racing," moaned Sean. "Is this bad?"

Candy buried her head deeper into the crook of his arm. When she caught her breath, she jumped off the bed and ran for the door.

"I'm going for your parents," she shouted over her shoulder.

"Wait!" pleaded Sean.

The memory of chasing Jimmy down to the lake Saturday night slammed Sean's senses. His hands started to shake.

The door to his room swung open. Sean studied the grim look on his parent's faces as they approached his bed.

"He's gone, isn't he?" blurted Sean.

Chuck solemnly nodded.

"Jimmy died out on the lake," said Chuck, sitting down next to his son. "He was laid to rest yesterday in the church cemetery not too far from your brother."

Chuck placed his hand on his son's shoulder. "I'm sorry Sean."

Sean looked up at the ceiling, shaking his fists.

"Why would God let something like this happen?" he cried. "Jimmy was my friend."

"My darling, don't question the Lord," consoled Lorraine, dabbing at her tears with a handkerchief. "Now is not the time to question your faith. If you like, we'll take you by Jimmy's grave so we pray and ask God to bless your friend."

"I'm not going to that cemetery ever," screamed Sean. "I'll never go there, never, never."

Sean swung his legs out of the bed.

"Please take me home," he said firmly.

"I'm not sure the doctors will let you go so soon," said Lorraine.

Chuck held up his hand.

"I have to agree with your mother on this one, Sean," commanded Chuck. "Lorraine get a wheelchair while I help Sean get on some clothes on. We'll wheel Sean down to the waiting room, there are a bunch of folks who want to see him."

When Lorraine returned, Sean stood leaning on his father, his hospital gown crumpled next to the bed.

"Hop in, Sean," said Chuck. "I'll drive. We'll get you out of this place as quick as we can. Getting you out of this room for a while will do you good."

Lorraine walked behind the wheelchair as Chuck pushed his son out of the hospital room.

"We'll have you home soon enough," said Chuck, leaning to kiss Sean on the cheek.

By the time the Gerards reached the hospital's waiting room, Veronica was approaching the Vineyard Beach town limits, maneuvering her Camaro through a mixture of ice and snow.

Dark bile churned in her throat.

She whipped her car into the lot next to the St. Joseph's rectory, throwing the door open with enough force to dent the passenger door in the car in the adjacent spot.

"You and me are going toe-to-toe," steamed Veronica, pointing to Father Paul Sterner's name emblazoned on a bronze plaque screwed to the rectory's mailbox.

Veronica banged on the storm door.

"Where is Father Paul?" yelled Veronica to the surprised housekeeper.

"He's in the garage working on his car," said the old woman, pointing to the building next to the rectory.

Veronica pounded her hands together as she stormed for the garage. She could see through the side door window that the priest was changing a rear tire on his beloved Riviera.

Veronica pushed through the door, not slowing to knock.

Father Paul stood up at the sound of approaching footsteps. "Well, well, if it isn't the pharmacist's whore," taunted the priest, spinning a tire iron in his right hand. "Sold any more condoms today?"

"Watch your mouth, old man," hissed Veronica, pushing her face within inches of the priest's chin. "I'm not scared of you."

"Don't talk to me in that tone," said the priest, taking a step back. "You better show me some respect or there will be consequences."

"We'll see about that," challenged Veronica. "After I go to the police about what you did to Jimmy Moran, no one in Vineyard Beach will ever respect you again."

The priest looked at her with surprise. "Who is telling lies this time?" he stammered, his face suddenly flush.

"Sean Gerard talked last night as he came out of a coma in the hospital," said Veronica, placing her closed fists on her hips. "He wasn't aware I was listening but I heard enough to figure out your misdeeds."

"And who did you share these wild accusations with?" demanded the priest.

"No one yet, I came straight here from the hospital, but you can bet the entire town will know in time," announced Veronica proudly.

"We'll see about that you misdirected fool!" screamed Father Paul.

The priest swung his arm with the speed of an attacking viper.

The last thing Veronica Maggione saw in this world was the pastor of St. Joseph's parish whipping a black crowbar directly at the middle of her forehead.

Three days later, when police found Veronica's car at the bottom of Lake Erie, her death was ruled an accident. The coroner determined that the deep contusion to the front of her head happened when her car slipped off a curve in Lake Boulevard due to the weather conditions, and plunged over the nearby cliff.

CHAPTER EIGHTEEN

Greasy and unkempt as always, Dell Pilot was a comforting sight to Sean, although, the actual location of the encounter did seem a bit out of character. The old fisherman wasn't known as the kind of man who liked to play bingo, but there he perched, legs curled under his folding chair, four bingo cards spread out in front of him on one of the many tables lining the length of St. Joseph's parish hall. A Camel smoldered in an ashtray by his side, the smoke helping to cover the faint odor of dead lake perch emanating from his work clothes.

Dell slid a pewter flask from the side pocket of his fishing vest and poured a liberal amount of Old Crow into a bottle of Coke wedged between his legs. He drank deeply, wiping his mouth clean on his green khaki shirt, the soda and bourbon smudge mark blending with the gray grime dotting the sleeve.

"B sixteen," announced the voice over the speakers encircling the hall.

Dell dropped his head and squinted at his cards. "Shit out of luck on that one." He picked up his cigarette and inhaled.

Smoke shot out of his nose.

"You care to tell me why you're here?" inquired Sean, his arms full of bingo cards. "My dad ordered me to come because the Knights of Columbus were short on volunteers. What's your story?"

"No story," replied Dell, looking up at his young friend. "I just thought I'd take some of that Coho prize money we split and invest it."

Tom Tozer

"Why not put your money into booze and smokes, you'd be better off," said Sean, turning to collect bingo fees from several fresh arrivals.

"Already did that. Got a case of the good stuff stashed back at my cabin with a couple of cartons of cigarettes for good measure. Makes waking up in the morning worth the effort."

"Stop cracking wise, old man," teased Sean. "You'll get yourself a comedy spot on the Ed Sullivan show."

"O thirteen."

Dell ran his finger down the O columns on his cards.

"Hey, I got a number!" yipped Dell, clapping his hands. "This could be my lucky night."

"Heck, any piece of luck I ever had was bad," grumbled Sean, waving the bingo cards he was holding at the smoke around Dell's head. "I think good fortune ran out of this town a long time ago."

"Maybe you should move on and take that black cloud with you," suggested Dell. "You might jinx me."

"G twenty-one."

"Look, my young charge, another one!" proclaimed Dell. "I'll be saying 'bingo' before your little butt can do any more whining."

The hall was just about full, hundreds of Vineyard Beach residents huddled over bingo cards competing for the $100 jackpots.

"The only people yelling 'bingo' around here will be my friends hiding outside in the dark," insisted Sean. "They love hearing the big moan go up when the crowd thinks someone has a winning card."

"Not that tired old trick," moaned Dell. "That cuts to a man's soul. Can't we do a little gambling without those shenanigans? Go outside and tell those knuckleheads to go home or I'll whip 'em with one of my fishing poles. I don't need to hear the caller say 'Hold your cards please,' and waste time figuring out it's not a real bingo, but some morons yelling by the windows."

Sean passed out the last of his bingo cards, folding the payments onto a thick wad of one-dollar bills held together with a rubber band.

"Let me turn this money in up front and I'll go outside and make sure nothing dumb happens," he said.

170

"Come back when you've done your good deed," replied Dell, pouring another shot from his flask into his Coke bottle. "You can help me with these cards, just no negative crap."

"Yes my captain," said Sean with a crisp salute.

"N twenty-two."

"Another number, my first mate," blurted Dell. "You better get your scrawny self moving if you want to see me cash in tonight."

Sean turned and sprinted for the caller's table, dropping off his money with the cashier on his way to the front entrance.

He stepped through the large double glass doors, spotting Johnny Pasquale and Buddy Trotz shuffling their feet in the snow just on the edge of light streaming from the hall's windows.

"Well, fellows, I guess there's no screaming 'bingo' tonight," claimed Sean, approaching his friends. "Sorry for the disappointing news."

"Why not?" demanded Buddy, the sound of his voice sending Johnny's hands up to his ears.

"Why not?" taunted Johnny, pushing Buddy to the ground. "Because with your mouth, everyone in that hall and all of downtown Cleveland will know it's you, Trotz."

"Dell Pilot is in there for God's sake and he wants to play without the distractions," replied Sean, flapping his arms across his chest to fight off the cold. "I guess we owe him one."

"I thought we're still The Caper Brothers," muttered Buddy, knocking the snow off his jeans as he stood up.

"We are, even though there's only three of us," said Sean, his breath creating small clouds of vapor in the night air. "But I promised Dell."

"That wouldn't stop Jimmy," challenged Buddy.

"Yeah, I know, but crazy Moran isn't here, is he?" said Sean. "So let him rest in peace. You guys go on and I'll catch up with you. We'll hold a monthly meeting soon. It's freezing and I'm headed back inside where it's warm."

Sean waved as he walked away.

"We better get together soon," shouted Buddy watching Sean approach the front doors. "We have to stick together, remember."

"Let's go," said Johnny, putting his arm around Buddy's shoulders. "Nothing is happening tonight."

Dell studied Sean weaving his way through the rows of bingo tables, wondering how his young friend was holding up under all the stress of the recent weeks. The boy looked thinner, his face in particular seemed gaunt and the furrows in his forehead ran deep.

Jimmy's suicide and now Veronica's death had the town on edge, not to mention the death of Sean's brother.

Sean slid into a chair next to Dell.

"So how's that Candy Delight chick treating you these days?" probed Dell, his eyes focused on his bingo cards.

"Her name is DeLane and she's fine. I haven't seen much of her since I got home from the hospital. She went back to California for part of the holidays to see some friends. She needed the break, but I really miss her."

"I hate the holidays," complained Dell, snubbing out his Camel. "My wife ran off just before Christmas. You can take all the bright lights, gift giving and ho, ho, ho and shove it up Santa's ass. But you Sean, enjoy your time as a young man, it won't last long."

Sean eased his wallet from a back pocket, his hands trembling slightly. He gently slid out a small color photo encased in plastic.

"Candy gave me this before leaving town," asserted Sean, beaming at the image of his friend from California. "She looks pretty good, don't you think old man?"

Dell's eyes popped open in wonderment. "Yikes, that's a great looking girl," remarked the fisherman, taking the photo from Sean. "That's the smallest red bikini I've ever seen. You ought to bring that girl around this summer and we'll all go out in my boat. It would give me a chance to throw you overboard and make my move. Gosh, having that naked lass around my pier would really boost business. Make all the arrangements, young squire."

"Fat chance, old man. One whiff of you and she would jump overboard."

"Well, it's good to know that the hit to your head didn't wipe out all of your senses," chuckled Dell. He suddenly turned serious. "Just don't go out and get your heart scarred by that pretty thing."

The mention of Sean's injury made him rub the small lump left on the crown of his head. "I can still smell a rat that's for sure," laughed Sean, holding his hand out for Candy's photo.

Dell slid the memento across the table.

"So are you in l-o-v-e with this girl?" asked Dell, rubbing his whiskers.

"I'd like to think so but lately we haven't had much time together."

"Well, take it from an old guy, love is a good boner in the morning. After that, if you can find a warm place to put your wanker, then thank your lucky stars."

"I can't believe you're sharing that," said Sean. "You just gave new meaning to the term dirty old man."

"B eleven."

"My good fortune is fading fast," said Dell flatly. "I'm not sure I can take anymore of this crap if the action doesn't pick up."

"It's bingo, Dell," said Sean. "If you want action go to Las Vegas."

"Good idea, my young charge," said Dell. "That would beat the hell out of Ohio in December. If it wasn't for a few crazy ice fishermen needing bait and gear, I'd starve to death."

Dell pushed two bingo cards in front of Sean.

"Here, pay attention to these and see what happens," ordered Dell, dropping a pile of chips into Sean's outstretched palm.

"I seventeen."

"Hey, this card is only two short of a bingo," said Sean. "Look at the diagonal running across the card. Maybe we will win something."

Dell lit another Camel, spitting out a piece of tobacco that clung to his lip when he inhaled.

"Well, shit in my overalls, my little friend, maybe something good will still happen to you this year," said Dell, twirling his cigarette in his hand. "God knows you've seen your share of trouble lately."

"No bad stuff tonight," warned Sean wearily.

"Oh, don't go sensitive on me," responded Dell. "I'm just getting warmed up to your company again."

"G twelve."

"Holy smoke and all the saints in heaven," squealed Sean. "Only one more number! Hundred bucks here we come!"

Dell pushed his chair over and put his arm around Sean. "You're a squall busting out on Lake Erie," said the fisherman. "Full of piss and vinegar and a lot of hot air."

"Come on 0 fourteen!" gushed Sean, pulling away from Dell and jumping to his feet.

Sean spun around in a circle. "Can't they call the numbers any faster? The waiting is killing me."

Dell dropped his cigarette butt into the now empty Coke bottle.

"If someone else gets 'bingo,' I'm gonna die," said Sean, dropping back into his chair.

"Hush, the announcer just pulled another ball from the machine," said Dell. "And if we luck up, slide that card back over here. You're too young to pick up the prize money and those Catholic sons of bitches will screw you for sure."

"0 fourteen."

"BINGO!" howled Sean and Dell in unison.

The sight of the old fisherman and his friend whopping and hugging brought some of the bingo players to their feet, their applause following the duo as they approached the winner's table.

"It's legit, go ahead and check the numbers," commanded Dell, when he reached the cashier. "I'll take that one-hundred dollars in ten-dollar bills, please and thank you."

Dell held out his hand, smiling as the bills started to pile up.

"I love this game," said Dell, bowing deeply at the waist to the acknowledgement of the crowd near the front of the hall.

Dell strutted from the bingo hall waving the money over his head. "Come on Sean, let's celebrate!"

The two raced for Dell's old pickup parked at the far end of the lot, Sean easily reaching the truck first.

As Dell finally tottered up, a passing car bathed the truck in light.

Sean turned to watch Father Paul Sterner's Buick Riviera slip around the corner of the parish garage. A shudder ran the length of his spine.

"Jesus, who just pissed on your head?" said Dell, breathing heavily as he unlocked the truck's side door. "Jump in and let's get out of this Catholic wasteland."

"Come on Myrtle, get us home," said Dell. He rubbed his hands over the dashboard, the truck coming to life with the first turn of the key. The radio blared soul music as the engine started up.

"Do you always turn white at this time of the evening?" asked Dell, placing the bingo prize money on the seat next to Sean. "If we're gonna have some fun tonight, you have to get that crazy look off your face."

"Sorry old man, it's just … it's just … ah, hell," sighed Sean, his mouth suddenly going dry.

"It's just what?" wondered Dell, his voice full of emotion. "You don't have to say it. I'll tell you. It's that old piece of shit pastor driving that fancy car of his. I say eventually the truth about that miserable bastard comes out and this town makes him walk the plank. I'd be happy to do the honors."

"The truth?" I don't understand."

"There's been talk for years about that old pain in the ass who calls himself a priest," fumed Dell, slamming the accelerator as the truck peeled from the parking lot. "Let's just say he's not such a holy roller as he claims."

"Meaning?"

"Meaning," said Dell, pushing his cap back on his head, "that it's time you know a man who likes to go to brothels shouldn't be telling others how to live their lives."

"He sees prostitutes!"

"I don't think he's just seeing them, if you know what I mean. He's been doing more than just looking."

"How's a story like that get started?" wondered Sean. "And why didn't you tell me that sooner?"

"I wanted to the last time we went fishing but the Coho got me distracted," said Dell. "It seems his car was stolen one night when it was parked out front of one of his favorite places. The cabbie who took him home recognized him, because the good father had baptized his daughter some twenty years back. The priest was sneaky though. He had on his street clothes and asked to be dropped off several blocks from the church."

"Jesus," said Sean, clearly incredulous.

"Jesus indeed," said Dell, turning the truck off the main road. "If you remember, I warned you about the good pastor's sneaky ways back this summer when you were having some trouble with him. Trouble you never shared with me."

"I remembered your advice about two-legged rats. That one I didn't forget."

The truck bounced along the pitted dirt road, coming to a stop at the foot of Dell's fishing pier.

"Come along Master Sean, I'll fire up the old stove and make you a cup of hot chocolate," said Dell, scooping the ten-dollar bills off the seat as he stepped out of the truck. "Of course I'll have my usual libation."

"How's the war going by the way?" inquired Sean.

"Beautiful," said Dell, "there just isn't a season I don't like killing rats. Winter, spring, summer, fall—it's all one big opportunity for me."

The mention of killing rats caused Dell to start dancing on his pier.

"You are one crazy old man," said Sean, pushing Dell towards his cabin.

"It's a little slow right now with the cold weather but I'm not dropping my guard. You be careful to keep your hands off the pier rails. I just put out a fresh batch of arsenic balls."

Dell slid a large key in the padlock securing the door to his cabin, standing aside as the slab of polished oak swung open.

"You first young man," said Dell, ushering Sean inside.

A lone bulb spread a circle of light over the sink.

Dell marched directly to the potbellied stove resting on a pad of bricks in the center of his one-room cabin.

"It won't take long to get the chill out," he said, opening the small door in the front of the stove and striking a match along the floor.

Soon, the shards of pine at the bottom of the stove kicked to life, their flames licking the hard woods placed on top.

"Old Mabel gives off good heat," said Dell, patting the side of his stove. "Better than any woman. At least I can trust my stove."

"What's with all the M names?" asked Sean. "There's Mary the boat, Myrtle the truck and now Mabel the stove. Your crapper probably has a name beginning with M."

"Right you are, boy genius. That little device is named Madeline in honor of my ex-wife. I take a dump on her every morning."

Sean's laughter bounced off the pine walls.

"The butler has the night off so you'll have to put up with my service," said Dell, pouring milk and chocolate syrup into a pan and placing it atop the stove.

Sean took off his parka. Soon he was sipping hot chocolate, the warm liquid and aroma energizing his senses.

"There is something to be said about a simple pleasure on a winter night," said Sean after a big gulp.

"You can be a profound young man sometimes, Master Sean," said Dell, lifting up the bourbon bottle next to his folding chair and filling a large metal cup. He leaned back and placed his feet closer to the wood stove. "Too people many make foolish decisions that lead to complications they can never imagine. Just stick with living a good life, it's a lot easier."

Dell drained his cup.

"Take my ex-wife," said the fisherman as he opened the stove door to throw in more wood. "She ran off with a stranger. Well, the illusion of love didn't last and it ruined a pretty good marriage. I lost my best friend, my home, and a business I had built for over 20 years. Not to mention my broken heart."

"That must have been really bad," said Sean tenderly.

"Well Sean, you're old enough now to understand that life is full of unexpected twists and turns," said Dell, waging his finger for emphasis. "Surely you realize that, after what happened to Jimmy and Veronica. Just enjoy the good times as best you can along the way. And stay away from guile and trickery, in the end it will ruin you just like everyone else."

"Did you ever forgive your wife and try and get her back?"

"No, she never gave me the chance. When I confronted her, she told me she didn't have a problem with adultery. Kind of hard to save a marriage once you hear that nonsense coming out of the mouth of someone you cherished. And time does not heal all wounds. I still miss her, every day, especially late at night."

"What ever happened to her?"

"She died in her sleep of a stroke in her fifties," said Dell, pouring more bourbon into his cup. "Oh gosh, she was something in her day."

The genuine grief in his voice moved Sean. "I'm sorry Dell about your loss," said Sean, his eyes welling with tears. "I feel the same way about Jimmy. I can't believe he's not around. It's a shame, pure and simple."

Dell placed his empty cup on the floor, smacking the right side of his head with such force the impact made Sean flinch.

"Damn tick, gets my eye fluttering so bad I can't see out of it," said Dell. "A good whack is the only thing that works."

Sean wiped his eyes on the sleeve of his shirt.

"Do you have any inkling as to why that red-haired wonder boy would ride out onto the lake like he did? That's something I'll never understand."

Sean looked over at Dell solemnly but did not answer. He crossed his arms and rocked in his chair. In his mind he could clearly see Jimmy riding off the edge of the ice.

"It was that trip to the rectory to see Father Paul," he finally said in a soft voice.

"What do you mean?" prodded Dell gently.

"Jimmy screwed up in class with one of the nuns and she shipped him off to have a talk with the pastor," said Sean, gazing down at the floor. "I lost my friend that day. The old Jimmy just slipped away after that."

"What are we going to do about the rat bastard?" Dell's words were becoming slightly slurred. "I'm getting loaded, but I'm not going to sleep without some response."

"Who can I trust?" pleaded Sean, placing his empty mug in the sink. "Who will believe me? It's still his word against mine and I already have a big strike against me for the stunt I pulled on the Fourth."

"So it was you who pushed the old priest in the pool. That's the biggest open secret in this little village."

"Yup, I'm screwed up," said Sean looking down at Dell. "The pastor got his revenge. He beat the crap out of me on the very day I found out my brother died—right out in my backyard in broad daylight."

Dell's blood-shot eyes turned to slits. He turned away to open the stove door and blow a load of snot out of his right nostril into the fire. He fought to catch his breath.

"That bastard!" screamed Dell, his face turning crimson. "Who does he think he is, mister high and mighty pastor."

Dell took down his .22 rifle from over the door and paced around his stove.

"Mark my words, Sean, my good friend, something has to be done," he said, furiously working the rifle bolt back and forth. "Keeping all this quiet is no longer an option. Secrets only make things worse."

"You can't just go out and shoot him," warned Sean.

"Wish I could, but I'm not doing any jail time for the likes of him," stammered Dell. "We need to have cooler heads and a good battle plan."

Dell plopped down hard in his chair, laying the rifle across his lap.

"We should proceed with care and caution," he said firmly. "As in any conflict, especially with rat bastards, we need to know who our allies are in our campaign."

"I did tell Father Ken about the beating back in the fall after my brother's funeral," offered Sean. "But nothing happened that I can see. I think Father Paul has him intimidated. We can't go to the nuns and we can forget my parents and the police. They are not gonna believe me against the pastor of the whole damn parish."

"I believe you Sean," said Dell, picking up Sean's coat as he ambled towards the cabin door. "Father Ken is the key right now. We need to know what he believes and where he stands."

Dell squeezed Sean's hands in a tight grip. "I promise you I won't let you down." He dug into his overalls and took out the bingo winnings.

"It's getting late and I do my best thinking while I'm asleep," he said, counting out fifty dollars. "We can't solve this problem tonight. Do you want me to take you home?"

"No," said Sean, slipping on his coat, "the wind's died down and the walk will give me time to think about how to approach Father Ken."

"But no heroics until we hear from the young priest and that's an order, sailor," said Dell. "Enjoy the jackpot. Fifty dollars is a lot of money to spread around Vineyard Beach."

"No promises," said Sean, stepping over the threshold. "Didn't you tell me once that when dealing with rats it all comes down to personal initiative."

"Don't worry, I haven't lost to a rat yet," said Dell, closing the door.

Sean paused for a moment on the pier, looking down at a pile of rags pushed up against the side of the cabin. He fished out a small swath that once was part of one of Dell's old work shirts.

As he walked towards the road, Sean slowed near the last pier support and carefully used the gray rag to lift one of the arsenic dough balls off the piling. He folded the rag neatly into a secure bundle, then pulled his parka open to drop the package into an inside pocket. Content with the secret tucked inside his coat, Sean smiled. He zipped the compartment shut and headed for Maple Street.

CHAPTER NINETEEN

Lorraine was perched at her usual spot in the Gerard kitchen, just to the left of the head of the table, her chair facing the window so she could look out over the backyard. Light snow fell.

The night before, the arthritis in her lower spine had flared, making sleep impossible. She adjusted the cushion behind her back and laid out two aspirin next to her cup, waiting for the coffee to finish brewing on the gas stove. The gurgling of the percolator was the only sound in the room.

As each minute passed, she became more and more agitated.

Her beloved Sean, once the light in her life, was now a silent, sullen mystery, rarely speaking to his parents at any length.

Lorraine's lower back went into a sudden spasm, the pain ripping down both legs. "God, I have enough burdens to carry," she wailed under her breath. "Please not any more of this, not now."

She poured her coffee, using the brown elixir to wash down the pain pills.

The St. Joseph's church bulletin rested on the table next to her cup. Lorraine had retrieved it from the early Sunday service she attended while her family slept. She ran her hand over the short announcement and photo on the cover.

Lorraine gritted her teeth as another wave of pain attacked her spine.

She dabbed at the sweat on her forehead as she read the announcement one more time. Her hands clammy, Lorraine picked up the bulletin.

Tom Tozer

FATHER KENNETH WASOWSKI TO LEAVE ST. JOSEPH'S PARISH

We are sorry to inform the parish that Father Kenneth Wasowski will be reassigned effective immediately due to a critical shortage of priests in Appalachia, announced Bishop Robert Imish, head of the Greater Cleveland Diocese of Catholics. Father Paul Sterner will take over all parish responsibilities until a replacement is found. Father Wasowski was credited with the successful launch of the football program in the first year of St. Joseph's High School. He will be truly missed. Father Wasowski has already left for his new assignment, any correspondence should be directed through Pastor Sterner. A mass honoring Father Ken will be said by Pastor Sterner, next Sunday, December 25 at 11 a.m. Because of the holiday crowd expected, please be on time.

Lorraine knew that the departure of the young priest would upset Sean. Just last night her son, in a rare moment of openness, had agonized about the need to speak with Father Ken.

The jangle of the telephone on the wall by the sink jolted Lorraine from her chair.

The bulletin fell from her hands and fluttered to the wood floor. She closed her eyes for a moment, inhaled deeply, and limped to the phone.

"Who's calling this early in the morning?" whispered Lorraine. "No more trouble, please."

Upstairs in his bed, Sean pulled the blanket over his head at the sound of the phone ringing. He wasn't ready to start his day just yet. Last night with Dell was a roller coaster of emotions but he felt better about sharing his secret with the fisherman. He hoped Dell would somehow protect him if the situation with the pastor turned any uglier.

"Yes, Father I understand," said Lorraine, holding the phone tightly. "You need Sean to help say the high mass in Father Ken's honor on Christmas Day. Yes, yes Father, I'll be sure my son shows up early to get the church ready for such a big day."

Lorraine couldn't control the shaking in her hands. She slipped her coffee mug onto the kitchen counter.

"Yes, Father, I understand it's a tribute for any altar boy. Sean will be pleased. I will tell him when he wakes. Yes Father, your blessing will be appreciated."

Lorraine made the sign of the cross. "Amen," she said into the receiver before hanging up.

When she turned around, Sean stood in the doorway, pulling up his droopy pajama bottoms.

"Who was on the phone?" inquired Sean, picking up the bulletin off the kitchen floor.

As Sean read, his right hand slowly closed into a fist. "This is the dirty work of Father Paul. I hate that man!"

In a rush of grief that stunned him with its violence, Sean tore the bulletin up and threw the pieces at his mother.

CHAPTER TWENTY

Sean awoke before dawn. He laced up his leather boots for the trek through the heavy snow blowing down on Vineyard Beach. He made one stop in the basement to look through his father's toolbox. He checked his watch for the third time as the sun broke through the cluster of gray clouds hanging over Lake Erie. The blanket of pristine snow sparkled in the faint light, a blemish-free layer of shiny crystals covering the town's imperfections.

The center of the village beckoned—the shops and small businesses that The Caper Brothers knew so well. Sean left a line of fresh tracks in the powder as he darted past the long dark shadows cast from the brick buildings congregated in the town's business district. Off to the left stood the Saddle Inn, the little hotel that catered to the workers at the nearby power plant, its Horse Tail Bar a lively spot on Friday nights. The marquee of the small movie theater next to the hotel proclaimed its provocative offering: "The Planet of the Apes." At the Ben Franklin Five and Dime, Sean paused to read the hand-painted sign in the door declaring "Bomb Hanoi." He continued on to the nearby Vineyard Beach Pharmacy.

Sean squinted through the plate glass window at the soda fountain and small counter where Veronica once poured Vernors ginger ale and entertained his troupe with her stories and the best titties along the shore. The interior of the pharmacy was bathed in an eerie light from a large, round electric clock on the far wall promoting Stroh's beer. The interior of the pharmacy was a lonely sight, its once brimming shelves of cold medicines, candy, bird feeders, and the occasional fishing pole, now barren except for a small pile of ice scrapers near the front door.

The sign taped to the inside of the bay window read: "For Sale Commercial Real Estate."

Sean stepped back to the curb for a better view, drinking in the details, from the horizontal stained-glass window embedded in brick over the door to the blocks of limestone that comprised the foundation.

"This place *is* closing," sighed Sean. He leaned forward and patted the brick facade. "I guess the old pharmacist couldn't make this place work without Veronica."

"Talking to yourself is not healthy," said Trotz, his voice echoing down street.

"Yes, and neither is sneaking up on your friend," said Sean warmly. "I know it's early for you boys to be out of your beds but it's actually good to see you both. Thanks for being here."

Buddy, Johnny, and Sean exchanged handshakes, stomping their feet against the cold wind, the loss of their favorite hangout darkening their faces. Johnny reached out and grabbed the handle of the pharmacy's front door.

"It's locked," he declared after several attempts at turning the knob.

Sean slid a large screwdriver from the sleeve of his parka.

"Step aside there my good man," he said, pushing Johnny away from the door. "Make way for a master thief, all in the honor of our missing Caper Brother. God bless the memory of Jimmy Moran all of our days."

Sean plunged the screwdriver with both hands into the door jam, working the shaft next to the lock mechanism. With a mighty jerk, he leveraged the shaft against the door, popping open the lock.

"Step inside for the last official meeting of The Caper Brothers," ordered Sean with a dramatic bow and wave of his arm.

"Ah, Sean, don't say that, we can still keep our group together," whined Buddy.

"Get off the street, now," barked Sean. "I want to be out of here before the sun gets all the way up and the security guard starts making his rounds."

The boys crept through the store in the dim light, stopping in front of the soda fountain. They each took their usual place on their assigned stool. Sean perched on the first stool, followed by Johnny and Buddy. The second stool was left open in memory of their dead friend. Sean poked the toe of his boot at a mouse piloting along the step in front of the counter.

"I'll get right to the point," said Sean, spinning to address Johnny and Buddy. "The three of us will always be friends, but The Caper Brothers are no more. Without crazy Moran and without this place, it just doesn't make sense to continue. Sorry for the bad news."

Johnny Pasquale jumped down and moved to Sean's side. "Don't be sorry, you and this whole town have been through a lot these last few months," said Johnny, his voice breaking.

"I was thinking of something," said Sean, placing his hand on Johnny's shoulder. "I was thinking we should do something that this town will remember for a long time, a very long time."

The boys flinched at the sudden anger in Sean's voice.

"Whoa, slow down there Sean, there's enough trouble already to go around," insisted Buddy.

Sean waved his hand in their faces. "I'm going this one alone then," he said, the determination in his voice quieting his friends. "The Caper Brothers can't end with a whimper. Jimmy wouldn't have it that way and I'm not either."

Sean walked his friends to the front door. "Go on now, I'll catch up to you soon."

"Not a chance," shouted Johnny. "Not this time, Sean Gerard. We're in this thing to the end. You are not ordering us out of whatever you have planned."

"That's right," added Buddy. "If you called us here this early in the morning and it's our last time together, then we're not leaving without you."

"Then what happens today stays our secret," conceded Sean. "Stay right where you are and get ready to run."

"Just what are you going to do?" pleaded Buddy.

"With all the protesting going on in this country right now, I thought I'd have my own little personal protest," offered Sean.

"Protesting what?" asked Johnny.

"Injustice!" proclaimed Sean.

Sean waited a few minutes, checking his watch again. It wasn't quite full light yet so there was still time.

He pulled the commercial real estate sign down from the inside of the glass and walked to the back of the pharmacy where several worn boxes were stacked against the wall. Sean pulled a Zippo lighter from his coat pocket and put the flame to the corner of the sign, dropping it on top of the boxes.

The three boys sprinted from the building.

By the time the security guard spotted the fire, the pharmacy's interior was gutted.

Two days later, the local newspaper reported that the fire was of suspicious origin but investigators had no leads in the case.

CHAPTER TWENTY-ONE

Dell had just cranked up his old truck about midday when he heard tapping on the driver's side window.

There in the cold and snow stood Sean Gerard.

Dell rolled down his window.

"I guess you heard the news," said Sean, gulping for air.

"About the young priest," answered Dell nodding.

"Yes, he just got shipped out of Saint Joe's," replied Sean. "You can bet that's the work of the pastor."

"Suppose you're right," said Dell. "Maybe the old bastard felt the new priest knew too much about his shenanigans."

"I need a favor," said Sean.

"Ask young man," said Dell.

"I just found out from my mother that I have to help with a service on Christmas Day to honor Father Ken," grumbled Sean. "And you know what that means. I'll be up there on the altar with the pastor of St. Joe's, good old Father Paul Sterner and I'll be at his mercy."

"Get in the truck," ordered Dell, flicking his smoldering Camel into the snow.

Sean climbed into the seat next to Dell as the old fisherman rubbed the gray stubble on his chin.

"Don't talk just yet," ordered Dell, picking up a Zippo off the dashboard. "Give me a minute to think. Catch your breath for now."

He fired up another cigarette, pushing his cap back on his head as he blew smoke rings.

"Well, what's your biggest worry?" prodded Dell, eyeing Sean with sympathy. "You'll be surrounded by parishioners for that mass, especially on Christmas Day."

"I'm not worried about when I'm on the altar," blurted Sean. "But what happens if he makes me go to the rectory for one of his little talks? Look how it ended for Jimmy Moran. I guess I'll just run off."

"That's not a plan," countered Dell. "How about I drive my truck down to the church parking lot and keep an eye out? If you get hauled inside the rectory, I'll be right outside with the motor running for a fast escape. And if you're in there too long, I'll just invite myself inside and speak with the pastor myself. Either way, you can stop worrying."

Sean reached over and patted Dell on the head.

"Good thinking, old man," he said with relief. "Just knowing you will be nearby is comforting. Are you sure you want to do this?"

"I'm your friend," said Dell. "What else did you expect, Master Sean? I'll be in the church parking lot sometime before 11 a.m. with bells on. Now, go and enjoy your Christmas Eve and I'll be seeing you tomorrow."

CHAPTER TWENTY-TWO

The luminarias snaked the length of the DeLane brick driveway from Lake Boulevard up to the double oak doors at the front of the mansion, beckoning the holiday partygoers as they arrived in their cars. An oversized wreath made of fresh evergreen sprigs adorned the double entry doors, and the grounds were awash in colorful outdoor lights hanging from the trees. Even the helicopter resting on its pad in the back of the property had bulbs dangling from its rotor and blades. The main house was set off with single electric candles burning in all twenty of the windows lining the marble façade. A sixteen-foot Christmas tree in the foyer, trimmed in green and gold bulbs with miniature white lights, was visible all the way out to the main road.

A valet stand near the garage welcomed the lucky guests invited by Weldon DeLane and his daughter, Candy, for Vineyard Beach's most anticipated social event of the year. Local caterers spread the word around the village that the food order alone was going to cost close to $10,000. Mouths were watering at the news that a mound of lobster tails would be piled on ice in the centerpiece of the buffet.

Weldon, tanned and looking relaxed in a black tuxedo, stood encamped near the front door, greeting visitors after the butler helped with their heavy winter outerwear. His face broke into a grin as Sean, in a blue blazer, gray slacks, and shiny black loafers, eased across the foyer's tiled floor. On his arm was his mother, Lorraine, looking radiant in a full-length red party dress; her hair piled high, accentuating the curve of her stately neck.

"Welcome and happy holidays," announced Weldon, thumping Sean on the chest. "I see you have a lovely escort for tonight's festivities." Weldon bowed to Lorraine, taking her hand and kissing it lightly.

"And where might I ask is the good Lieutenant tonight?"

"He has a touch of the flu, I'm sad to say," offered Lorraine.

Sean shot a disbelieving look at his mother.

"Well then, it will allow me the opportunity to spend some time with you, Lorraine," remarked Weldon. "Once most of our guests arrive I'll be free to move about and chat. And I'd love to hear more about your beloved France, one of my favorite spots."

"Then we will have a nice little talk, *mon cheri*," said Lorraine, softly touching Weldon's cheek. "It's been some time since I shared my thoughts about my homeland with someone who shares my passion for Europe. I look forward to the moment."

Sean cleared his throat, drawing the attention of Weldon.

The host pointed his finger to the ceiling.

"I imagine you're wondering where the hostess is tonight?" observed Weldon. "Candy flew in this morning from California. She's upstairs putting on the finishing touches. Sean, the wait will be worth it. The trip has been good for her. I haven't seen her this happy in quite some time."

"I'm really looking forward to seeing her!" exclaimed Sean, stepping forward as more guests came through the door.

Lorraine smiled back over her shoulder at Weldon as her son led her into the banquet room dominated by a two-story stone fireplace, flanked by custom floor-to-ceiling windows offering a majestic view of Lake Erie. Oak logs crackled on the hearth.

"My dear son," said Lorraine, straightening the collar on Sean's dress shirt. "I appreciate you not saying anything about your father. And thank you for coming with me tonight. I had to get out of my house."

"I understand," said Sean.

A butler glided up holding a tray laden with full champagne glasses. Lorraine nodded to the servant as she reached for one.

"Sean, on this occasion, you may have a drink of champagne," she said, handing a goblet to her son. He followed his mother's example and held the glass by the stem.

"To the holidays! May they be peaceful and be over as quick as possible," he said, clinking his glass with Lorraine's. They both sipped.

"*Hmm*. Weldon knows his champagne," said Lorraine, savoring the flavor in her mouth. "This is excellent."

The sudden dark look on Sean's face concerned his mother.

"What is wrong my little one?" she inquired. "Can we not have the light come back in your eyes for one night. How I miss your old sparkle."

"I can't even think straight, my head is so crammed with bad thoughts," mused Sean, twirling the glass nervously in his hand. "I mean, I miss my brother terribly, but with Jimmy's death, then Veronica's accident. Life seems just a mess."

"I know," insisted Lorraine. She gulped a mouthful of champagne. "Remember your prayers, Sean."

"Prayers," he sighed. "I don't think anyone is listening to mine. Not God, that's for sure."

"Oh, he's watching over us. Never doubt that. But right now we just have to be strong and focus on positive things."

"Like what?" challenged Sean.

"Like this wonderful evening we are about to enjoy with friends and neighbors on Christmas Eve," replied Lorraine, taking the glass from Sean. "Let's work our way over to the buffet table and put our troubles aside."

Sean unbuttoned his blazer and let out a small belch.

"That champagne had a kick to it."

"Don't forget your manners," said Lorraine, waging a finger at her son. "Let's get something to eat and mingle with the guests. But I don't want you staying up too late. You have an important day tomorrow with the holiday and the special Mass for Father Ken."

"Yeah, it will be special alright," complained Sean. "Special like a bad dream."

"Now Sean, you've worked Mass before many times," sighed Lorraine. "No need to worry about one more."

"It's the good pastor Sterner I can't stand," muttered Sean, slamming his hands together.

"Sean Gerard!" snapped Lorraine. "Can't you find it in yourself to be a humble servant? He is, after all, the pastor of our church and on top of that, it's the holidays. No more negative talk about our pastor."

"You know, you are so quick to defend him. Every time I bring up his name you're jumping to his defense. If only you knew the truth."

"Father Paul will be here tonight and you should take up your grievances with him," demanded Lorraine. "I expect you to patch things up with him so there's no trouble tomorrow. Christmas Day will be hectic enough. Now, not another word on this subject."

"Parents are all the same," grumbled Sean, his face flushed. "I bring up something important and you can't deal with it. It's like what I have to say doesn't even matter."

Lorraine headed for the buffet leaving Sean clutching his fists.

Sean jumped when a hand landed on his shoulder.

"Just breath, take a deep one, all the way down into your lungs."

"God, you scared the hell out of me," uttered Sean, quickly relaxing at the sight of Candy.

Sean took a step back, savoring the vision of Candy, decked out in a strapless black dress that showed off her trim, athletic body. Her golden hair, parted perfectly down the middle, fell in long rolls of curls. He hugged Candy, the smell of her musk perfume adding to his intoxication. He slid one hand down her back and gently squeezed her butt.

"Hey, watch it there, smarty pants," murmured Candy with a wink. "This might be Christmas Eve but you're not getting any free tours of this gift package."

"I missed you something terrible," gushed Sean. "You sure look better than the last time I saw you in that nasty school uniform."

Candy chuckled as she scanned the banquet hall to make sure no one was staring.

She moved closer to lock her lips on Sean's mouth, flicking her tongue inside for a brief moment.

"I thought about you every day," whispered Candy, pulling away. "I didn't miss Ohio when I was on the West Coast, but I did want to be with you the minute I got back."

Candy took Sean by the hand.

"Let's go," she said, leading him towards the kitchen and the back stairs to the second floor.

At the threshold to her room, Candy spun and pushed Sean past her door, swinging it shut with her foot. She jerked the dead bolt in the door lock and faced the center of the room, where Sean stared at her, smiling.

"You just gonna stand there with your mouth open looking dumb?" taunted Candy, slowly walking across the oak floor.

She stopped several feet in front of Sean, reaching back to lower the zipper on her dress.

"Close your eyes," she said softly.

"Close my eyes?" wondered Sean. "Why do I have to do that?"

"Because there's something I want to show you, silly boy," said Candy confidently. "Don't you trust me?"

"I guess I trust you," answered Sean. "Why wouldn't I?"

"Why wouldn't you indeed," offered Candy, impatiently tapping her foot on the floor. "You trusted me down at my pool last summer when we kissed for the first time, and I took off my swimsuit top, now didn't you?"

"If that's the kind of trust you're talking about, then I'm the guy you can count on," declared Sean, pulling off his blazer and tossing it on a chair.

"Close them and put one hand over your eyes for good measure."

Sean did as he was told.

Candy inched closer, slowly lowering the zipper the rest of the way. The black garment slid silently to the floor. She unsnapped her bra, letting it fall off. She kicked her dress onto her bed and put her arms on her hips, her perfect breasts pointed slightly to the ceiling. She preened in her blue panties with a small red balloon emblazed across the front, her calves accentuated in her high heels.

"Keep those eyes closed now or you'll ruin my surprise," instructed Candy as she approached Sean.

Her lips were now inches from Sean's.

She trembled as she guided his hands to her breasts.

"It's okay to look now," she said softly, giving Sean a quick kiss.

"I guess there really is a Santa Claus," exclaimed Sean, admiring the tanned girl.

"That's as far as you go," warned Candy, spinning around. "I just wanted you to see how the California sun has returned the glow to my skin."

"I'll say it's a mighty fine job," remarked Sean pulling Candy back into his arms. "I haven't seen you like this since we were down by your pool. You can bet I think about that every day."

Sean moved his left hand to the back of Candy's neck as their tongues interlocked. He slid his other hand down her back and under her panties, fondling her.

Candy squeezed Sean in return, feeling his excitement. She started rubbing.

In minutes, Sean released a loud groan.

"Oh Sean," cried Candy, laying her head on his shoulder. "I missed you so much."

She moved away, crouching on the edge of her bed.

"Did you like my little present?" she teased, crossing her legs.

"That was better than anything I ever found under my Christmas tree. I mean ever. Are all the girls from California as wild as you?"

Candy laughed as she slipped on her bra and dress. She motioned to Sean.

"Zip me up please."

Sean encircled Candy from behind when he finished with her dress.

"I love you," he purred.

"I love you too, very much. Now, you should clean yourself up while I find us some champagne."

"Can we talk for a minute?" insisted Sean.

"But nothing too heavy, it's the holidays my friend," she said.

"Screw the holidays," blurted Sean. "I gotta be around Father Paul tomorrow during the Christmas Mass. I can't stand it."

The mention of the pastor sucked the color from Candy's face.

She held up her hand. "Don't mention that name around me ever again," she ordered. "As in, the rest of my life. I'm still trying to forget what he did."

"I'm sorry, I won't let it happen again," said Sean in defeat. "I'm really sorry."

Sean picked up his blazer and tossed it over his shoulder

"Do me one favor tomorrow," inquired Sean. "Please come to the mass I have to work. Wear something bright and sit up near the front so I can see you. I'll feel better."

"I'll try," she said. "But only because it's Christmas."

Candy unlocked the door and led Sean down the hall to the guest bathroom.

"You might want to throw some water on your face to cool down those bright red cheeks," advised Candy. "I'll meet you down at the buffet table. I don't want anyone seeing us coming down the stairs together."

Sean kissed Candy gently on the lips.

"I love you."

"I know, I heard that already tonight," giggled Candy. "See you soon."

Sean took his time in the bathroom. When he felt it was safe, he opened the door, peered down the empty hall and stepped out.

By the time Sean reached the kitchen, the adjacent banquet hall was overflowing with guests, so many in fact that he had to circle the room to avoid the crush near the buffet table in the middle of the room.

When he found Candy, she was balancing two glasses of champagne and a plate with a perfectly shelled lobster tail and a small silver cup of warm, melted butter.

She handed the champagne to Sean and dipped a piece of lobster into the cup.

"Here, open your mouth," she said. "After what happened upstairs, you need to get your energy back." Her laugh erupted deep in her throat.

Sean threw his head back and accepted the morsel, the flavor exciting his taste buds.

"That's my first lobster," he marveled. "I can see now why people make a big deal out of that stuff. You know, I'm getting one hell of an education hanging out with you."

"Well, tomorrow is Christmas after all, we should have some fun," observed Candy.

Carolers streamed into the far side of the banquet room, each one carrying a single red songbook. The sound of "Silent Night" was soon drifting over the hum of the crowd and the clicking of plates.

The two friends watched the holiday pageant, holding hands and drinking champagne.

"Here comes your dad," said Sean, pointing at Weldon weaving through the crowd. He waved at the pair.

"I'll be there in a minute," he yelled above the noise.

Weldon turned around to speak with someone, his large frame obscuring the identity of the partygoer from Sean and Candy.

When Weldon started back towards Sean and Candy, his arm was draped over the shoulder of Father Paul Sterner.

Candy dropped her champagne glass, the impact sending tiny shards across the floor.

"I can't believe *he* is in my house," blurted Candy. "I'm leaving."

Sean tried to grab Candy but it did little to slow her escape. She pushed Sean's arm away and fled the hall.

"Where's Candy going?" wondered Weldon as he approached.

Sean shook his head.

"I guess she's not interested in spending any time in his company," challenged Sean, gesturing towards the priest.

Weldon eyed Father Paul suspiciously.

"Am I missing something?" he demanded.

"You are missing nothing, my good man," commented Father Paul. "Except for some tall tales from Mister Gerard."

"Are you calling me a liar?" shouted Sean.

"Watch your tone with me, young man," he said sternly. "What I am saying, exactly, is that you cannot be trusted. Period."

"Look, this is Christmas Eve," interrupted Weldon. "Why don't you both shake hands and let's move on."

Father Paul gulped deeply from his martini.

"Not to worry, it *is* the holidays," said Father Paul, his voice suddenly warm and friendly. "Sean, I'll see in you church tomorrow and after Mass, we can get together in my office and hash things out."

The priest patted the side of Sean's face and smiled sweetly.

"Now, go enjoy the party," he said softly. "Your mother is looking for you. She too wants us to meet and put the past behind us. Just ask her."

CHAPTER TWENTY-THREE

Christmas morning broke cold and clear. Sean scooped his prayer book off the nightstand next to his bed, a gift from his parents on the day he received his first Holy Communion in the second grade. When he snapped open the missal, a prayer card fluttered to the floor. Sean could see the image of St. Jude on the front. He turned the card over.

"To be said when problems arise or when one seems to be deprived of all visible help, or for cases almost despaired of."

Sean fell to his knees.

"Dear Saint Jude, now is my time of greatest need," prayed Sean. "Please give me courage or all is lost."

When he finished reciting the St. Jude prayer, Sean dressed for church in dark slacks, a white shirt and his black dress shoes. He took his parka off the hook behind his door, quickly checking on the secret package he had hidden inside a zippered pocket.

Sean headed for the kitchen, passing the Christmas tree in the living room ablaze in colorful lights, a ring of presents encircling the base. Lorraine wiped lipstick off her coffee cup as Sean entered the kitchen.

"Good morning and Merry Christmas my son," announced Lorraine. "I hope you are fine on this holiest of days."

"I'll survive I guess," muttered Sean.

"Would you like something to eat before Mass or are you going to wait 'til we have brunch afterwards and open our gifts?"

"I'll just have some juice and get down to the church," replied Sean, putting on his coat. "I want to get there early because I have some set-up work to get done before the service."

"Good enough, my son, I hope the Mass goes well. I'll be in my usual seat near the front. Be sure to wave and wish Father Paul merry Christmas for us. This is a good time for you two to patch things up."

"Right, I'll just do what the pastor tells me to do. Isn't that what you want?" said Sean smugly, heading for the door.

"Sean, just have a good service. Do you want me to drive you to the church?"

"No, I'll walk. Dad not going today?"

"He's still asleep," said Lorraine, walking over to her son. "Maybe he'll go later in the day."

Lorraine kissed Sean on his forehead.

By the time Sean reached the side door to the church a few early arrivals worried about the holiday crush were moving across the parking lot. He glanced at his watch. The start of the service was thirty minutes away. As he started to pull the door open, Sean heard the familiar rumble of Dell's truck. Sean returned the fisherman's wave as he guided his pickup behind the garage next to the rectory and cut the engine.

Sean entered the church, going directly to the altar boys' room to hang up his coat. He started the pre-service ritual, donning his vestments, then lighting the candles throughout the church. Next he needed to pour the sacramental wine into a glass pitcher that would be consecrated during the Mass. Entering the priest's chamber, his heart thumped deep in his chest. He checked his watch again; there was still enough time before Father Paul arrived. Inside the supply closet, Sean held the pitcher under the spout protruding from a large wine cask resting on a shelf. He turned the valve, watching the red wine flow smoothly into the pitcher. He carried the container back to the altar boys' room where his parka hung. He carefully lifted the dirty rag out of the inside pocket and using a penknife, sliced a piece off the arsenic dough ball that he had hidden there, placing the sliver into the container. He put in the stopper and shook the pitcher until the dough dissolved. He walked the wine pitcher out to the side table near the altar and placed it next to a pitcher of water and the chalice holding the communion wafers.

The church was starting to fill up. Sean spotted his mother in her usual pew but he could not find Candy anywhere in the crowd. Sean decided to stay out on the altar, moving his seat so he could see the entrance to the priest's chamber. Sean scanned the congregation hoping that Candy would show up.

When he looked back, Father Paul was standing in the doorway, his hands on his hips. "Come over here, young man," snapped the priest, gesturing with his finger.

Sean crept towards the priest.

Father Paul stared at Sean menacingly.

"You look nervous on this blessed morning," he observed. "What could be bothering you?"

"Nothing Father," retorted Sean, wiping sweat off his nose. "I guess I'm just heated up getting the church ready."

The priest moved out of the doorway, motioning for Sean to come into the vestibule. Frankie scrambled for his little bed under the crucifix. As Sean passed the threshold, the priest flung his arm around the boy's neck and pushed him into the room. He spun Sean around and shoved him up against the wall. He gazed down into Sean's eyes, his face contorted in anger. The aroma of alcohol overwhelmed Sean.

"Let me go!" yelled Sean, trying to break free.

"Stop squirming and listen to me and nothing will happen to you," ordered the priest.

Sean relaxed enough for the priest to release his hold.

He started to step back but the priest lunged and grabbed the front of his robe.

"Get this straight," hissed the priest. "No shenanigans today, young man. I have a homily for Father Ken to deliver and this Mass will go smoothly."

"Yes, Father, yes Father, you are right," said Sean coolly.

The priest released his grip and smiled sweetly. "Let's get ready for this Mass on this day of all wonders," he said in a tender tone. "I hope

Christmas will bring you peace and we settle our differences. After Mass, we'll go to the rectory and work things out, once and for all."

The priest walked to where his vestments had been laid out on a table near the portrait of St. Joseph. When he finished putting on his sacred garments, he turned to Sean. "I assure you, Sean Gerard, you will thank me when we've finished our business today. Remember, I want close attention to detail, no missteps."

Sean mopped the moisture off his forehead with his sleeve, the sense of dread rising in his throat.

"Is everything ready on the altar? The wine, water and communion wafers?"

Sean nodded to the priest.

"Then it's time for this Mass to get started."

Sean followed as the priest marched out onto the altar.

The congregation stood up at the first sight of the priest coming through the side door.

Sean checked the church again for Candy. No sign of her. He nodded to his mother and began his duties, kneeling to the side of the altar as Father Paul began the service. He tried to concentrate during the different stages of the Mass, hoping to block what might happen when it came time to consecrate the wine. Father Paul's homily to the young priest had some in the congregation dabbing their eyes with tissue. As the service dragged on, sweat rolled down Sean's back, soaking into the top of his underwear.

The priest consecrated the host, holding it aloft so the parishioners could see the symbol of the body of Christ.

He turned to the side of the altar holding his golden chalice. Sean rose off his knees and went to the side table to secure the wine pitcher. He pulled out the stopper and carried the pitcher back to the altar.

His hands trembled as he poured the wine.

"A little more, please," whispered Father Paul.

Sean emptied the contents into the cup.

The priest placed the chalice on the altar and bent his head in prayer.

"Take and drink all of this, for this is the chalice of My Blood, the mystery of faith, which shall be shed for you and many unto the forgiveness of sins."

The priest continued with the communion ceremony, breaking off a piece of the consecrated host and placing it in his mouth.

He placed a communion plate under his chin and raised the chalice brimming with wine to the congregation. "May the blood of our Lord Jesus Christ preserve my soul to life everlasting."

Sean made the sign of the cross.

Father Paul put the chalice to his lips and drained its contents, lifting a starched linen napkin off the altar to wipe the last drop of red wine from his lips.

Sean studied the pastor throughout the rest of the service, Father Paul's face slowly turning bright red as the Mass neared its end.

The priest raised his right arm to the parishioners. "May the blessing of almighty God, Father, Son and Holy Ghost descend upon you and remain with you forever. Amen."

The pastor stayed on the steps to the altar, wishing happy holidays to the churchgoers as they filed out. Once the church had emptied, Father Paul returned to his chambers. Sean waited in his street clothes.

"I'll be out of these vestments in a minute," said the priest wearily. "I'm feeling a bit sickly. Go and change out of your altar clothes."

When Sean returned, Father Paul seized his arm firmly and led him out the side door, Frankie following close behind. At the steps to the rectory, the priest suddenly stopped.

"You're trying to ruin my reputation and I'll have no more of it!"

The priest abruptly fell to his knees, vomit blowing out of his nose and mouth.

"Oh my God," wailed the priest. He held his hand up to the light. "That's blood! I'm bleeding! Jesus Christ!"

Sean stepped over the pool of vomit.

"I need to get to a doctor immediately," moaned the pastor. "I don't know what's wrong with me!"

The priest rose and stumbled up the stairs to his residence.

Sean bolted for the road, sprinting all the way down Lake Boulevard and up the driveway to the DeLane residence. He slowed near the garage, trying to catch his breath. He leaped up the steps to the front door, two at a time.

Sean slammed both hands on the front door.

Weldon opened the door, a look of alarm spreading over his face.

"Where's Candy?" yelled Sean.

"Sean. Calm down. It's Christmas."

"She was suppose to be at the Mass I just helped with," demanded Sean.

"I don't know what happened," said Weldon, scratching his chin. "She wasn't talking to me this morning. But she was dressed for church when she went out the back door."

Sean started backing up.

"Sean, look something happened last night I'm not quite sure about," blurted Weldon. "Candy started telling me about Father Paul and calling him dirty and evil but it was late and I had several drinks and it was Christmas Eve and…"

"You didn't listen to your own daughter?"

"I tried to but she just started crying and saying I wouldn't understand or ever believe her," stammered Weldon. "I feel terrible that I let her down but I was only trying to…"

Sean turned and raced down the steps, not hearing the last part that Weldon was trying to get out. He scrambled around the side of the mansion.

Fresh tracks in the snow led from the kitchen door to the stairs leading down to the beach.

Sean followed the trail to the edge of the cliff. He looked down to the bottom landing, recognizing Candy's black overcoat folded neatly on the last step. He climbed down, picking up the garment to examine it. The tracks were harder to find in the jumble of ice and snow pushed up along the shore's edge. Sean scaled the icy wall, shielding his eyes against the wind.

Sean covered his mouth with his hands at the sight of Candy creeping slowly out on the blue ice.

"God Almighty!"

Sean tried to sprint but it was hard to get his footing on the frozen surface. By the time he closed in on Candy she was almost to the edge of the flow. Lake water rushed by, seeping onto the ice.

"Please stop," howled Sean.

Candy spun around in panic. "Leave me alone!"

Sean edged gingerly towards Candy, holding out his hand as he inched in her direction.

"Don't move, just don't move," pleaded Sean. "You could fall into that water and the current will pull you away."

Candy froze.

Sean reached the girl, wrapping his arms around her.

"Let's get back on shore and out of this cold," he said tenderly.

Candy rested her head on his shoulder as they stepped away from the water's edge.

A loud crack suddenly rumbled under their feet.

Sean squeezed Candy tighter, fear covering his face as the ice flow they were on ripped free of the main body and moved into the lake.

"What's happening?" cried Candy.

"I'm not sure," stammered Sean. "Just hold onto to me."

The ice flow jerked into the current, spinning in a circle.

Water rushed over the top, lapping at their ankles.

"God, the water is so cold," moaned Candy. "What should we do?"

"Nothing," whispered Sean. "There's nothing we can do now. We're stuck on this small piece of ice."

The water kept rising, sending shivers through their bodies.

"Oh, Sean, I'm so sorry," sobbed Candy through chattering teeth. "I made another bad decision. You shouldn't have come out here. Why did you do that?"

The water reached their knees.

"There's no way off this piece of ice now," sighed Sean.

He looked at Candy, tears streaming down his face.

"I'm sorry too," he cried, taking off his heavy coat and draping it over her shoulders.

Candy screamed hysterically.

They both closed their eyes.

Sean picked Candy up so she was clear of the water. Their small island of safety slowly drifted further into open water.

Sean squinted back towards the shore at the sound of a large engine starting up.

Off the back of the DeLane property rose a helicopter.

"It's your dad, Candy! He sees us! Hang on! Hang on!"

Within minutes, a rope ladder was swinging overhead, secured to one of the runners along the bottom of the helicopter.

Still clutching Candy, Sean lunged for the ladder with his free hand, pulling it down on his first try.

"You have to help yourself now, Candy," hollered Sean over the roar of the helicopter. "Get up that ladder! Do it now!"

Sean held the ladder tight as Candy climbed several rungs. When she was high enough, Sean scampered onto the bottom of the ladder. The helicopter immediately turned for shore. When the copter cleared the cliff, it hovered over a large bank of fresh snow. Sean jumped clear, the snow softening his fall. Candy followed.

With the two safely on the ground, the helicopter descended onto its landing pad at the far side of the DeLane property.

Sean lifted Candy up out of the snow.

"I guess this still might be a merry Christmas," sighed Sean, holding onto Candy as he stumbled towards her home.

Back at St. Joseph's church, Dell watched intently as Father Paul, carrying Frankie, climbed into his Riviera. He started up his truck, following closely behind the pastor as snow started falling in blinding waves.

Father Paul accelerated along Lake Boulevard, heading east towards Cleveland. Dell gunned his truck to keep pace, losing sight of the priest's car as it rounded a curve. Ahead, the priest had stopped suddenly, the bile in his stomach rising uncontrollably. The priest threw open his door and leaned his head out to vomit in the snow. At that moment, Dell came upon the scene, speeding in his truck. He braked hard and swung the wheel to the left in an attempt to avoid the Riviera. Dell's truck slid sideways down the icy road, the back end hitting the stopped car with such force it decapitated the priest and ripped off the side door.

Frankie dashed off the front seat, running after the rolling head of Father Paul, spitting blood as it spun around in the fresh snow. The dog's little feet left a line of red paw prints down the street. When Frankie reached the priest's head, he curled up and licked the blood off the cheek of the pastor of St. Joseph's Church.

Dell got down out of his truck, lit a Camel and made his way to where Frankie lay in the snow. He looked down at the dog, pulled back his steel-toed work boot, and kicked Frankie high over the snow bank running the length of the road.

Dell returned to his truck and sat in the open door smoking his cigarette while he waited for the police to arrive.

EPILOGUE

Father Ken Wasowski slumped in his leather chair behind the desk in his rectory in Euclid, his head propped up with his right arm. His neck and upper chest were still encircled in his long purple stole. An empty coffee pot and two mugs rested on a silver tray just out of his reach.

Sean studied the face of his confessor.

The room was dark except for the small beam of light thrown off by a brass lamp near the door.

Sean checked his watch. Midnight. It had been almost seven hours since he had first entered St. Thomas Aquinas Church looking for Father Ken. He rubbed the back of his neck with both hands, trying to get out the kinks that had settled in while he had sat across from the priest.

Father Ken leaned forward on both elbows. He looked at Sean thoughtfully but did not smile.

"The big question, and the real reason I've come this far to seek out a simple truth," offered Sean, "am I bad and damned for all eternity?"

"We all have the capacity for evil or we wouldn't be human," answered Father Ken. "It's not in your character to be mean. I saw your kindness as a young boy and I believe you wouldn't have pursued a career in law enforcement if you didn't want to take the right path. And you sure wouldn't be here today trying to clear your conscience if you were inherently bad."

The priest took a sip of cold coffee.

"But this is still a confession so we have more to discuss."

Sean braced in his chair.

"It's the biggest regret in my life that I didn't do more to stop Father Paul," said the priest sternly. "But when I was sent to West Virginia, I just put my head down and tried to be a good priest. I didn't want to get a label as a problem in the church. Then the pastor died and I went on with my career and ended up here."

"My guilt is immense," sighed Sean. "What happened in Vineyard Beach still haunts me."

"That was profound loss for someone your age," conceded the priest. "Jimmy's suicide, your brother's death."

"Everything changed in a hurry," whispered Sean. "When my dad moved us after Father Paul's death, Vineyard Beach, and all my friends, just became a part of my life in the rearview mirror."

"Did you keep up with any of your old gang?" prodded the priest.

"I talk with Buddy Trotz once and a while," said Sean. "But that's about it."

"What ever happened to the girl from California?"

"Candy DeLane? Her dad moved on to the East Coast to get her to a safer environment. We wrote for a while but we were just kids. Last I heard, she married a doctor and lives in North Carolina of all places. Considering I'm on wife number three, it's a good thing she settled on someone else."

"Sean, your recovery has started now with this admission and you're headed in the right direction, finally," counseled the priest. "Keep working on yourself."

"I've got a ways to go before I'm free from all my obsessions," answered Sean.

Father Ken rose from his chair and walked around his desk to stand near Sean.

"We know a lot more today about clergy sexual abuse that we did back in the sixties," claimed the priest, putting his hand on Sean's shoulder. "We learned after his death that Paul Sterner was a serial offender with scores of victims, both girls and boys. The church had a large settlement with most of his victims. That doesn't justify his death on that icy road back in Vineyard Beach. But you did not set out to kill the pastor, only impede him from hurting you."

"Sean, the police ruled his death an accident, and I feel that you have paid enough of a price over the last forty years. You should accept that finding," stated Father Ken. "His death was an accident."

"But Father Ken, what I did was wrong," insisted Sean.

The priest held up his hand.

"Sean, I've been a priest a long time," he said softly. "A long, long time." Father Ken massaged his chin with both of his hands.

"Sean, I can't count the number of times someone from my parish has sat where you are now, right there in that leather chair you've occupied for the last several hours, and complained about how their life had turned out because of a stupid mistake. And I've heard it said from embezzlers, adulterers, drug addicts, the full spectrum of life. If only I had known, they say."

Father Ken patted Sean's arm.

"Sean, people rationalize all the time," he said emphatically. "They think no one will find out or they'll never get caught. That's the allure of sin talking in their heads. Then when the result of their missteps are fully realized and out in the open, it's devastating. So they come here and ask me why their life turned out the way it did."

The priest returned to his chair.

"My answer is always the same," lamented the priest. "Without a doubt, if you had known at the beginning how sin would essentially alter your life, you would not have strayed from the righteous path. No one would."

"Was my trip to Ohio in vain then?"

"Not at all. You have officially rejoined your Catholic family and sought the forgiveness of your church and of God."

Father Ken raised his right hand and made the sign of the cross.

"May Almighty God bless you, the Father, Son and Holy Spirit. Sean Gerard, you are absolved of your sins. Go in peace."

Sean strode towards Father Ken.

"I'd like to give you a hug."

The two men embraced.

"I know the only way to recover is to actually deal with the truth and stop the denial," asserted Sean, smiling at the priest. "I also realize that

I can't make it all the way back without help. Thanks for offering me forgiveness."

"You're not free and clear just yet," said the priest, taking off his stole. "Have you forgotten the part in confession about penance?"

"Right, I'll do as you say," nodded Sean.

"I want you to follow my instructions then," ordered Father Ken. "You must return to Vineyard Beach and visit Jimmy's grave in the St. Joseph's Church cemetery and talk to God on a personal level to complete your penance."

Sean looked down at the priest and shook his head.

"You're making this hard. I guess you know about the promise I made never to go anywhere near that place. I was so hurt by his death."

"Yes, I know, that story made the rounds through the village," interrupted Father Ken. "I want this to be hard. You need to work to cleanse your soul. So it's time to let go of your promise and complete your journey."

The priest slowly rose from his chair and extended his hand.

"You're allowed to mourn Sean, for one more day, but stop moping and get on with your life."

"More good advice," replied Sean, shaking the priest's hand. "I'll never forget this."

Sean turned towards the door.

"One last thing," said Father Ken. "I always wondered about that fancy brass bell Sister Mary Martin liked to ring in her classroom. Goodness, she made a fuss when it disappeared. She grumbled about it that entire first year in the new high school. The rumor around Vineyard Beach was you had something to do with its demise."

Sean held the door open as he broke into laughter.

"I see that damn bell all the time, dear Father Ken," exclaimed Sean. "It sits on my nightstand. I ring it every morning before I get out of bed!"

"Well, ring it one time for me then," chuckled Father Ken with a wave.

Sean returned the wave as he closed the door.

He raced for the rental car parked in the side lot, pausing to pull his knapsack and a flashlight from the trunk. The drive to Vineyard Beach would take about an hour, time enough to reflect on his days in that small village and the effect on his life. Sean felt lighter as he drove through the snow, a sense of achievement lifting his spirits. He flicked on the radio, tapping his fingers on the steering wheel to the oldies on the classic rock station. As he approached St. Joseph's Church, a sight he hadn't seen in decades, he smiled.

"I will not be afraid, ever again," he exulted, banging the top of the dashboard with his fist. He pulled over in the corner of the parking lot nearest the cemetery, the stone grave markers off in the distance sparkled against the snow in the moonlight.

The cell phone in Sean's right front pocket suddenly vibrated. He flicked open the cover and hit the "talk" button.

"Sean Gerard, Detective Sean Gerard?"

"Yes, this is me chief, I recognize your voice. Go ahead."

"Hate to bother you while you're on leave but something has come up."

"What exactly?"

"Another body has turned up."

"A boy?"

"Yes."

"Staked to the ground like the other one?"

"Yes."

"I will be there tomorrow. Have my reinstatement papers ready. I have just one thing left to do here." He closed his phone.

Sean picked up his knapsack off the passenger seat and headed off for the short trek. The flashlight beam revealed a large snowdrift running through the middle of the cemetery covering most of the burial sites, including his brother's grave. He paused outside the fence near the spot he knew Terry was put to rest. Thoughts of his deceased parents, and that day of terrible grief when they said goodbye to their son, rushed through his memory. He wiped his tears on the sleeve of his parka.

Sean pulled open the iron gate and crossed over to a large granite marker near an oak tree. Someone had recently visited the grave, the snow was cleared and a pint of bourbon, topped with a red ribbon, rested in front of the marble headstone. Sean could clearly read the name chiseled in letters eight-inches tall: JAMES ELLIOTT THOMAS MORAN.

"Jimmy, I'm finally here to see you old friend," sighed Sean.

He reached into his knapsack and pulled out the nun's brass bell, lifted it over his head and shook it mightily.

The sound of the little bell drifted across the church property.

"Getting me to steal the nun's precious bell was one of your best ideas," shouted Sean. "I was proud to be your Caper Brother!"

Sean gently placed the bell on top of the grave maker.

"Jimmy, you deserve to have this!"

Sean knelt in the snow.

"Dear God, thank you for guiding me this far," whispered Sean, running his hand across Jimmy's name. "I promise to change my ways and ask for your help every day. And please take good care of my friend until I see him again."

Sean picked up the bottle to read the note taped to the side.

"Happy birthday, Jimmy. You would have been fifty-four. We Miss You, Buddy and Johnny."

Sean folded the paper and slid it into his coat pocket. He pumped his fists into the night sky.

"Friends to the end!" he yelled.

He twisted the top off the pint and deeply inhaled its contents. Sean studied the bottle for a few minutes, then poured the bourbon into the snow. He threw the empty pint into the shadows.

On the way out of the cemetery, Sean stopped at a small granite marker barely sticking out of the snow. He knelt to clear the space in front so he could read the inscription: Dell Pilot, Master Fisherman, 1907-1972.

Sean leaned over and kissed the top of the stone.

Made in the USA
Lexington, KY
19 September 2018